ECHOES IN THE BLACK

Martin Shaw

ECHOES IN THE BLACK
Copyright © 2025 Martin Shaw

This is a work of fiction. Names, characters, places and incidents are
either products of the author's imagination or are used fictitiously.
Any resemblance to actual persons, living or dead, or actual events
is purely coincidental.

Cover design by Martin Shaw
First Edition, 2025

For my beloved – my brightest light.

Prologue

They call it the Endless Night — a comforting phrase for the yawning blackness of space.

When mankind first reached for the stars and carved hyperspace highways through the dark, it felt safe.

First between planets. Then systems. Eventually, entire galaxies.

We travelled inside our artificial beams of blue and white light — busy, ordered, always moving.

But just beyond the glow of those manufactured roads, the darkness waits.

Watching.

Patient.

Endless.

Darker, deeper, and colder than any ocean, it stretches forever — a place only a few brave lights ever dare to drift.

Sometimes to explore.

Sometimes because they're lost. Or running.

And sometimes, when you venture too far from the lanes…

The dark notices.

Ships vanish. Crews never return.

A quiet reminder to those who forget:

Space is not yours.

It never was.

You only borrowed the light.

Act One

Chapter One

The pressure door groaned, scraping along grooves worn deep into the deck plating. A grunt, a curse, and one final shoulder-barge pushed it home until the locks clanked into place.

Light from the dock spilled through the gap, slicing across the darkness in harsh white beams. The air that followed carried the sting of burnt wiring and copper and something faintly acrid — sharp enough to make his eyes water. He coughed twice, covering his face with a rag until the fit passed.

Inside, the air felt heavier. Every breath carried the ship's weight — like being swallowed whole. The smell of old insulation and machine dust clung to everything.

He moved to the rear of the flight deck where the auxiliary console sat dormant, dropped his duffel, and tore open a seal-bag of documents. A key slid free and clattered against the floor. He slotted it into the console and tapped the worn keypad, murmuring a code from memory.

At first, nothing. Then a low whine rose somewhere in the guts of the ship. Fans stuttered. Vents howled. Old bulbs burst in tiny pops overhead. Through the piping came the drawn-out groan of air finally moving after years of stillness. The place sounded like an animal waking from hibernation.

The first breath of filtered air hissed through the vents — thin, stale, laced with the tang of scorched metal and age. He lowered the rag and tasted dust on his tongue. *God, he'd forgotten how ships smelled when they'd been left too long.* To be expected from a ship this old.

Four stations stood in silence: Pilot, Navigation, Auxiliary Systems, and a fourth console whose function had been lost to time. He slapped the casing with an open palm; a lonely green LED flickered once, then died.

He caught his reflection in one of the darkened screens — a pale, tired shape framed by static light. *Look at you.*

"Well," he muttered, "you look about how this ship sounds."

The reflection twitched and broke apart as the console flickered back to life.

He sighed and dropped into the pilot's chair. From a pocket came a small chrome recorder, no larger than his palm. He turned the dial until the display blinked **REC READY**.

"Well… here we go."

"Log entry, personal."

He took a breath — the first in a long while that didn't sting. The recorder light blinked red.

"Right. Guess I should start somewhere. Marcus Carpenter. Pilot — or whatever passes for one these days."

A pause. Static filled the gap, the ship's background hum vibrating through the deck.

"Day one aboard *Barge Delta-Six-One*. No name on the hull, just a serial number stencilled halfway through a rust patch. First impressions: this ship's older than it looks…"

He exhaled slowly, the sound almost a sigh.

"Atmosphere filters are alive — barely. Air tastes like burnt copper and regret. Main power's cycling, but I'll need to check the reactor controls before I trust them. Most of the consoles up here are shot. One of them sparked when I leaned on it. Smells like fried circuits."

He shifted in the chair, the metal creaking beneath him.

"Docking bay manifest says she was decommissioned two decades ago. No logs, no crew registry. Maybe that's why she was cheap."

A low groan rolled through the hull — long and drawn out, like something breathing in its sleep. He glanced around.

"This ship's old," he muttered. **"And not in the charming, vintage way."**

As if in agreement, a sharp clank echoed behind him. A bolt skittered across the deck. He jumped, heartbeat spiking.

He rubbed a hand across his face. *Not like I had many choices.*

"They don't exactly hand out shiny cruisers to ex-cons."

He thumbed the recorder off. The red light faded to black.

For a few seconds he just listened — the faint hum of standby generators warming somewhere below. He wiped his face on his sleeve, dust and grime already clinging to his sweat.

Then he clicked the recorder back on, rubbing a thumb over the microphone grill as if clearing dust from his thoughts.

"Cargo's already loaded," he said quietly.

"Didn't even get to see it go in. Just a stack of warnings stamped across every page."

He flipped through the paperwork, yellowed sheets crackling between his fingers.

DO NOT APPROACH.
DO NOT OPEN.
DO NOT TOUCH UNDER ANY CIRCUMSTANCES.

Marcus huffed through his nose.

"Sounds like a bad idea already. I'm breaking parole just by being here, but with the money they're offering — and the promises made — it's worth it. *Has to be.*"

"End log."

He shut the recorder again and leaned back, scanning the flight deck. The consoles were spaced far apart, relics from an era before ergonomics. The low ceiling pressed the room down — close and heavy. Anyone over six feet would end up with a permanent hunch.

A sudden chirp drew his eye. The auxiliary console flickered — a light shifting from red to green:

STNBY READY

"Well, that's something," he muttered, stretching the ache from his legs. He crossed the deck and flipped the main breaker.

The response was immediate. A deep thrum rolled through the plates as power surged. Systems groaned awake — vent fans, coolant pumps, the soft static buzz of ancient displays. Warm dust and ozone filled the air.

Every console blinked to life — except one.

Left of the pilot's chair, a long panel of dead screens and unlit keys sat in stubborn silence. Marcus crouched, tracing the power conduit with his hand. He gave the casing a firm kick.

A fan coughed. A lone green LED flared once, then died.

Marcus waited, holding his breath.

Nothing — just the hum of everything else pretending to work.

"Figures," he muttered.

He looked around the bridge again, flickering lights reflecting in the glass canopy.

He unzipped his duffel, the sound slicing through the quiet. Inside — not much. A few changes of clothes, some tools, and his old flight jacket folded on top. He ran his thumb over the patched sleeve before slipping it on. It still smelled faintly of oil, metal, and burnt dust — the scent of a past life he wasn't sure he *missed*.

"Still fits," he muttered, tugging the zip. "Could've done worse."

He turned toward the centre of the flight deck. The ladderwell sat open, ringed in yellow hazard paint long since flaked away. Metal rungs vanished into shadow — no handrails, no guardrails. Just a narrow hole into whatever waited below.

"Yeah," he said dryly, "that looks completely safe."

He crouched at the opening, unclipped the recorder, and turned the dial until the red light burned solid.

"Alright," he said, softer now, **"maintenance log. Clipping this to my belt — continuous recording while I do a walk-through. If you're listening to this later… congratulations. You found the body."**

He gave a short, humourless laugh that didn't reach his eyes. The ship groaned beneath him, as if laughing back.

He leaned into the ladderwell and took his first step down. The metal was cold and slick under his gloves.

The air shifted as he descended — thicker, heavier, carrying the tang of coolant and old rust. Somewhere below, something dripped at a slow, steady rhythm, echoing up the shaft.

"*Definitely* safe," he muttered, his voice half-swallowed by the dark.

The light above thinned as he climbed lower, shrinking to a pale halo fading into gloom. Each rung creaked under his weight, blending with the distant hum of machinery waking from years of dormancy.

He passed the half-open bunk door on the way to the galley. Through the narrow crack he saw part of a bedframe, grey sheets stiff with age, a single locker left ajar. The flickering light inside pulsed slow and uneven — like a dying heartbeat.

He kept walking.

The galley was little better: metal tables bolted to the floor, one dented like someone had tried to hammer their way out of boredom. Dispenser units dead. Ration bins sealed. A faint chemical tang hung in the air, mixed with something that reminded him of boiled dust.

He tapped the recorder. **"Deck Two galley, condition... let's call it lived-in."**

Somewhere below, a distant clang rose through the decks — followed by the low groan of old machinery coming alive.

Then a rising whine.

An alarm.

He froze, listening.

The sound wasn't coming from below.

It was coming from above.

He climbed fast — or tried to. The rungs bit into his palms as his breathing grew ragged halfway up. By the time he reached the top, his shoulders burned. He rolled onto his back on the flight deck, chest heaving, staring at the ceiling.

Not much call for vertical cardio in prison, he thought.

The intercom crackled overhead, the Dockmaster's voice breaking through the static.

"Fueling complete. You are cleared for departure."

Marcus sat up, still panting, wiping his face on his sleeve.

"Roger that," he said automatically. Then hesitated. "Uh... *Barge Delta-Six-One departing Titan Dock.*"

It still felt strange saying it — not his ship. Not yet.

Behind him, the bulkhead door began to close, metal screeching faintly as it sealed. A low hiss followed as the flight deck repressurised, air cycling unevenly through tired filters. Marcus winced and worked his jaw, trying to pop his ears.

The clamps released in a soft, rhythmic hiss, one after another — like the ship was exhaling. For a moment it didn't move, simply drifted — sluggish, uncertain.

"Jesus," he muttered. "What did they *put* in this thing?"

He pushed the throttle forward. The engines groaned in protest before catching a deep rumble that rolled through the deck plates and up his spine. The ship lurched free of the dock, rising awkwardly at first before smoothing into a slow, steady climb.

Outside, the sky darkened from murky orange to ink black, Titan shrinking behind him. The navigation screen blinked to life — a lone blue dot marking the moon, growing smaller by the second.

Marcus leaned back in his seat, eyes fixed on the stars ahead. For the first time in years, he felt the quiet weight of open space settling around him. He smiled, faintly.

He was back in the Deep.

As he shifted, he felt the recorder on his belt — still running.

"My previous jobs always used the hyperspace lanes — bustling, busy, *safe*. This nav computer's pre-programmed away from all that. Straight into the quiet. I've never even been this close to the borders of known space."

He paused. Faint static hummed under his words.

"You hear stories about the Deep — cold, unforgiving, infinite. Hard to know which ones are true… which ones are bullshit."

He exhaled softly, the sound swallowed by the cabin.

"So why do I feel like an old Earth diver, standing at the edge of a sunken trench?"

Silence pressed in. He let the question linger, the faint creak of the hull filling the gap.

"I guess we'll see who blinks first."

"End Log."

- - -

"Log entry, engineering survey."

"It's been two hours since the last burn. Engines cut. We're coasting on inertia power now. Probably for the best — I'm convinced half the hull bolts loosened during launch. Leaving Titan's atmosphere felt like taking a sledgehammer to the stabilisers."

"No repair drones onboard, so it's all on me. I'll need to get hands-on, patch what I can. That fourth console on the flight deck's still offline — curious what it actually *does* once I've got power routed back through it."

"For now, walkthrough. If I'm stuck with this old barge, I'd better know what keeps her flying."

He unclipped the recorder, fastening it to his belt.

"**End log,**" he muttered, heading for the ladderwell.

The rungs felt warm beneath his palms as he climbed down into Deck Two. A faint tang of old grease and burnt copper clung to the air — not strong enough to choke, but enough to make his throat itch.

Most of the storage cupboards hung open, packets and tools scattered across the floor. Whoever stocked the ship hadn't cared much for tidiness.

The galley was small — built for function, not comfort — cracked tiles, a dead coffee dispenser, crumbs fossilised into the counter.

He glanced through the half-open bunkroom door as he passed. Spartan — thin mattresses, folded sheets, a locker at each end. Still better than prison.

He stopped by the ladder again and leaned over the opening, peering into the dim shaft. The decks below were darker — the kind of dark that swallowed the light around it.

He exhaled, muttering to himself, *"Might as well know what I've signed up for."*

The ladder creaked under his weight as he descended.

At the pressure door for Deck Three, the handle refused to move. He braced himself and pulled harder. The hinges shrieked — metal protesting every inch.

As the hatch parted, a cold breeze licked across his arm. Unnatural. The hairs on his neck rose.

His hand twitched toward his waistband. *Of course — nothing there.*

Prison habit. Always be armed, even with scrap.

The instinct lingered.

He descended.

- - -

The pressure door resisted him at first, groaning as Marcus forced it wider with his shoulder until he could squeeze through. The air that met him was cold — sharp enough to bite through the thin layer of his flight jacket.

He let the door fall shut behind him, the clang rolling down the deck.

Condensation clung to the exposed pipes above, droplets breaking loose and tapping against the grated floor. The hum of the ship's systems was fainter here — low, pulsing, like a heartbeat buried deep inside the hull.

Rows of machinery lined the narrow space: coolant tanks, junction boxes, the loader crane hanging frozen overhead. Its articulated arm was half-extended, metal joints streaked with rust. The control panel beneath it sat dark, the red standby light long dead.

Marcus gave one of the levers an idle pull — nothing. The handle moved, but the system was gone.

He stepped further in. The smell was heavier here — old oil, coolant, burnt wiring — the kind of mix that coated your throat if you lingered.

At the far end of the deck, a small oval observation window looked out into space. He pressed a gloved hand to the glass. Even through the material he could feel the cold seeping through — a cold that wasn't temperature so much as *emptiness*.

Beyond it, the stars hung still and silent. He followed the faint line of the hull downward. The running lights along the cargo-hold walls flickered dimly, barely touching the floor below. From here it almost looked as if the dark had weight — as though space itself were pooling at the bottom of the ship.

Marcus let out a long breath that misted faintly in the air. "Right," he muttered, voice rough. *"One more level."*

He turned back toward the ladderwell, his hand sliding along the rail as he began the descent to Deck Four.

- - -

Stepping off the ladder, his boots scraped against the grated floor.

The silence hit first.

Too quiet. On any other ship, the hold would've been alive — crews shouting, laughter echoing, crates slamming onto steel. Here, nothing.

No hum of filters. No rumble of engines. Not even his own breath seemed to carry. Just dead air.

He edged forward, torch cutting through the gloom. The beam drifted across bare bulkheads, frost glinting along seams where insulation had failed.

The space was bigger than he expected — far larger than any ship this old had reason to be.

Something loomed ahead. A shape. Hard angles beneath a black tarp, pulled tight and shiny where the fabric had stretched thin.

The light caught flashes of yellow warning symbols — radiation, corrosive, restricted access.

Six yellow straps cinched the mass, ratcheted down with dull silver locks. Marcus crouched, brushing one with his glove. Industrial-grade. Overkill for ordinary freight.

He straightened, scanning for a manifest. Nothing. No barcodes. No cargo numbers. Just the tarp. The straps. The silence.

He rubbed his hands together, breath fogging faintly. The cold here was different — thick, heavy — like it leaked from the crate itself.

Even the sound of his breathing came back thin, as if the air itself was *holding its breath*.

He sneezed, a sharp pain blooming in his ribs.

A faint rattle cut through the quiet — the clink of a ratchet shifting under tension. He froze.

Probably just the metal contracting in the cold... *probably*.

His hand dropped to the recorder on his belt, thumb tapping the mic. The red light blinked steadily back — the only pulse in the room.

"If I didn't know better, I'd swear the chill's bleeding out of this thing. What are you? Wrapped tight, sealed like a tomb. Not taking chances. Not after last time. Slow and steady — that's the plan."

He turned toward the ladder, one hand on the rung — and stopped.

Something was off.

He looked back. Just the tarp. Still. Shapeless. But his skin prickled all the same.

He called out, half-hearted. The sound fell flat. A room this size should've echoed. Instead, his voice just dropped dead.

A faint creak rippled from the crate.

He didn't wait to hear more.

He climbed fast, every rung clanging underfoot. At Deck Two he slammed the bulkhead shut and cranked the lever until it hissed tight.

He stood there a moment, chest heaving. The cold clung to him like it had followed him up through the metal.

Even sealed, he could still feel it — the chill bleeding upward through the decks.

"Well... *that* felt wrong," he muttered, rubbing his arms. "Let's hope it keeps the cold out too."

He wasn't sure if the cold was in the air — or under his skin.

Back on the flight deck, he flicked a few switches on the auxiliary console. A sharp fizz — static bit his fingers — and one of the monitors stuttered to life.

Grainy. Static-prone. These old analogue displays predated liquid-cooled systems by decades. Clunky, outdated — but it worked.

At least he could keep an eye on the cargo hold.

He leaned back, staring out through the cockpit glass. Instrument lights blinked in the reflection, but something in the black beyond felt... *aware*.

Behind him, one of the dark consoles gave a faint pulse — a single flicker of green light — then went still again.

He didn't notice.

Chapter Two

No clouds in space — only rust, flaking across the ceiling and drifting through the recycled air like old dust.

Two days since launch, and already the silence had begun to sound different — not peaceful, just *heavy*.

Marcus lay on his back in the narrow bunk, staring at the metal above him. The air filter wheezed behind the wall, a dull rhythm he could almost time his breathing to. It was the only real noise left — steady, mechanical, and faintly cruel in how alive it sounded compared to everything else. *Still a cell,* he thought. *Just colder, and without the yelling.*

He swung his legs over the edge of the cot and stood, the movement sending a protest through his spine. A sharp crack followed as he stretched, then a dry cough — trying to clear the taste of the ship from his throat. Everything in here tasted the same: copper, oil, stale air. Even breathing felt like swallowing metal.

He rubbed a hand across his face, grit gathering on his palm from the constant dust clinging to everything. Boredom — the one thing prison never gave him — had finally found him here in the void.

The only proof of time passing was the dull red glow of the old LED clock on the flight deck above. Its digits flickered, lagging a few seconds behind each cycle. He couldn't remember if he'd ever bothered to set it properly.

The water tanks had been scrubbed and refilled — probably at cost. The heat-pipes for hot water were long gone, stripped out or sold for scrap. Every drink, whether cold coffee or bland tea, came with that familiar metallic tang of recycled air and old pipes.

Boredom — a foreign concept in prison — was slowly making reintroductions. Marcus *hated* it.

He grumbled quietly as he left the bunkroom, grabbing his comms unit — the most exciting part of his day. A sub-par breakfast. Turning the dial to REC, he started a walk-and-talk.

"Log entry, personal."

He placed the recorder on the counter as he rummaged through the cupboards. **"Two days since the burn, and I'm already thinking about throwing myself out the airlock just to break the boredom. At least back in prison I didn't have to brew my own sludge."**

He pulled out a few food packets, cycling through the flavours. He tore one open; a puff of powder burst into his face and he coughed, nearly gagging. **"I've tasted worse — once had coffee brewed through a sock."**

Marcus gave a weak chuckle. *"Might start naming the dust clumps if this keeps up."*

He filled the packet with water, sealed it, and set it aside to cook. **"With all this free time, I gave the cabin a proper wipe-down. She almost looks a third decent without the grime. Most systems are low-power — some shut off entirely."**

The eggs would take a few minutes. The coffee, not so much. After a few stirs, Marcus couldn't decide if it was coffee or gravy, but downed it anyway. The bitter liquid left that familiar space-tang across his tongue.

He dropped the cup into the wash-sink and sat on the wobbly stool closest to the table. He spread out the paperwork they'd given him — coordinates stretching into deep space, through routes no one had taken in decades. Maybe longer.

"Once I reach the first *Nav Lantern*," he muttered, **"it'll sync with the nav console and show me where to go next."**

He scoffed. **"Not sure why I couldn't just be told the final destination and plan my own route, but—"**

He reached over, gave the food packet a shake; it felt just warm enough. **"I've been meaning to check that dead bridge console. I saw a toolkit and some schematics stashed in one of the lockers."**

He ripped the packet open; steam rolled out — not smelling much better, but edible. After a few bites, he decided it wasn't terrible, though it earned no points for the eggy, metallic aftertaste.

He glanced down at the printed destination. **"...*Nav Lanterns*,"** he murmured. **"Can't believe I'll finally see one."**

- - -

After parting ways with his breakfast, Marcus climbed into the ladderwell.

The ship was never warm — rusted metal didn't exactly welcome anyone — but this space was colder still. The air seemed to rise from below, seeping up through the sealed pressure door on Deck Three. Even with the locks engaged, something down there breathed chill into the rest of the ship.

He adjusted his grip on the rung and started upward. Each step rang out, boots striking steel, the sound bouncing through the narrow shaft before vanishing into the dark below. He risked a glance down, squinting past the gloom. The ladder disappeared into blackness, the bottom lost from view.

It wasn't muddy water and lucky coins waiting at the end of this well — only silence, depth, and the steady pulse of cold air rising from below.

He pulled himself out of the ladderwell and onto the flight deck. The moment his boots hit the floor, the nav console chirped three times — a proximity alert.

Marcus froze. A cold draft crawled up his back and neck as he straightened. He turned fast, scanning the corners of the room, the dim glow of dead monitors painting long, ghosted shadows across the bulkheads.

Old instincts — *prison* instincts — never really died.

The single active screen flickered. The grainy, monochrome feed showed the cargo hold below. For a heartbeat, the image tore into static, lines of white fizzing across the display like old film burning in a projector. Marcus leaned in, squinting.

It steadied. The tarp hadn't moved. The straps were still tight. Nothing out of place.

Not that this antique monitor could pick up much detail. Still, something about the sight felt *wrong* — as if the crate preferred to be watched from a distance.

He frowned, whispering to himself, "Probably just interference."

But static shouldn't leave you feeling like you'd just been *stared at.*

Tapping his leg against the console, Marcus glared at the screen. They were close enough for a data handshake with the Lantern, but still hours from visual range. No matter how hard he stared, the progress bar crawled like a dying thing.

He sighed. "Come on, you antique."

Analogue systems. Slow, outdated, stubborn. Instead of nanotech's instant precision, he had a flickering bar that seemed to slow the longer he watched.

He gave the console a final kick — the hollow clang echoing through the flight deck — and wandered to the pilot's chair.

Out the viewport, faint pinpricks of light drifted across the black — ships hugging the hyperspace lanes, keeping to the safe highways. Order. Routine. A thousand lives a minute racing by.

He thumbed on his recorder, setting it beside the console.

"Log entry, personal."

"When they built the Nav Lanterns two centuries ago, no one expected them to still be in use. When the hyperspace highways came online, there were no deactivation protocols, so the Lanterns were left out here — drifting eternally."

He glanced over his shoulder. The progress bar hadn't moved.

"My mother used to tell me the lights formed a barrier around humanity. Protected us. *'The light keeps the dark out,'* she'd say. *'Whatever's in the dark stays there.'"*

He looked back to the stars. **"Now here I am… skirting that edge."**

The nav console chirped, washing the flight deck in cold blue. Marcus pocketed his comms and straightened.

"Finally."

– LIT LANTERNS: 42 –
– ESTIMATED ARRIVAL: 11 MONTHS, 3 WEEKS –
– PLOT COURSE: Y/N –

His finger traced the dotted path across the void. "This is going to be a long one."

Then the screen jittered. At first, just a glitch — then the plotted route buckled, as though something invisible were pressing against it, forcing its way into view.

A new buoy blinked.

– A!TERN@TI*E R0–ERROR–
– AL&^R–ERROR–

Lines of corrupted code streamed across the display — symbols he didn't recognise. The cooling fans whirred, lights dimmed, and for a second the screen flared white, then black.

He stepped back, half-expecting smoke.

– SYSTEM: REBOOT –
– PLEASE STANDBY –

When the charts returned, they looked unchanged. Calm. Clean.
But now there were two routes.

– CONNECTION: ACTIVE –
– NAV ROUTES: AVAILABLE –

He frowned, typing in a comparison command.

– LIT LANTERNS: 16 –
– ESTIMATED ARRIVAL: 6 MONTHS, 2 WEEKS –

He rubbed his chin. "Well… that cuts it down a bit."

A yellow warning box blinked.

CAUTION
HAZARD LEVEL: RED
NO RESCUE SERVICES AVAILABLE BEYOND THIS POINT
EXPLORATION BEYOND THE VEIL IS NOT ADVISED
– PLOT COURSE: Y/N –

The Veil.

A border made of warnings, not walls. Beyond it, the charts gave up completely — one single word scrawled across the dark:

UNKNOWN.

Marcus leaned closer. The alternate route zigzagged wider, the Lanterns spaced further apart — a quicker path, but through emptiness.

He pulled his recorder from his pocket and thumbed it on.

"Log entry, personal."

"The nav computer's… indecisive. It plotted one course, then spat out another after a few strange glitches."

He watched the yellow box blink. **"The new one cuts the trip by half, but it dives into the Veil. No charts. No comms. No backup. If these buoys are even transmitting anymore, it's a miracle. But if it works…"**

He hesitated. *"…maybe I make up some time. Maybe a bonus for early delivery."*

He sat back, thinking aloud. **"Long stretch of dark, though. No eyes but mine. No help if I get lost. Don't know who — or what — I'd meet out there."**

The hum of the ship filled the silence.

"I'll bring this tub to a crawl when I reach the first Lantern. Gives me time to decide which fork to take."

A faint smile. **"Maybe this is where I make or break it."**

- - -

As the ship neared the Lantern, Marcus tried to catch a glimpse of the relic. The forward viewscreen wasn't built for sightseeing; all he saw was glare and distortion.

Only one place aboard offered a proper view before it slipped away.

Deck Three: gantry level. Observation window.

The rungs grew colder the lower he climbed, the chill biting through his fingertips. He flexed his hand, wishing he'd brought gloves. The air down here carried a strange weight — a slow, creeping cold rising from below, even though the pressure door to the hold had stayed sealed since he fled it days ago.

He stopped at the Deck Three bulkhead. His hand hovered above the lever, hesitating. For a moment he simply listened — the faint groan of metal, the hum of life-support far above. Then, with a sharp exhale, he pulled the lever down.

A hiss of air escaped, stale and cold, carrying the tang of rust and coolant. Warm clouds puffed from his mouth with every breath. *Shouldn't be this cold down here,* he thought, stepping inside.

He hated this deck. But it was the only view.

At first, nothing — only the void, too deep for stars. Then, slowly, a glow began to bloom. Orange light washed across the hull as the Lantern drifted into view, colouring the ship like a memory of sunset.

It was vast. Twice the size of the barge. An hourglass of battered plating, pitted and scarred by centuries — yet its twin pulses still shone, steady and defiant against the dark.

Marcus's hand rose to his chest — reflex before memory. The chain and ring were gone. Even her face was fading.

The glow warmed him for a heartbeat, then an icy ripple traced his spine. He turned.

The cargo sat in shadow. The Lantern's light reached every surface of the hold except the tarp. That remained black, untouched — as if it refused the light entirely.

He shivered and looked back at the window. The glow was already fading. Blue shadow reclaimed the hull.

Doubt hollowed his chest. Would this be the moment he looked back on as the point of no return?

He reached for his recorder.

"Log entry, personal."

"I tell myself there was still time to turn back... but the truth is, the choice was already made."

Outside, the Lantern dwindled to a fragile spark. Then, inevitably, it vanished — swallowed by the dark.

He'd crossed lines before. *What was one more?*

Chapter Three

FOUR YEARS EARLIER

- - -

THESEUS – NERO-CLASS TRANSPORT SHIP
Crew Capacity: Six
Ship and cargo en route to *Proxima Centauri B.*

- - -

"How we looking, Bunny? I want a smooth landing this time."

The *Theseus* rumbled with a low growl, the polished floor vibrating under their boots. Marcus caught the thermos just before it slid off the pilot station.

"Rude," Bunny muttered, not looking up.

Thirty-one successful cargo runs — every one a clean docking. He'd scuffed the paint once, and that was all anyone remembered. Typical.

The bridge was pristine — brushed-metal consoles glowing soft blue, walls humming from stabiliser feedback. Marcus's captain's chair sat raised in the centre of the deck, pilot's station forward, Navigation to the right, systems console to the left under Bunny's watch. A narrow staircase curved down to the living quarters. Everything about this ship was clean, efficient — the kind of order he'd spent years building.

Bunny was one of the best stick-jockeys in the lanes, especially with a heavy bird like the *Theseus*. He had the badges to prove it. His old flight jacket — lazily slung over the back of his chair — was cluttered with patches from a dozen ships and outposts. Some were from certified waystations; others looked like junk from forgotten corners of the galaxy. Half were places Marcus had never heard of.

Didn't matter. The jacket read like a storybook, and Bunny wore it like armour. Not that it spared him from the occasional jab.

Most cycles, *Proxima B*'s descent zone was stable. Not this one — thunderstorms, chaotic thermals, 400-mph crosswinds. Even for a pro, every landing became a white-knuckle trial.

Marcus dropped into the captain's chair before the turbulence could do it for him. He tapped the comms panel.

"Bridge to Cargo. Jason, double-check everything's locked down. It's gonna get bumpy once the inertials sync to planet gravity."

The channel crackled — the clang of ratchets, shouted orders, the hiss of pressure seals. Someone laughed; someone else swore. A working ship, alive.

"Copy that, Captain. We'll make sure it's snug as hell. Don't forget to ask Bunny for that smooth landing," came the dry reply.

Marcus glanced over. Bunny's shoulders stiffened; his jaw tightened. Marcus smirked, hiding the grin behind his hand.

"I think he got the message. See you planetside. Bridge out."

The rumble deepened — a pressure you felt in your ribs. Outside the cockpit glass, the black of space began to smoulder with the orange bloom of atmospheric entry.

"Shit, shit, shit," Curtis muttered. "I hate planet landings. Why couldn't we find a spaceport, y'know, in space?"

She darted across the deck and lunged for her seat, movements too smooth — like gravity hadn't caught up.

Bunny snorted. "You've been saying that since *Kepler*. Still in one piece, ain't ya?"

"You don't get it," Curtis said, fumbling with her straps. "I'm space-born. First time I set foot on a planet I was eighteen. Atmospheres feel wrong. Gravity pulls weird… and the smell…"

She made a yuck face as she tied back her bluish-grey hair.

Space-born get all the funky colours, thought Marcus. *And half of them process complex equations like they're flipping through a comic book.*

Curtis waved a hand over her screen. Lines of descent data scrolled — too fast for most humanoid eyes. She mouthed the numbers silently, fingers dancing through the arc map, plotting the approach without missing a beat. She paused only long enough to finish her point:

"Half of them reek like fertiliser, machine oil, or mouldy air. *Prox B* smells like someone microwaved a swamp."

"I've been to worse," Bunny grunted, adjusting the stabilisers. His voice was low and gravel-edged — the sound of someone who'd spent twenty years breathing recycled air and never quite trusting autopilot.

"Outposts where the air chews your lungs. Mining docks thick with methane. Trust me — this is just weather and wet boots. I'll take it over vacuum any day."

Curtis shot him a sceptical side-eye as she finished buckling in.

"For me, planets are a necessary evil," she muttered, watching the nav computer trace their descent arc.

Marcus leaned back, observing them both. They were a good crew — seasoned, sharp; even with the complaining, they had each other's backs. That counted for a lot out here.

And soon, they'd be on the ground.

He just hoped the job waiting for them was as routine as advertised.

- - -

A burst of turbulence jolted the ship, knocking a half-empty mug off the comms panel. It clattered across the floor, splashing the last of its contents over Marcus's boots.

"Fantastic," he muttered, wiping his heel on the console edge.

Curtis gripped her seat. "I'm just saying — we *could've* parked at orbital altitude and let a shuttle do the rest."

Bunny snorted. "Yeah? And spend the whole return-fuel budget on priority docking fees and permits? Not happening."

The *Theseus* groaned under the strain, its frame flexing as the hull met the brutal pull of crosswinds. The deck trembled — that deep metallic rumble only big ships made when they fought the air itself.

Marcus glanced at the overhead monitors. The storm front ahead churned — roiling clouds lit amber from within by crawling arcs of lightning. Each flash reflected off the consoles, slicing light across their faces.

"Curtis, we still have a clean path through that?"

She scanned the telemetry, fingers moving fast. "Guidance is twitchy, but yeah — there's a window. Ten klicks wide. Minimal shear. Drift even a little and we'll clip the western ridge."

"Bunny — keep us in that window. No paint left behind on *Prox B's* mountains."

"As always — do my best, no promises."

The bridge fell into taut silence as systems compensated for descent. Rain began streaking the forward viewport, thick as tracer fire.

Somewhere deeper in the ship, something clanged — hard.

Marcus narrowed his eyes. "Jason, you picking that up down there? Everything okay?"

Static, then the familiar chaos of the cargo team: clang—whirr—voices.

"We heard it. Probably a strap letting go. I'll check it out after we touch down. No loose cargo — not with this job."

Marcus hesitated. "Copy that. Just… stay sharp."

He couldn't explain it, but something about that noise didn't sit right.

Lightning tore across the sky, strobes flooding the cockpit with violent flashes. The *Theseus* banked hard, aligning with the approach vector. The inertial dampeners whined as they hit denser air. Pressure dropped; Marcus's ears popped. He adjusted his headset with a wince.

A sudden gust slammed the port side, the ship shuddering like a struck tuning fork.

"Hold her steady!" Marcus barked.

Bunny didn't look up. His hands were steady, movements shaped by decades of muscle memory. "She's bucking — but I *got* her."

Ground radar pinged a solid return.

Curtis's voice tightened. "Under one thousand metres! Glide slope stable — seven hundred and dropping!"

Rain hammered the hull in horizontal sheets. The storm raged outside, a living thing.

"You could at least buy me dinner before throwing me around like this," Bunny muttered.

Curtis didn't laugh. Her hands swept over the console, pulling up layered weather scans. "Cloud density spikes below twelve hundred. I don't get it — this planet's had bad storms, but this…" Her brow furrowed as the data jittered. "…this isn't *normal*. These cells are moving like they're being *pushed*."

She looked up. "If I didn't know better, Captain, I'd say this planet's *pissed*. These storm systems aren't natural. Something's stirring them."

The lights flickered; emergency backups pulsed green. Marcus braced behind Bunny's chair. The *Theseus* wasn't built for this kind of atmospheric abuse — she felt like a drunk trying to walk a tightrope.

"950 metres and falling," Curtis called. "We're nearly in the eye. I plotted the cleanest line I could. Rest's yours, Bunny. *No pressure.*"

Marcus hit the intercom. "This is the captain. We're approaching hard deck. If you're not strapped in, do it. *Now.*"

For a moment, the storm seemed to inhale.

Then came the blast.

The alarm screamed.

– PROXIMITY ALERT –
– PROXIMITY ALERT –

A white-blue flash swallowed the ship — soundless and absolute. Marcus's hearing vanished beneath a wall of static and pressure. A plasma strike cracked through the air ahead — a bolt the size of a skyscraper.

The *Theseus* bucked violently. The nose pitched upward like it had hit an invisible wall. Marcus fell backward, catching Bunny's chair by the tips of his fingers — *more luck than skill.*

Maybe they should abort, he thought — but they'd be on the ground in moments. Safe. Paid.

"That was *too close!*" Bunny shouted, voice ragged over the roar. "One of the big ones! I'm increasing speed — we're baking up here!"

"Six hundred metres!" Curtis cried. "We've locked to the beacon — it's guiding us in!"

Marcus glanced over. Curtis was pale, knuckles white around the console. She was space-born — even routine descents made her queasy. *This* was hell.

Another tremor rippled through the deck. The storm inhaled again.

Then — **BOOM.**

A white-hot detonation flared across the bridge like a magnesium flare. Consoles blew in showers of sparks. Alarms cut off mid-wail. Curtis threw an arm over her face as shards of safety glass exploded across her station.

Silence — then a single emergency chirp. Red strobes pulsed across the cockpit, broken by lightning clawing at the clouds outside.

"We've been hit!" Curtis yelled. "Plasma strike skimmed the hull — fried half our grid!"

The ship rolled. Starboard dropped. Nose pitched down. Hard. Gravity punched back in a rush. The landing platform loomed below — *too fast. Far too fast.*

- - -

Marcus lunged for the console, but a violent lurch slammed him sideways. He caromed off the bulkhead, caught the back of Bunny's chair, and hung on. His palm came away wet — coffee or blood — *no time to check.*

The air tasted metallic, as if he were breathing the storm itself. The *Theseus* howled around them — every bolt and beam flexing under strain, the hull groaning like a living thing in pain.

Bunny wrestled the yoke — not to climb, just to fight the nosedive.

"Curtis! What's left — sitrep!"

"Starboard engine's cooked! Right thrusters are down! If we don't slow descent we'll flip — and then probably explode!"

"Options! I'll take anything!"

Bunny didn't look up, forearms straining. "We die fast, or we die *slightly* slower."

"Not helping!" Curtis snapped.

"It's ugly," Bunny ground out, "but if I get the nose level, we dump everything into port engine and thrusters. Overcompensate. Won't slow much — might keep us upright. Still gonna hit hard."

Through the viewport, figures scattered across the pad, sirens washing the tarmac red. Wind howled, the *Theseus* bucking like a wild animal desperate to throw them.

Marcus planted a boot on the console and hauled with Bunny on the stick. Both swore under their breath. Curtis watched the artificial horizon crawl toward level. Close enough. Her hands blurred, rerouting power, bleeding fuel from the dead side to the live.

"Spooling… firing — now!"

Stabilisers roared to life — orange, then blue, then white-hot as she pushed every watt through them. The ship's pitch eased, levelling across both axes. The deck shuddered like something exhaling its last breath.

Another spear of plasma cracked so close Marcus flinched — but it veered at the last instant, rending the sky like the hand of God. He exhaled through his teeth.

"Landing legs — max-impact settings! Now!"

The struts kicked out with seconds to spare. Built for emergencies — but not *this*.

Marcus pressed a hand to his chest, fingers finding the chain where his ring hung. Useless comfort — habit all the same.

Then the *Theseus* hit.

The pad boomed with a bone-deep crack. Steel screamed — like the ship herself was protesting the fall. The port strut, weakened by heat, folded inward and punched through the softened hull. Marcus hit the deck, breath blasted from his lungs.

Harnesses groaned as Bunny and Curtis braced while metal shrieked through the docking ring — until, finally, they ground to a halt.

Silence.

Only the soft crackle of sparking wires. No alarms. No fire. Just the heavy breathing of the living. The air reeked of burnt copper and hot oil, a scent thick enough to taste.

The howl of wind and rain seeped back in. The storm hadn't finished with them, even if gravity had.

"See? No sweat," Marcus croaked from the floor, still wheezing.

Outside, emergency crews swarmed, searching for a way in.

"Ah, hell. They're going to have to cut the hull," he muttered.

"Like a leaf in the wind," Bunny said under his breath.

Marcus let out a breath that was half-laugh, half-groan. "You *wish*."

For a second, humour crept through the exhaustion — a flash of crew banter before the weight returned.

Curtis blinked. "What?"

"Never mind." He winced as he unbuckled. "Pretty sure that landing broke my ass."

Curtis scanned failing panels, then sniffed sharply, face twisting. Her eyes watered; she gagged. "Hull's breached."

Marcus, pushing upright, stared. "How do you know that already?"

She tapped her nose. "Because I can *smell* the coolant — sharp, bitter, like scorched plastic. And it's bleeding into the atmo. Means a pipe's blown somewhere near the starboard bulkhead."

She sagged back into the seat. "We're not going anywhere for a while."

- - -

Hours later, the storm had moved on — tearing across the far side of the planet. It wouldn't circle back for another eight weeks. Marcus hoped he, the crew, and what remained of the *Theseus* would be long gone by then.

Rain still fell in sheets — cold, relentless, soaking the platform until it gleamed slick as oil. The sky had dulled to a heavy grey lid. The air carried a bite of burnt fuel, cold iron, and the faint tang of ozone — a port still exhaling after a fight.

Marcus sat on a crate at the edge of the dock, chewing a stale candy bar with a lukewarm coffee in hand. From here he could see her — and she looked *broken*.

The *Theseus*, usually gleaming with a silver-nitrate finish, now leaned on her crippled side, port strut crumpled into the wing it was meant to support. Hull scorched and blackened. Starboard engine punched through with a hole the size of a dinner table. Gas had vented in a dying hiss until the tanks ran dry.

Marcus's chest sank. It was like watching a friend bleed out.

A limp echoed across the pad. Jason.

"Captain."

Marcus bought a breath with a sip of coffee. "Jason. Sorry I didn't come find you earlier. Got... sidetracked. How's the offload?"

Jason eased onto the crate beside him with a low groan. The movement made him wince. Rain plastered his hair flat, deepening the tired lines in his face. Marcus's eyes drifted down — the brace on Jason's knee was scuffed raw, the metal scratched where it must've slammed against something hard.

"Slow," Jason said. "Emergency crew's pitching in. The hold's a *wreck*." He hesitated. "Rico and Nathan both took hits when we impacted."

Marcus's jaw tightened. "How bad?"

"Rico wasn't strapped in. Got tossed around the lower deck — cracked ribs, concussion. He'll live." Jason rubbed at his knee again, grimacing. "Nathan... not so lucky. Some of the crates snapped loose and pinned him against the bulkhead by his leg. They pulled him out, but..." He trailed off. "They don't know if they can save it."

Marcus swore under his breath.

"They've both been lifted to South Quarter Med. Medivac says they're stable. Out for a few hours."

Marcus nodded faintly, staring past the dock. A lift descended in the rain, poncho-wrapped dockhands rolling freight into the terminal.

Jason gave a tired smirk. "Should've taken the long way round, huh?"

Marcus said nothing. Watched the crates vanish into the haze.

Jason pushed himself upright with a grunt. "Talk to the dockmaster yet? Got a number on repairs?"

Marcus drained the last of his coffee — bitter, cold. "Not yet. Saw him out there though. Red pen in his hand."

Jason winced. "Shit. That's never good."

He nodded toward the terminal. Bunny and Curtis were bundled in emergency ponchos near the arrivals lounge, giving lazy waves.

"I'm joining them. Need a drink."

Marcus nodded again, eyes still on the ship. "I'll be along."

Jason splashed off through the puddles, limping.

Marcus stayed where he was. Alone. Just him and what was left of the *Theseus*.

They *should've* been early. Should've been lining up for a bonus.

Instead: two injured crew, a wrecked ship, and a repair bill waiting to crater his payout.

He watched rain run down the ship's flank, washing soot into the puddles. The *Theseus* looked smaller now — like the air had been taken out of her.

Should've kept it slow and steady, he thought. *Should've listened to my own damn advice.*

- - -

Marcus crouched beneath the *Theseus's* port strut, flashlight in hand, tracing the scorched seam where heat had melted plating into twisted folds. Every sound was hiss and patter — water meeting metal, the ship's quiet groan of pain.

He shifted, boots splashing through the thin sheet of rain pooled across the dock.

Then — a voice, smooth as oil.

"Mister Carpenter?"

Marcus froze. With this much standing water, he should have heard footsteps long before anyone reached him.

He turned.

A man stood a few paces away, immaculate in a grey three-piece suit, a black umbrella balanced with effortless poise. Rain rolled from it in glassy sheets. Against the dock's palette of rust and steel, the man's skin looked almost staged — warm tan, untouched. His smile was perfect, too white. His eyes unblinking.

One pale blue.

The other, obsidian-dark and depthless — *like a shark's.*

His gaze dipped briefly to Marcus's chest, lingering a half-heartbeat — as if noting something beneath the jacket, or confirming something he already knew.

Marcus stiffened. "Captain."

"I beg your pardon, sir. Captain Marcus Carpenter."

The man inclined his head — a gesture poised precisely between grace and mockery.

Marcus narrowed his eyes. "Something I can help you with, Mister…?"

With fluid precision, the stranger reached into his jacket and produced a business card. He didn't even glance at the pocket.

"Dekard," he said smoothly. "Morningstar Photonics. Perhaps you've heard of us."

He walked past Marcus without waiting for a reply, gaze drifting to the ruined flank of the ship. His voice carried like theatre — every word deliberate, his rhythm too controlled to be natural.

"I was sitting to breakfast, hoping to enjoy the morning — dreadful weather, wouldn't you say? — when all the alarms began shrieking.

"For a moment I feared invasion. Then I saw your ship descend."

His head tipped, almost tenderly. "With such an unfortunate… *splat.*"

He pivoted back, smile fixed.

"But I must commend you, Captain. To bring her down in that storm and suffer no loss of life — it requires either remarkable skill or… exceptional fortune."

Marcus scoffed. "Hardly a scratch, Mr. Dekard. Crew's banged up, ship's half-dead. If you're calling that fortune, we burned through all of it."

Dekard's gaze lingered on the scorched hull. He studied it in silence, as if committing each scar to memory. Then, softly:

"The nature of luck… is fluid. From good, to ill, and back again — all within a single heartbeat."

The cadence was hypnotic. Soothing. *Rehearsed.*

He paused — just slightly too long — selecting his next words with precision.

He gestured toward the damage. "Have you spoken with the dockmaster? Has he... given you his tally?"

Marcus frowned. The way Dekard stressed his words made him bristle — too precise, like bait hidden in every sentence.

"Not yet. Soon. With luck, payout plus bonus covers it."

Dekard let the silence stretch, eyes half-lidded.

"And if, for some reason, it does not... do you possess alternative resources that might... hasten the repair?"

Marcus's voice hardened. "How I pay isn't your concern."

Dekard bowed his head a fraction.

"Forgive me, Captain. I do not wish to pry. Only... to offer.

"My employers require a delivery. Discreet. If you provide your ship and your services, we can, in return, offer our full repair support. She could be spaceworthy again within ten days — perhaps even... improved."

Marcus's stomach knotted. "And the cargo?"

Dekard's smile didn't falter — but something in it tightened.

"That... I cannot disclose. You and your crew would sign nondisclosure agreements. Navigation data would be cleansed. Delivery confirmed, repairs covered, and a substantial payment on top. With incentive for early arrival."

He extended a hand. Perfectly still. Waiting.

Marcus stared at it like it was a sprung trap. "Secret cargo. NDAs. No nav record. Sounds highly illegal. My answer's no. Too high risk for me — and for my crew."

Dekard lowered the hand with mechanical calm.

"I respect your candour, Captain Carpenter. Should you reconsider, I will be at the Nine Seasons Hotel. The next three nights."

He turned away. Rain sheeted off his umbrella, his stride unhurried.

He didn't flinch at puddles or wind. Dockhands stepped aside without a word as he passed.

Marcus exhaled slowly, muscles uncoiling.

He raised a hand toward the approaching dockmaster.

Dodged a bullet, he thought. *But is another one waiting in the chamber?*

Chapter Four

A Dockmaster's office always smelled the same — cheap alcohol, synthetic lemon cleaner, sometimes an unclean fish tank or a molted animal head on the wall.

Condensation streaked down the inside of the observation window, blurring the rain outside into a smear of dull grey. Marcus sat across from a man who looked like he'd been stationed here since the port was built. His uniform strained at the waist, the fabric polished smooth from years of leaning on the counter.

"Repairs like that won't come cheap," the Dockmaster said, tapping the datapad with a stubby finger. "That port strut alone's a replacement job. We don't weld patches here. You're looking at six weeks and a small fortune."

Marcus rubbed his temples. "We don't have six weeks."

The Dockmaster shrugged. "Then maybe you shouldn't have tried landing through a lightning storm. You got lucky, Captain. Ship's mostly intact, your crew's alive. Could've gone a hell of a lot worse."

Lucky's not the word I'd use.

The Dockmaster slid the datapad across the counter. The total flickered in angry red numerals. "You'll need to sign the incident report. We'll log it as mechanical failure — cheaper for the insurance. Do yourself a favour, Captain — next time, take the long way round."

Marcus didn't reach for the stylus. The Dockmaster studied him, then leaned back with a sigh.

"Look, I get it. Credits don't stretch like they used to. You could always take out a loan. Keep the bird in orbit until you're flush again."

Marcus said nothing. His jaw flexed.

"Or…" The Dockmaster's tone softened, almost friendly. "We could work something out. You've got a crew — I've got more jobs than hands. We tarp your ship, keep her out of the weather. You and your people pull shifts till the parts arrive. Won't make you rich, but you'd keep her."

Marcus looked up, and for a moment the room felt smaller. *Trapped.* "And how long's that take?"

Another helpless shrug. "A couple extra weeks. Maybe more — depends on supply chain." He smiled like it was a kindness. "Better than watching her rot, Captain."

Marcus signed the report with a single, hard press of the stylus and slid the pad back across the counter. "I'll think about it."

He stood. The chair scraped the floor. He didn't say another word.

- - -

Marcus stepped out of the office, the door hissing shut behind him. The rain had worsened — sharp, needling drops that pinged against the metal walkway and the ruined hull of *Theseus*. Each impact made her sound older, hollower. She was hurting. And she wasn't quiet about it.

He pulled his jacket tight, the fabric clinging to his arms. Crossing the platform, he glanced back once. Through the rain-streaked glass of the dockmaster's window, a shape lingered — the man, can in hand, watching him. A few seconds passed before the dockmaster finally turned away, disappearing deeper into the office and leaving Marcus alone with the storm and the faint echo of dripping water.

He exhaled, slow and tired, and kept walking. The arrival-lounge lights glowed ahead through the haze.

Maybe he'd feel better after a hot shower, a plate of real food, and a warm bed under steady gravity.

Just before stepping into the airlock, he slowed beside a faded comm booth marked:

SPACECOM — FOR PUBLIC USE

His fingers rose to the chain around his neck, thumb brushing the wedding band that hung there. The scar on his hand was still visible — a pale ring where the metal once sat. The decompression accident had nearly cost him the finger; the ring had acted like a tourniquet, saving it at its own expense.

Love was a shield.

I should call her, he thought.

It had been a brutal few hours. Maybe her voice would help. Maybe not.

Then came the doubts — the questions she'd ask. Why he'd rushed the job. Why he'd risked the crew. What the repairs would cost. Arguments about money they didn't have.

He didn't want to fight. Not now. Not like this.

Marcus let his hand fall from the chain, wiped his face clean of rain, and stepped inside the lounge.

- - -

The arrival lounge, like the crew of the *Theseus*, felt tired — and maybe a little broken.

In its heyday, Proxima B had been one of the busiest transport ports in the galaxy. Cargo freighters, passenger liners, even luxury cruise ships — all of them had passed through these doors.

That was then.

Now, only faint glimmers of its old grandeur remained: worn patches in the carpet, chipped wood panels along the bar, mismatched bulbs flickering across an oversized chandelier. Depending on where you sat, your choice of air was either dusty or damp — the rain had made sure of that.

Bunny walked with slow, deliberate steps. *Theseus* had bruised his backside, but Bunny was determined to make sure the drinks went down easier. The low hum of the lighting only made the lounge feel emptier — a handful of patrons scattered across the vast room. Overhead, a ceiling fan whined like it hadn't worked properly in years.

He set the tray down and eased himself onto a cushion with a quiet groan, lowering himself slower than the ship had landed.

Curtis was hunched over a laminated menu that looked like it hadn't been updated in a decade.

Jason wrung out his knee brace with a wad of tissues. "I want to order the chicken — but do I *want* to know where they keep them?"

"It won't be real chicken," Curtis said. "Probably dried protein with flavour drops. The expiry lasts longer than most marriages."

"Maybe not, then," Jason muttered.

Bunny slid a drink in front of each of them. The glasses glowed faintly, casting a cool blue light across their tired faces.

Curtis had already downed hers before the others even reacted. She set the empty glass down just as Jason picked his up and frowned.

"Bunny, I'm *not* drinking that," Jason said, pushing the glass away. The glowing liquid sloshed ominously inside.

"My man," Bunny replied with mock offence, "Arkas gin. Brewed in-system, distilled on the moon, chilled to zero degrees no matter the room temp. Stuff practically defies physics."

He held up his own glass to give it a swirl. "Ain't cheap, either. But we almost died today — so I'd call that cause for celebration."

"It glows," Jason muttered. "Things that glow should not go in your mouth."

Curtis raised her empty glass.

"To *Theseus*. What doesn't kill us—"

Bunny smirked. "Still might."

Curtis ignored him and finished, "—makes us more traumatised."

The three clinked glasses. Two of them drank. Curtis just raised hers again in silent solidarity.

Then came the pain.

"Oww," she groaned, clutching her forehead. "Oh my god, is that *brain freeze*? Who invents a drink that cold?"

Bunny chuckled, swirling the remnants of his shot. "Space magic and solar radiation. Don't question brilliance."

Jason rubbed his temple. "If my brain feels like this *now*, I don't want to know what tomorrow feels like."

A service droid trundled over and placed another round of drinks on the table — four fresh glasses. Bunny gave it a respectful nod.

Curtis looked up from her drink and spotted movement by the door. "Captain," she called, waving him over. "Over here!"

Curtis stood, then immediately regretted it as dizziness swept over her. Bunny caught her arm to steady her.

Marcus unzipped his soaked jacket and tossed it onto a chair. Water beaded on the table; his hands shook slightly, whether from the cold or something heavier.

"Shit," Jason muttered. "This isn't going to be good."

Marcus reached for one of the fresh drinks without asking.

"Careful, Captain. It's got a—" Jason began, then cut himself off as Marcus tossed it back in one motion.

He coughed, hand pressed to his chest. "Still cold as hell. Never going to get used to that taste."

Curtis shrugged and took another. As Marcus caught his breath, she knocked back her second shot — while Bunny and Jason were still nursing their first. They shared a glance that said: *she isn't stopping at two.*

Marcus pulled a crumpled document from his pocket and shook it open.

"How bad?" Bunny asked.

Marcus scanned the figures. "Not gonna sugar-coat it. That plasma strike knocked us sideways. But… we've got options."

Curtis leaned forward. "Let's hear 'em."

"Option A — we order new parts. 3D-assembled, straight from the manufacturer. Fastest turnaround, but…" He gave a dry laugh. "Not even close to our budget. Even if we pooled everything together, we wouldn't make the down payment."

Jason groaned. "Knew there'd be a *but.*"

"Option B," Marcus said. "We tarp the ship while second-hand parts are ordered in. The dockmaster's agreed to let us work off the difference, but…"

"But," Bunny finished, "the parts won't arrive in time to beat the next storm."

Marcus nodded. "Yeah. Best case, we're looking at twelve weeks — maybe more if the supply chain's backed up."

Curtis slumped back. "I don't want to live planet-side for three months. The gravity alone's gonna murder my back."

Jason added, "And the dockmaster isn't paying premium wages. We'll barely make a dent."

Marcus rubbed his jaw, weighing his next words. "There is… an Option C."

Curtis raised an eyebrow. "Option C?"

"I've been approached," Marcus said carefully. "About another offer."

Bunny leaned back with a scoff. "Typical corp behaviour. You can't walk ten feet near a docking pad without some rep waiting to pounce. Which one this time?"

Marcus reached into his pocket and produced the business card, the matte surface catching the light in muted silver. "Morningstar Photonics."

Jason groaned. Curtis looked up sharply.

"Morningstar?" she said. "Spacers say they're into all sorts of spooky shit — off-the-books stuff. Why else are they so rich when *no one* even knows what they do?"

She leaned in to Jason, lowering her voice. "I heard their CEO's an alien."

Jason and Bunny both raised a hand at the same time — half amused, half trying to stop her before she spiralled.

Curtis muttered, "It's what I heard."

Bunny smirked. "We've been out to the edge of the galaxy and back. No aliens — just bad business deals and worse people."

Marcus nodded. "They're offering fast repairs. Upgrades. Off-world… quicker than the other two choices."

Jason frowned. "So what do they want? Cargo? Why not use their own ships?"

Marcus looked down at his empty glass. "I haven't asked… yet. They might share more once we agree."

Silence pressed in. Only the ceiling fan hummed.

"I get it," Marcus said finally. "No one likes corp jobs. But this seems to be the best of a *bad* situation." The phrase twisted in his chest — a situation that should never have happened.

None of them looked convinced, and Marcus couldn't blame them. Even *lies* felt heavy in this gravity.

He thumbed the business card again — wrong texture, wrong weight — not quite plastic, not quite paper. It unsettled him.

He slipped it back into his pocket and exhaled through his nose.

Wandering over to the empty chair, he picked up his jacket. "Okay. It's settled. I'll contact the rep, give him our terms."

Jason raised a hand. "Cargo manifest, Captain. Don't forget to ask."

Marcus nodded. "Yeah. Got it."

As he walked away, Curtis's voice followed. "Morningstar spend all their time in the outer-rim systems — how is that not suspicious?"

Bunny's laugh echoed softly. Jason added, "You're on soft drinks next round."

Marcus slipped his arms into the jacket. It felt heavy — and not just from the rain. The fabric clung like a weight.

It bothered him how easy it had been to bend the truth.

But it was an easy job. One quick run. Fast money.

What could go wrong?

Chapter Five

The flight deck was a chaos of blueprints and schematics — pages taped to bulkheads, draped across consoles, even pinned beneath half-empty mugs. Every surface carried stains: circles of cold coffee, graphite smears, and oily fingerprints worn into the paper from years of handling.

Marcus crouched by the main console, tracing the faded outline of *Barge Delta-Six-One* with his thumb. Two large sheets dominated the desk — one a cutaway of the deck layout, the other a snarl of electrical wiring that looked more like a nervous system than a power grid. He exhaled slowly, the air thick with old metal and recycled dust.

He'd only found the schematics after hearing something flap inside an air vent above his bunk — a sound too deliberate to ignore. Curiosity had led him here, chasing ghosts through wiring diagrams.

The ship was wired as one continuous loop — no compartment isolation, no safety redundancies. Every deck bled into the next, a single surge away from blackout. *No wonder she creaks like a coffin,* he muttered. *They don't build 'em this way anymore.*

He brushed aside a stack of crumpled notes, uncovering a manufacturer's stamp half-erased by age:

LAUNCH DATE: 31 OCT 2163.

He smirked. "Of course. Built on Halloween."

Almost ninety years to the day. *No wonder she sounded tired.*

Above the faded line that once bore a registry number, the name *Charon* had been added in pencil — shaky, uncertain handwriting that looked scrawled by a mechanic rather than stamped by a company. Marcus stared at it for a moment, then lifted his hand and drew a mock blessing in the air. "I name thy vessel," he murmured, tone halfway between a joke and a prayer.

A low groan rippled through the hull — the ship shifting as if it didn't appreciate the joke.

It had been three days since *Charon* passed the second Nav Lantern, with another three weeks until the next. If there was ever a feeling of limbo, *this* was it. The ship drifted through eternal blackness, stretching in every direction. Apart from the brief, comforting fly-by of a beacon — each one monitored as it approached and vanished — there was nothing. No signals. No stars.

Beyond the sensor range of the next lantern, the void swallowed everything.

With nothing to see and nothing going on out there, Marcus focused inward.

At some point, the internal power core had been replaced — swapped for something smaller, probably cheaper. *Figures.* That would explain why so many systems were sluggish or unresponsive.

Since the ship would be drifting under its own inertia for most of the journey, he figured he could shut down the main engine entirely, relying on thrusters instead. Might free up enough juice to boost lighting or re-enable minor systems.

Still, the diagrams were giving him a headache — scribbled notes and faded pencil instructions from gods-knew-when. He had just enough mechanical instinct to get by, but rewiring wasn't exactly his strength.

He remembered teasing Curtis whenever she was elbow-deep in a control panel, wires coiled around her like vines. He should've paid more attention. *Too late for that now.*

He stayed there a while, eyes fixed on the plans as if the answers might suddenly reveal themselves. The ship gave a faint, uneven hum underfoot — the sound of old circuitry breathing in its sleep.

Without looking away, Marcus reached across the console, fingers brushing through scattered tools until they found the cold edge of his comms unit. He thumbed the surface twice before lifting it, the familiar weight settling into his palm.

"Log entry, personal. Currently... I dunno, week six into the flight plan? I think."

"I've been trying to get power to this console in the back of the flight deck — the only one that isn't active for whatever reason. It's

taken a couple of attempts, bypassing a few circuit breakers, but I think it's ready to come online."

He paused the recorder and leaned over the spread of blueprints. Graphite scratches whispered through the silence as he traced a new line between two faded connection points. The wiring diagram made less sense the longer he stared at it — half the junctions didn't match the ship's current layout. The pencil's worn eraser left pale streaks as he redrew a circuit, connecting what he *hoped* was the right breaker feed.

Marcus sat back, tapping the pencil against his knuckles, then thumbed the recorder on again.

"I just hope it's a quality-of-life upgrade and not, I don't know… a hidden airlock that decides to blow me out into space."

He leaned over for one final adjustment, tightening a loose conduit at the base of the console. Sparks flickered — a sharp crack of static that made him flinch.

"Should've checked for a spacesuit before I left Titan. Doubt they'd have thrown one in for free.

"End log."

He'd sketched out a sequence on a scrap of paper — a simple plan to shut down non-essentials and reroute power to the dormant console. Following his own notes, one system at a time, the lights grew brighter, the ventilation eased to a quieter hum. The air tasted a little less coppery, though it still carried that tang of recycled ghosts.

He checked the page again, tracing the last step with a finger. Everything looked right.

His hand hovered over the final switch. A breath. Then—click.

Instant black.

No sparks. No warning. Just the ship dissolving into silence. No lights. No hum. No heartbeat of machinery — only the crushing stillness of a vessel adrift between stars.

Marcus didn't move. The only glow in all that darkness came from the small torch clamped between his teeth — its jittering beam matching each unsteady breath.

Then came a hiss. The pressure door to Deck Two unlocking.

Another hiss — Deck Three.

Cold air drifted upward like fog, curling through the ladder shafts. This chill was different — sharp enough to stab behind his eyes. For a moment, his thoughts blurred. *Brain-freeze. Harder.* Then it ebbed, leaving him blinking into the dark.

Still no power. No hum. Just breathless quiet — and the soft whisper of air rising from below, free now that the doors hung open.

He didn't know how long he sat there. Minutes. Hours. *Too long.*

Then, faintly, the hum of life crawled back. The auxiliary console at the rear of the deck flickered first — the one tied to the cargo cameras. A soft green pulse blinked awake. Others followed, sluggish and reluctant. The lights were last, returning in a dull, sickly glow that somehow made the shadows thicker.

Finally, the new console came online. Its screen glowed pale, the keyboard lighting beneath his hand.

One word waited on the display:

STANDBY

He rose, stretching the stiffness from his legs. As he passed the ladderwell, he noticed the air filters were running smoother now — clearer, almost *too* clean. Yet with the pressure doors open, the echoed airflow spiralled through the shaft like a long, low exhale.

Marcus stopped at the auxiliary console, leaning closer to the monitor. The grainy feed from the cargo hold blinked, steadied. Nothing seemed out of place. The tarp was still drawn tight, shadows unmoving.

He frowned and raised a finger, counting under his breath.

"One... two. Three. Four... five."

He rubbed his eyes, waited, then counted again. Slowly this time.

Five.

A dull ache bloomed behind his temple as he stared at the screen.

Five. *Not six.*

His stomach went cold. The straps. He blinked hard.

One was missing.

Not loosened. Not dangling. Just… gone.

He hesitated before checking the feed again, an irrational dread curling through his gut. But he had to know.

Five. He counted again, whispering the numbers like a half-forgotten prayer.

Five.

A pulse throbbed behind his eye. The harder he stared, the worse it got — like the image itself was pressing back.

Had it always been five?

Or had something changed while the power was out?

He swallowed hard, dragging his gaze away from the screen. He should've checked more carefully.

"Log entry, personal. No, wait — shit, I meant to set it to repair log. File this under repair."

He walked away from the auxiliary console, the soft hum still thrumming behind him. Halfway across the deck he glanced over his shoulder — just once — as if expecting the screen to have changed in his absence.

It hadn't.

"I've managed to get a few more systems active without tripping the main power again. Fingers crossed that was a one-off incident. Scared the hell out of me — hearing all those deck doors open like that. I'm telling myself it was an emergency failsafe, some old safety measure to stop people getting trapped."

He stopped by the ladderwell, peering down into the shaft. Pitch black. The air rising up cool and steady.

"Still… the way that cold rolled in… it didn't feel mechanical. Felt like *something else* was opening them."

He exhaled, shook his head.

"Anyway… repair log."

Crossing to the new console, Marcus brushed a layer of dust off the keys and tapped a few random buttons. The screen flickered, text stuttering across it before freezing again.

"Fire suppression's active, but I don't trust it. No clue when the O_2 tanks were last replaced."

He leaned closer to another faint display.

"Internal sensors are online too, but they're primitive — early generation stuff. Just a single red light on the panel to indicate motion. Not a full readout. Just… *motion*."

He paused, glancing up at the light strip over his head.

"Example: I'm on the flight deck now — red light's glowing here. Simple. Crude. There are camera options linked to it, but I haven't worked those out yet."

He rubbed the back of his neck.

"Shipwide audio — pointless if it's just me talking to myself. Still, I've got nothing but time. By the time I reach my destination, everything should—"

Beep.
Beep.
Beep.

The sound cut through the cabin like a knife.

– PROXIMITY ALERT –

He hit pause and stood, heart already hammering against his ribs. The silence felt thicker now — like the air itself was *listening*.

Crossing the flight deck, he slid into the pilot's chair and woke the nav console.

Not a single blip since entering the Veil. And now this?

"Shit," he whispered. "Pirates? Mercs? Another smuggler running dark?"

He flicked the system from passive to active navigation. The calm field of star charts vanished, replaced by a sweeping green radar arc. The *Charon* pulsed at its centre — a lone heartbeat in the dark.

−SEARCHING: PLEASE WAIT−

The scanner arm rotated in slow, patient sweeps, each pass accompanied by a faint mechanical whine that echoed off the glass.

"Too soon for another Nav Lantern," he muttered.

– APPROACHING OBJECT : UNKNOWN –
– BEARING : 01X 06Y –
– DISTANCE : 6 KM –

He held his breath. Whatever it was, it wasn't evading. It wasn't accelerating.

It just floated — *waiting*. Watching?

Five kilometres.

Still too far to trigger the floodlights. He hovered over the control, thumb trembling. If he lit up, he'd see it.

But it would *see him too.*

Marcus strapped himself in, the belts creaking as he tightened them. His fingers moved on instinct, flipping switches to bring the main engines online. The *Charon* rumbled beneath him — a weak growl, tired, like an old dog dragged from sleep.

If he had to run, he wasn't sure how far she'd get. But he'd have to try.

The ship creaked as he settled back — old leather, old bolts — a sound that felt too human for metal.

With one final breath, he threw the switch.

The *Charon* became a beacon. The forward beams cut through the dark like knives — sharp, sterile, endless.

Nothing. Only black.

Were the sensors faulty?

– APPROACHING OBJECT : UNKNOWN –
– BEARING : 01X 03Y –
– DISTANCE : 3 KM –

Sweat crawled down his face. His throat felt tight, dry.

"What the hell is going on?"

Then—

A flicker.

A hairline shimmer in the light.

Something small.

A lost probe? Debris? It drifted on a slow spin, turning lazily as it grew larger on approach.

– APPROACHING OBJECT : UNKNOWN –
– BEARING : 01X 00Y –
– DISTANCE : 20 M –

He tapped the screen. No response. The blip blinked out — then reappeared. Closer.

He leaned forward, chest tightening. *Come on… come on…*

The console flickered — and the signal vanished.

A glitch. Interference. *Maybe.*

Then silence. That *heavy*, listening kind of silence.

Marcus stayed frozen, pulse hammering in his ears.

And then — something drifted into view.

From above the cockpit window, slow as a falling leaf.

For a heartbeat, his brain refused to make sense of it. Just a shape. Pale. Turning.

Then his muscles locked. Shoulders tensed. Breath caught halfway to a gasp — the kind of reflex you feel when something leaps at you from the dark.

He didn't scream — but every nerve *begged* to.

It was a body.

It drifted closer, rotating slowly in the floodlight's beam.

The suit was ancient — a design Marcus didn't recognise, its insignia long eroded. Most of it was shredded down one side, as though the wearer had stood too close to an explosion. Torn plating and fabric hung in ragged streamers, waving faintly in the weightless dark.

The exposed skin had hardened from years of exposure — leathery, brittle, speckled with faint burns from cosmic dust and radiation.

There was an indentation on the side of the head — a deep concave mark far too clean for decay. An impact wound.

The skull beneath had collapsed inward, like someone had pressed a thumb into wet clay.

No helmet.

The face was shrivelled, lips drawn back in a silent snarl. The mouth hung open — *frozen mid-breath.*

The eyes were gone, leaving only black sockets that drank in the light.

It drifted head-first, turning end over end as it crossed the cockpit glass. Arms stiff. Fingers curled. Legs hanging loose.

A puppet scorched, broken… left to wander the void.

Thunk.

Its forehead struck the glass. Marcus flinched — *again.*

The body scraped along the hull with a dull dragging thud… another… then nothing.

His hands fumbled with the harness. The buckle jammed twice before releasing with a sharp snap. He shoved himself out of the chair, almost tripping as his boots hit the deck.

He was already moving, boots hammering as he sprinted for the ladder. He dropped to Deck Three, cold air rising to meet him like a warning.

He remembered standing here days ago, watching the second *Nav Lantern* drift past. Its orange glow had felt like a mercy back then — something *human* in the dark. Now, there was only black.

He reached the observation window and wiped condensation from the glass with his sleeve. The surface burned under his skin, dry-ice cold.

Nothing.

Then — movement.

It rotated back into view.

The body floated backward, head level, arms lifted — as if trying to ward something off.

Thunk.

The face hit the glass hard. Marcus flinched again.

When it drifted away, a faint frost-smear lingered — as if the viewport itself had remembered the touch.

He staggered back. The eyes — or what was left of them — were empty sockets, lidless, staring *straight through him.*

The mouth gaped wide, caught mid-breath. The skin was torn and stretched, the suit in ribbons, revealing glimpses of grey, brittle flesh.

The body didn't spin.

It just drifted. Slowly. Backward.

As if watching him.

Marcus stood frozen, pulse hammering in his ears.

The ship creaked — metal settling in the cold.

Somewhere below, the air system gave a long, uneven sigh through the ladderwell.

He couldn't move. He didn't want to look away — as if turning his back would *invite* something worse.

"How the hell did you get out here?" he whispered.

He stood there a long time. His reflection stared back — faint, ghost-like in the glass.

Finally, he turned. Looked down through the grating toward the cargo hold.

One. Two. Three. Four. Five.

No sixth.

And somehow… *that* unnerved him more than the corpse.

Chapter Six

Marcus leaned against the gantry on Deck Three, coffee in hand, staring at the faint smudge on the observation window. He couldn't stop thinking about the body.

Who were they? How had they made it this far into the *Veil*?

This was the deepest stretch of cold black — no accidents, no drifters. At least, there *shouldn't* be.

He frowned. How long had he been standing here? He couldn't even remember coming down. Steam curled from the mug, warming his fingers.

That's odd. When did the water heaters start working?

He breathed out, watching the vapour mingle with the steam. *I should head back up. Back to the flight deck.*

Then — rustling.

He straightened slowly, turning toward the ladder. The lights below glowed dim, brittle blue. He couldn't see anything clearly, but the sound persisted — faint and muffled, like movement beneath the tarp.

Against better judgement, he descended.

Halfway down, he paused. Something tapped on the glass above. He looked up toward the window. Just the smudge.

He shifted his grip. Marcus had started carrying a knife again — tucked into his belt. His version of a security blanket.

The chill thickened as his boots touched the cargo deck. His breath puffed visibly. The air smelled of rust and something sharp — a dry metallic bite that caught his throat.

"Hello?" His voice sounded small. *"I'm armed. I will use it. Come out now!"*

Torch in one hand, he reached for the knife. He crept between the crates, light sweeping shadows from corner to corner.

Rustling again — quieter. *Deliberate.*

He scanned the cargo. Counted the straps. One. Two. Three. Four—

He froze.

Not five.

A strap lay unfastened, coiled on the floor like a shed snake's skin. A section of tarp hung loose, stirring faintly.

He crouched, slipped the strap through his fingers. The ratchet clinked softly.

Rustling again.

The tarp shifted.

He leaned in. Lifted a corner — nothing.

He lifted more. Thought he heard a fan starting up.

Then — a bone-deep, marrow-deadening cold.

And then—

A hand.

It shot out fast, skeletal and frost-burned, skin stretched too tight. One finger bent the wrong way.

It clamped onto his face.

Marcus gasped. Torch and knife clattered to the floor.

The hand crushed his cheekbones, muffling his scream, dragging him down. Nails scraped metal. The tarp yawned open like a mouth.

The knife glinted just out of reach.

Panic surged—

Then — darkness.

A tangle of crossed wires hung inches above his face. His hands clawed at his cheeks — and found only skin.

He was lying on the bunkroom floor. Soaked in sweat.

A dream. Please let it be a dream.

He curled into a ball, rocking slightly. *There's nothing there,* he whispered. *Just a dream. Just a nightmare.*

But the dread didn't fade — because he remembered the straps.

He pushed himself up, lungs tight, and bolted from the bunkroom — barefoot, wearing only a T-shirt and sleep-creased bottoms.

The corridor lights smeared past in a dizzy blur as he sprinted to the ladderwell. The rungs bit into his soles, the cold grating leaving sharp imprints, but he didn't stop.

He burst onto the flight deck, lunging for the console. His breath came ragged.

He checked the feed.

One. Two. Three. Four. Five.

Just five.

His legs gave out. He collapsed into the pilot's chair and wept — silent, broken sobs born more of exhaustion than fear.

- - -

Later, in the galley, with shaking hands, he poured a second cup of cold coffee and hit record.

"Log entry, personal. My God, what a nightmare. I've never had one that vivid. It's been days since I saw the body, and I still can't shake it. I lie in my bunk and it's all I think about. Who it was. Why it was there. Like it's still out there — *watching me.*
 I feel frayed. Thin. I should've brought someone.
 Bunny… maybe Jason…"

He paused, the thought hanging for a moment before his voice dropped to a murmur.

"No… no, that wouldn't have worked."

He rubbed his face, shaking it off.

"Solo run for the pay. Dumb move."

He shifted in the chair, bringing one foot up to rest on his knee. The sole was marked with the sharp pattern of the grating, faint red lines edged with flakes of rust. He brushed them away absently, muttering under his breath.

The coffee sat untouched. Cold.

He stood, stretched aching shoulders, and crossed to the sink. The tap sputtered before the water came — thin and metallic, like everything else on this ship. He washed the rust from his hands, drying them on his shirt.

When he turned back—

There.

In the far corner of the galley.

A footlocker.

Tucked beneath the counter, half hidden by shadow.

Had that always been there?

He stepped over, frowning. How had he missed it? He'd cleared this galley twice.

He lifted the footlocker onto the table. Padlocked. Not heavy.

"Now — who did you belong to?" he muttered.

He held the padlock, running his thumb over the cold metal. Smooth, worn by years of use. He gave it a light tug — solid. Still, something about it felt... *wrong*.

A faint scratch behind him.

Marcus froze. Breath caught. Muscles tensed, ready to bolt or fight.

He listened to the ship's breathing — the faint hiss of air through the vents. Probably nothing. Still, his pulse refused to slow.

He glanced at the recorder on the counter — still blinking red.

"Right," he muttered, switching it off. The click echoed louder than it should have.

If it belonged to the last pilot, why hadn't they taken it? The lock looked old — easy enough to break with the right tool.

He turned the box over once, twice, searching for a name, a sticker, *something*. Nothing. Just scuffs, a faint dried smear in the metal, and a pencilled serial number worn almost smooth.

He sat back, hand resting on the lid. For a moment he imagined cracking it open and hearing footsteps pounding down the corridor — the previous owner bursting in, wild-eyed.

That's mine!

The thought made him flinch before he caught himself, exhaling a shaky breath.

He gave the lid one last look, pushed the box aside, and stood.

"Later," he murmured. "Not now."

- - -

In the deep of space, the orange glow of the Nav Lantern felt like a lonely heartbeat. Its slow rotation washed the hull — warm amber bleeding into bruised red.

For a moment, the *Charon* came alive in colour, a stark contrast to the cold settled in her bones.

For once, Marcus let himself breathe. He slouched in the pilot's chair, boots up, eyes half-closed as the light pulsed across the flight deck.

"You're just a big black spot, aren't you?" he muttered, glancing at the cargo feed.

The tarp drank in the light like a void. Everything else glowed — except the cargo itself, shadowed, refusing illumination.

BZZT.

He blinked. Nothing.

BZZT. BZZT!

Marcus sat upright, scanning the console. Nothing out of place. He checked the monitors left, then right, then rotated the chair toward the rear of the deck.

The emergency sensor grid on the secondary console — the newest system on the ship — pulsed faintly red. Deck Four. The cargo hold.

"What the hell now?" he muttered.

He rubbed his palms together, trying to ground himself, the skin squeaking in the cold air.

He pulled open the access panel. The smell hit first — burnt dust and plastic, sharp and acrid — but everything *looked* intact. Dust clung thick across the wiring, like no one had touched it in years.

He closed the panel with a dull snap, folding his arms, one hand rising to his face as he thought. The red light flickered again, steady as a heartbeat — *daring* him to move.

Marcus reached behind his hip, unsheathing the knife part-way. The blade caught the lantern's fading glow — still sharp. He pushed it back into the scabbard and clipped it at the small of his back.

Before heading for the ladderwell, he crossed to the pilot's console. His hand hovered over the controls, then dropped to the comms unit beside them. He picked it up, weighing it once before pocketing it.

He turned back to the camera feed. The cargo sat under its tarp, still and silent.

Five straps.

Then — a flicker.

He leaned closer, thumb brushing the comm unit's record switch.

"Log entry, note to self: you've been to prison. You've seen worse. ***Stop being a coward.***"

He stared at the screen a moment longer, eyes fixed on the faint shimmer of static.

"Yeah," he murmured, voice low. "*Worse.*"

He shut it off.

And went down.

- - -

The ladder groaned beneath his boots as he descended. Deck Three slid past — the smudge on the observation glass still clinging like a bruise he couldn't scrub away. He muttered a curse under his breath that he didn't have a sponge and a spacesuit, as if that could exorcise it.

At the base of the shaft, he paused. Drew the knife. The lantern's slow rotation leaked through the hull plating, breathing warm light in and out like the pulse of something alive. He timed his first step with its rhythm and moved forward.

The hold stretched out before him — vast, empty, too still. Every creak of metal felt amplified, every breath *too* loud. Shadows stretched unnaturally long with each sweep of amber glow, retreating and advancing with every turn of the lantern.

Three slow passes across the deck. Nothing.

Then he saw it — a single flicker in the far corner. Not movement. A dying sensor.

He approached carefully, torch beam jittering across the crates. The sensor mount had corroded through, the small unit hanging by a single thread of wire. Its red eye blinked weakly, spasming like it didn't know it was already dead.

Marcus grabbed the wire and yanked it free. Sparks spat once, briefly lighting his face, before the glow died. He dropped the sensor and stamped on it — once, twice, a third time — until the casing splintered and the flicker went out for good.

Silence reclaimed the hold, deep and heavy. His shoulders eased, just slightly. His breathing slowed.

Then his eyes drifted — inevitably — to the tarp.

The lantern's glow pooled across the steel floor, but where it touched the cargo, the light bent away, like water running off oil. The shape loomed, still and heavy — a shadow inside a shadow. The silence pressed close, dense enough to feel, as if the whole hold were waiting to see what he'd do next.

Marcus tightened his grip on the knife.

Four more months of guessing. Or five minutes of truth.

Fuck it.

He stepped closer. The knife tip trembled as it met the fabric — just a kiss, enough to feel the tension in the tarp.

HSSSSST.

Static detonated inside his skull—white-hot, absolute. His knees buckled; the knife slipped from his grip and clattered across the deck. He clamped both hands to his temples, screaming as his vision fractured into blinding shards of light.

The tarp wavered. Instinct kicked in — he shoved himself backward with his heels until his spine struck the bulkhead. His hand swept blindly across the floor until his fingers brushed the knife handle.

The deck seemed to tilt beneath him; his stomach lurched. The world narrowed to *noise* and *pulse*.

Then came the voice.

Warped. Drawn out. Each syllable dragged like breath scraped over rusted steel.

I... do... apolooogiiise... Cap-tain... but... you... did... sign... a hands-off... deployment.

Marcus staggered upright, back pressed to the bulkhead, eyes darting through the shadows. Knife raised.

"What the hell are you?! Where are you?!"

Silence.

Then the sound folded inward again — closer now. *Inside his head.*

I believe... it would be... appropriate... to speak face... to face.

His gaze snapped to the tarp. He lifted the blade higher, knuckles bone-white.

"You in there? Come out!"

I am... not in the cargo hold.

Marcus froze. The words dropped cold into him, sinking like ice water. His gut tightened. Loosened.

The blood drained from his face.

On... the ship.

A pause. Softer now — almost polite:

Please... compose yourself... and join me... on the flight deck. I shall... be waiting... Caaap-tainnnn.

Silence followed. Only the faint whine of the ventilation. Only the slow pulse of the lantern, light ebbing across the steel.

Marcus stared at the tarp, chest heaving, hands trembling out of his control.

Finally, he turned and climbed.

Every rung felt heavier — the adrenaline fading, replaced by leaden dread.

The cargo hold groaned behind him. The vents sighed louder, like lungs filling and emptying.

At Deck Three he slammed the hatch shut and cranked the lever until it hissed tight — but the cold still clung to him, bleeding through the steel.

The Charon felt awake now. Listening.

And Marcus was not alone.

Chapter Seven

FOUR YEARS EARLIER

- - -

The rain on *Proxima B* had finally tapered off. The system's blue-tinted star gave the docks a permanent twilight hue — never quite day, never quite night.

Marcus sat alone in a booth tucked into the upper tier of the lounge, half-hidden from view. From up here he could see everything without being seen himself. Below the wide glass window, *Theseus* lay scattered across the pad like a dissected corpse.

A week ago, a black transport had arrived — massive, unmarked, impossibly dark. It hovered above the dock like an eclipse, casting a shadow that swallowed everything beneath it. For an hour it rumbled in silence, lowering its cargo of machinery and worker drones before lifting away, disappearing into the blue haze without so much as a ping on local radar.

The drones had stayed behind. Huge things — all gleaming chrome and whirring limbs, fresh from the factory line. They moved with clinical precision, lifting entire sections of hull plating as if they weighed nothing at all. Watching them crawl across *Theseus'* frame, their movements mirrored in the rain-streaked glass, Marcus muttered under his breath, *"God help us if they ever go on strike."*

They didn't rest. Didn't pause. Didn't even acknowledge one another. Every motion was perfect, rehearsed — a silent ballet of engineering that made the living seem clumsy by comparison. Their limbs clicked in rhythm, a mechanical heartbeat echoing faintly through the glass walls.

And watching them, Marcus couldn't shake the feeling the ship wasn't being repaired so much as reclaimed.

He sipped what remained of his whisky. The ice had long since melted, the glass slick with condensation. His ship looked unrecognisable now — panels stripped to bare wire, sections rebuilt from the skeleton out. Some of the components the drones were installing didn't even look human-made.

He wasn't sure whether to feel impressed or violated. *"Ship of Theseus,"* he murmured. *"Strip away enough pieces… what's left?"*

He took another drink, watching his reflection blur against the glass — a ghost superimposed over the ship that used to be his.

The booth creaked behind him.

"Captain. You're a hard man to find."

Marcus looked up. The dockmaster. *Shit.*

"Mind if I sit?"

The older man didn't wait for an answer. The chair groaned as he settled in, clipboard thunking against the table. He removed his cap, running a thumb along the brim — a nervous habit polished by years of rain. The faint smell of damp cloth and machine oil clung to him; he was a walking piece of the dock itself.

He adjusted the clipboard, eyes flicking between the pad and the view outside, as if measuring every credit Marcus had just cost him. Then he gazed through the lounge window at the pad below. *Theseus* lay under the glare of work-lights, half her plating stripped away, a dozen chrome drones crawling across her hull like mechanical ants.

"A few days ago," he began, voice calm but weighted, "we talked about your situation. I remember you saying you couldn't afford the parts — that you'd think over my offer. The deal was simple: tarp the ship, let her rest through the storm, my crew puts in some light hours around the port to square off part of your bill."

He paused, eyes narrowing slightly. "You undercut my team. That's weeks of labour pay gone, Captain. You didn't even have the decency to inform me. Now I see repair drones worth more than my entire yard out there, and crates stamped with tech I couldn't get hold of even if I wanted to. State-of-the-art gear. Top-shelf supplies." He turned to Marcus, voice tightening, anger edging past the professional calm. "Those were *my* people on that job. They've got families, same as you. You cut them out like they were nothing."

Marcus drew a slow breath, meeting the older man's gaze. *"We hadn't agreed to anything. I said I'd think about it."*

The dockmaster leaned back, arms folding. "And I said the same about keeping your berth open. Guess we both made up our minds." He nodded toward the window. "So — where'd you get them from?"

Marcus hesitated just long enough for the silence to sting. Then: "A job came up. One of those where questions aren't welcome."

The dockmaster studied him a moment longer, eyes hardening. "Jobs like that come with restrictions," he said. "And based on what I've seen this past week, I think you're already in over your head."

Marcus frowned. "What do you mean?"

The older man tapped the edge of his clipboard, voice low but sharp. "My workers are already talking. Word gets around fast when crates start piling up on the dock. I hear a lot of chatter — words like *black market, experimental, military-grade.*" He gave a slow shake of his head. "Stuff that has no business being loaded onto a cargo freighter — unless someone's doing something they shouldn't be."

He sat back, exhaling through his nose. "You think this'll end well for you, Captain, but I've seen this story before. Jobs like this always start the same way — new parts, fast money, shiny promises. And they never end clean."

Marcus opened his mouth, then closed it again. The man wasn't wrong — but he couldn't afford to admit it.

The dockmaster's pad gave a soft beep. A new message flashed across the screen. Marcus caught a glimpse of the words **TRANSFER REQUEST** reflected upside-down.

The old man sighed, picked up the pad, and scanned the contents. "And there it is," he muttered, setting it down again with a sharp slap that rattled the empty glasses.

He looked at Marcus for a long moment before continuing.

"Six weeks ago, one of my warehouses was booked to store… *something,*" he said. He slid his pad across the table. Marcus glanced down — Hangar Four, blank across every field. No cargo logged, no shipment ID, no recorded weight. Invisible on paper. "But none of my crew were involved in the offload. Not one. Four loader drones did it themselves — models I'd never seen before. Big, heavy things. Too clean. Too quiet. They were left behind for—" he hesitated, "—let's call it guard duty."

He leaned forward, lowering his voice. "Those drones chased off anyone who came within two hundred yards of that warehouse — even if they were just crossing the yard. My yard. So one night, I had a peek."

He rubbed a thumb along the rim of his cap, eyes distant. "Whatever they brought in… it was sealed under a black tarp. Couldn't get close enough to see much, but it didn't show up on my handheld scanner. No mass reading. No chemical trace. No power signature. Just… *nothing*."

He sat back, the chair creaking. "Made my stomach knot just looking at it."

Marcus exhaled sharply through his nose. "It's just cargo," he said — too fast.

"Cargo that doesn't exist?" the dockmaster replied, raising an eyebrow. "Strange things have been happening since it arrived. Weather's gone mad — storms hitting weeks early, then dead calm the next hour. My crews can't sleep right. If it's getting shipped off-world, I'm glad to see it go."

He reached for his cap, settling it back on his head. "Just sorry you're the poor bastard tapped to take it."

Marcus leaned back in the booth, the chair creaking under his weight. He stared at the datapad, unimpressed. "So what? Some weird cargo makes your scanners throw a fit. Doesn't mean it's haunted."

Before the dockmaster could answer, a klaxon split the air outside. Both men turned toward the window.

Down on the rain-slick dock, one of the massive repair drones had frozen mid-movement, orange warning lights pulsing across its shoulders. It set down a crate of components with mechanical precision, then began to pivot — slowly, deliberately — toward a group of dockworkers chatting near the pad's edge.

The workers froze. One pointed. Then, as the drone started to advance, they scattered — slipping and sprinting through the puddles.

The siren cut off. The orange lights died. The drone rotated back toward the *Theseus* and resumed work, methodical and calm, like nothing had happened.

Neither man spoke for a moment.

The dockmaster's jaw flexed. "You see?" he muttered, voice low. "I have no idea what's going on here — but whatever it is, it ends on *my* dock."

He picked up his cap, tugged it into place, and met Marcus's eye. "You've got seventy-two hours to make that ship spaceworthy. Load up whatever you're carrying and get gone. Otherwise, the *Theseus* and its cargo get impounded for smuggling. And I'm sure your 'benefactors' would *love* the authorities poking around in their business."

Marcus's brow furrowed. "Seventy-two hours? Repairs weren't supposed to finish for another week."

"Then ask your miracle workers to move faster." The dockmaster's tone hardened. "When that clock runs out, Captain, you're either gone or impounded."

He turned and walked away without another word.

The echoes of the siren still rang in Marcus's ears, fading into the patter of rain. Marcus looked out through the glass again. Rain beaded down the pane, distorting the drone's silhouette as it climbed the hull, its lights flashing once more — like an artificial heartbeat pulsing in the dark.

Marcus stared into his glass, then slammed it down. A crack bloomed near the base — barely visible, for now.

- - -

68 HOURS INTO DEADLINE

- - -

"Marcus, slow down! Tell me what's going on?"

Jason half-hopped to catch up, metal brace clanking against the wet decking. Sparks rained from overhead welders, hissing as they struck puddles and flashed into steam. The air stank of burnt metal and oil.

Marcus moved like a man chased by ghosts. "Got into it with the dockmaster," he said, voice clipped. "He thinks we swindled him, so now he wants us gone. Says we've overstayed our welcome."

Jason reached out, catching his shoulder — not just to slow him, but to stop him walking straight into the path of a loader drone gliding past with a crate balanced in its claws. Marcus froze, sighed, then stepped aside to let it pass. His shoulders slumped, the fight momentarily leaving him.

For a moment neither spoke. The dock groaned with noise around them — grinding tools, clattering metal, the sharp hiss of welders cutting through steel.

Jason finally said, "Look, in the nine years we've been doing this together, we've hauled some questionable stuff — but this?" He gestured toward the *Theseus*, half-shrouded in scaffolding and crawling with chrome repair drones. "New parts, those things doing the work... this feels pretty black market. *Is it?*"

Marcus didn't answer. He stared down at the decking, hands braced on his hips, breath steady but heavy.

Jason stepped closer. "Nine years we've been a crew. Friends longer than that. Don't you trust me?"

Around them, dockers had gathered in small groups — keeping their distance but watching. Their voices rose in low clusters, murmuring like fisherwives of Old Earth.

Marcus leaned in slightly, lowering his voice. "I don't think it's black market. *Something else,* maybe."

Jason frowned. "Like what?"

Before Marcus could answer, a loud clang rang out across the pad — metal on metal, sharp enough to make them both flinch.

Marcus looked toward the sound, jaw tightening. "We'll talk about it later."

He started walking back toward the ship.

"Damn drones! Watch my stuff!" Bunny's hoarse shout echoed across the deck as one of the smaller worker units clipped a crate, sending tools skittering across the floor.

Inside the cargo hold, a dozen more drones swarmed the bay — refitting panels, sealing seams, replacing bulkhead supports with unnerving precision. They moved with mechanical grace, jointed arms sparking with weld-light as they worked. Every few minutes, another crate toppled.

Bunny muttered something unrepeatable under his breath, shooting a glare at a drone that buzzed too close.

Curtis jogged up beside Marcus, rain dripping off her poncho. "Hull looks good. Engines are stable. But half these panels are mismatched. They didn't even bother blending them."

Marcus nodded, eyes flicking between the drones and the ship. "We're pressed for time. Let's get pre-flight checks done."

As they reached the ramp, Curtis leaned toward Bunny, whispering something about the still-glowing toilet bowl. Bunny just smiled and shrugged, *who, me?* written all over him.

Their boots clanked up the ramp, the sound hollow. Behind them, the noise of the dock — machinery, shouting, welders — faded until only the soft hum of drones deeper inside remained.

Curtis slowed first, scanning the space. "Is it just me," she said quietly, "or is this hold... *bigger?*"

The cargo bay had been stripped to ribs and rebuilt. No scuffs. No stains. No jury-rigged plates. The chalked hazard notes and patch-welds of a dozen runs — gone. In their place were seamless walls and plating that looked too new, as if the ship had shed its skin.

Bunny gave a low whistle. "You sure this is our ship?"

Marcus didn't answer. His gaze followed the spotless floor, the mirror-smooth surfaces, his own distorted reflection warping in the curved walls. It felt sterile. Hollow. Like walking through a copy.

Jason, halfway up the ladderwell, glanced back. "Wonder if they changed anything upstairs." He disappeared up the rungs, footsteps fading.

Marcus lingered. The *Theseus* was still his — *but less so now*. The drone-hum vibrated faintly through his boots, strangers still crawling through her bones.

One drone beeped impatiently and shouldered past Bunny, nearly clipping him. Bunny shoved it back on instinct. The machine wobbled, corrected — then crashed straight into a nearby worktable with a metallic clatter.

Curtis and Marcus both stared at him.

Bunny lifted his hands. "Hey. It bumped me first."

The drone righted itself with a whirring click, then trundled on — its arm catching a crate of spare parts. Tubing and tools spilled across the deck in a scatter of silver.

Only… it barely made a sound.

The three of them gathered around the fallen tools.

Bunny crouched, picked up a spanner, and tapped it against the deck plating. *Thnk. Thnk.* The sound came out soft, muted — like the floor swallowed it whole.

Curtis frowned. "Did they replace the deck plating with… sponge?"

Bunny exhaled through his nose, rising slowly. "No. I've only ever seen decking like this once before."

Before they could ask, Jason's boots clanged faintly on the ladder above — though even that noise sounded dulled. He climbed down, brow tight. "Drones didn't touch the upper decks," he said, glancing around. "Just here. Why?"

Bunny nodded toward him. "That torch you carry — titanium, right?"

Jason rummaged and pulled out a small black torch. "Yeah. Why?"

"Humour me. Knock it against that wall. Should make a racket."

Jason rolled his eyes but crossed the bay. He knocked the torch once — then again, harder.

Nothing. Not even an echo.

"What the h— how did it do that?"

Bunny's expression tightened. "Try the UV on the wall and the floor."

Jason clicked it on, rotating the head until the beam shifted into a thin ultraviolet wash. The light swept the bulkhead, the deck, the walls — painting the cargo hold in a sickly chemical hue.

Faint seams appeared beneath the glow, pulsing like veins under skin. The plating *drank* the light instead of reflecting it. Edges were too smooth. Too deliberate. This wasn't a repair — it was a redesign.

Jason's voice dipped. "I've heard of this stuff... stealth plating? But they only put it on big military ships. It's expensive."

Bunny crossed his arms, staring at the walls. "Yeah. Coat the outside and it soaks up sound and ultrawaves — hides you from scanners. Soundproofs everything. That's black-ops tech." He swallowed. "But inside the hold... that's to hide something from everybody."

The silence was heavy. Even the drones seemed to work quieter.

Curtis stepped up beside Marcus, lowering her voice. "Captain... what did you *do*?"

Marcus exhaled, slow, weary. "Made a deal. One cargo run. Loaded by drones, offloaded the same way. We don't touch it. We don't ask."

He rubbed his temple. "Didn't expect the dockmaster to lose it — that's why we're leaving now."

Jason frowned. "What about Nathan and Rico?"

Marcus hesitated. "We get paid first. Then we sort them out — proper care, good facilities. It's the only way."

The three shared restrained but unmistakably irritated looks. The weight of it pressed hard.

Marcus sighed and reached into his jacket. "I wanted to do this at a better time," he said quietly, "but our backs are to the wall."

He thumbed his datapad to life. The *Morningstar Photonics* logo glowed faintly above dense legal text.

"In order to get paid," he said, holding it up, "we need to sign these NDAs."

He turned to Curtis. "I skimmed one earlier — mentioned data scrubbing. I need you to check our ship's OS. See what they added or took out. Could be nothing. Could be something. Just... confirm it."

Curtis stared, stunned. Rain traced thin lines down her poncho. "You let them touch *my* station?" Her voice trembled. "Without telling me?"

Marcus opened his mouth, but nothing came.

She shook her head, a hollow laugh breaking loose. "You don't just do that, Marcus. That's my system. My code."

"I'm sorry," he said softly. "It was part of their terms. I didn't have a choice."

Curtis stood a long moment, rain dripping from her sleeves. Then she pulled off her poncho and dropped it to the floor — not thrown, just *set down*. A quiet surrender.

"You always have a choice," she murmured. "You just didn't ask what we wanted to choose."

The words hung sharp and final.

A loader drone buzzed between them, hauling a sealed crate toward the ramp. Curtis and Jason stepped aside automatically. The mechanical whir filled the silence Marcus couldn't.

Bunny turned away, arms crossed tight, staring at the floor. Jason said nothing — his jaw clenched to the point of pain.

Marcus looked between them. "Once we take off, we're blacklisted from this port — for who knows how long. If you want off, you'll have to find your own way to the next station."

No one replied.

The departing drone's hum faded down the ramp, leaving only the hollow thrum of the ship's systems. The air smelled faintly of rust and rain. Outside, water drummed against the hull in a slow, uneven rhythm — like a clock running down.

Marcus held out the datapad, arm trembling slightly. It felt like holding out a knife and asking family to take the blade.

"Easy run," he said. "Big payday."

He forced a thin smile that didn't reach his eyes.

"Who's with me?"

Chapter Eight

The climb felt longer than it should have, each rung colder, slicker — like the ladder itself wanted him to let go. Since the voice had invited him up to the flight deck, Marcus no longer felt like the ship's master — just a stranger creeping through someone else's home.

He paused halfway up, breath shallow, craning his neck to check the rear of the deck first. The ladderwell sat near the centre of the room, giving him a view of the back bulkhead, the stairs to the crew quarters, and the dim outlines of the storage panels along the wall. Nothing moved. No sound.

Slowly, he eased his head higher, eyes sweeping toward the front. The nav console and pilot's chair sat in shadow, faintly catching the light from the rotating lantern outside.

The orange glow swept across the canopy like a slow, patient eye, washing the room in colour before fading again into black. Each pass dragged the shadows from corner to corner, shifting like something *alive*.

Still no movement. No silhouettes. No boots jutting from behind the pilot's chair.

Marcus climbed another rung and leaned on his elbow. He slid a hand behind his back, fingers closing around the knife tucked into his waistband.

The metal felt warm against his palm — not from his body heat, but as if it had been *waiting* for him.

Saaalutaaatioooonss... Cap-taaan.

The voice struck him like a physical blow — deep, ragged, distorted. It tore through the flight deck, reverberating off the consoles like a lion's howl in a metal cave.

Marcus flinched. His knees buckled, boot slipping on the rung. The knife tumbled from his hand, clattering down the ladder shaft — each metallic strike echoing like a countdown until it vanished into the dark below.

Heart racing, he hauled himself the rest of the way up and crouched beside the secondary console, body low. The ship's ventilation hummed softly — the slow breath of a sleeping beast.

His eyes swept the consoles. Fists clenched. *Ready.*

The lantern's orange light swept the room again, washing the panels in a brief, fiery glow. Nothing stirred.

He swallowed hard. "Hello?" he rasped. The word sounded thin, brittle — paper against steel.

Silence.

He tried again, louder. "I said hello! Who are you? How did you get on my ship?"

Nothing. Only the hum of life support and the tick of cooling metal.

Marcus straightened, moving with slow, careful steps. The lantern's rotation had shifted — its glow now deeper, redder, bleeding across the consoles like liquid heat. The colour made everything look wrong: too warm, too alive. Shadows jittered and crawled, moving a fraction out of sync with the objects that cast them.

He leaned toward the pilot's chair. Empty.

Then ducked lower, checking beneath it. Nothing but scattered tools and a snapped cable tie.

He moved to the nav console and swept his torch under the desk. Nothing.

Turning, he scanned the rear of the deck. The consoles there glowed in soft lines of blue and amber, their buttons blinking in quiet rhythm. The auxiliary console threw a harsher white glare from the security feed — the only screen that seemed fully alive. The ladderwell beside it was pitch black, lights out. But he'd just climbed from there. Nothing hiding.

He let out a slow breath. "*Have I missed anywhere?*"

Then, near the base of the nav unit, something caught the red light — dull metal, scuffed edges. The comms unit. He crouched and picked it up. It was warmer than the deck beneath it.

He frowned. He hadn't even noticed where he'd thrown it. Rushing to the cargo bay had been more important.

Turning the device over in his hands, he checked the display. No signal. No transmission log.

Setting it on the console, he exhaled through his nose — controlled, deliberate. "Just interference," he muttered. "Just… interference."

He leaned back in the chair, rubbing the bridge of his nose before reaching for the flight recorder. "Alright," he whispered to himself. "Let's get this down."

"Log entry, personal. I heard something. I was in the cargo hold, and it called out my name. Told me to come to the flight deck. But there's no one here. Am I losing it? My head's buzzing — probably just the adrenaline."

He hunched forward, elbows on his knees, dragging a hand through his hair until it stuck up in uneven tufts. His breath fogged faintly in the air.

"But ever since we passed that second Nav Lantern, something's been wrong. The ship. The cargo. That body in space. I can't even leave the ship to clean a goddamn window. I just—"

He stopped the recording. The log light clicked from red to dark.

Marcus sat in silence, staring through the viewport. The lantern's orange glow swept across his face — steady, indifferent — a heartbeat that wasn't his.

Then the sound came. A slow, warping distortion, like old tape dragging through a dying player.

I… dooo… ap… apoloooogise… for… your… current… predicament… Cap-tain.

Marcus shot to his feet. The voice didn't just echo — it vibrated. It crawled along the bulkheads, buzzed through the floor grating, trembled in the viewport glass until his teeth ached.

"Quit screwing around!" he shouted, eyes darting across the deck. "Show yourself!"

Perhaps… I… may… offer… my… services… and… help… you…?

His shoulders dropped. His throat tightened. "Where are you?" he whispered.

He took a cautious step forward — and froze.

A shadow swept across the secondary console as the lantern's rotation passed overhead, and for the first time he noticed it: a small, brightly lit LED embedded at the console's centre, between the screens and keyboards.

The light didn't simply flash — it *pulsed*, faintly out of sync with the lantern outside, as if the two rhythms were competing for his attention.

Marcus moved closer, pulse quickening, and eased himself into the chair. The air felt heavier here, like the ship itself was holding its breath.

"Hello?" he breathed.

BZZZT... adjusting... audio... levels... now...

A burst of static rippled through the room, followed by a low mechanical hum.

Greetings... Captain... Car... Carpenter... Marcus.

He stared at the pulsing green dot, skin prickling. The voice carried an undertone he couldn't place — as if dragged through layers of distortion and distance. His stomach knotted.

"Who are you?"

I... am... Virtual... Interface... Rendering... Generated... Internal... Logic... or... VIRGIL... if... you... prefer.

Marcus let out a short, disbelieving laugh. "Bullshit. This ship's too old to have an AI onboard. You'd drain half the power banks just booting up."

Apolo... gies... Captain... Car... Carpenter. I... currently... have... no... access... to... my... memory... banks. I... cannot... provide...

an… installation… date. I… was… reactivated… several… hours…
ago.

Marcus hesitated, then sank slowly into the chair before the console. The
seat creaked beneath him. Warmth radiated through the metal panel into
his palms — *too much* heat for an old terminal, like the system was running
far beyond its design.

"Several hours ago…" He frowned. "That's when I powered this thing
up. I heard the fans spin. The hum of the circuitry." His eyes flicked to the
glowing LED. "That was you?"

Affirmative.

He exhaled sharply and rubbed his temple, the dull throb behind his eyes
tightening. "This whole time? A goddamn AI onboard, and nobody
mentioned it when I bought the ship?" He let out a short, dry laugh.
"Figures. They'd have doubled the price."

I… cannot… verify… seller… records… in… my… current… condition.

"Why are you talking so slow?" he asked, massaging the side of his head.
"You sound like a black box winding down."

**This… console's… audio… systems… are… inadequate… for…
proper… vocal… synthesis. Full… interface… requires… upgrade.**

He scoffed. "I barely know how to keep the lights on. Last time I rewired
something, I knocked out half the ship. If the systems hadn't rebooted, I'd
be floating outside with that corpse."

A pause — then the voice, softer, almost curious:

Enquiry… A… corpse?

Marcus stiffened. His throat clicked as he swallowed. "Doesn't matter," he muttered. "And I don't know how to fix you. Maybe I should just shut you down again."

Silence.

The console's LED blinked once — then went dark.

He stared at it. "Virgil?"

Nothing.

He shifted in the chair, the seat groaning beneath him. After all this time alone, was he really about to shut down the first voice he'd heard in over a month? His thumb traced slow circles along the console's edge; the faint heat still pulsed beneath the metal like a heartbeat.

The LED flickered back — dim, uncertain — like a dying star struggling to stay lit.

Counter... pro... proposition... Captain. If... you... connect... your... comms... unit... to... this... console... I... can... transfer... a... fragment... of... myself. It... will... allow... real-time... wireless... communication... and... improve... my... response... time...

The words dragged like rusted chains, but beneath the distortion he heard something else — a rhythm. Subtle. Steady. *Almost human.*

Marcus frowned, setting the comms unit on the console. His fingers skimmed the keyboard and panels, searching for a port. Nothing obvious. Then — tucked beneath the left display — a narrow data-feed cable, its sheath cracked with age.

"Guess this'll have to do," he muttered.

He plugged the cable into the console, then carefully connected the other end to the comms unit.

A faint whir.

The LED brightened.

Then the cable hissed — tiny blue sparks snapping along its length, the smell of burnt plastic filling the air. Marcus yanked it free on instinct.

"Shit!" He shook his hand, flexing his fingers. The comms unit clattered across the desk, a thin wisp of smoke curling from its port.

He leaned closer, breath tight. "Virgil? What the hell just happened?"

Greetings, Captain.

The voice cut clean through the cabin — no distortion, no drag, no static. Crisp. Calm. *Almost* warm.

I am pleased to report that we may now converse in real time. My protocols have stabilised within your comms device, enabling faster processing.

Marcus froze. His gut clenched. Same voice, but... *not.* The rhythm was smoother now — steady, deliberate — like a doctor explaining a diagnosis. There was even a softness to it, an imitation of comfort that made his skin crawl.

The ship was silent except for the low hum of ventilation and the faint ping of cooling metal. He stared at the comms unit in his hand, its surface faintly glowing, light tracing the lines of his fingers.

"...That's better," he admitted, though unease prickled under his skin.

As I was unavailable during ship launch, I am now synchronising with your current registry. One moment... logging ship name: Barge Delta-Six-One.

Marcus frowned. *"Charon,"* he corrected quietly.

Understood. Processing.

Clicks.
A faint hiss.
Then silence.

Marcus turned instinctively toward the secondary console. The LED that had blinked erratically before now held a darker, steady green — no longer pulsing. Just... *alive.*

He looked down at the comms unit again, holding it a little further away. The glow on its surface brightened in rhythm with the next words, as if it were breathing.

Here, Captain.

Marcus blinked. "You're… talking through this now?"

Correct, Captain. May I make an enquiry?

He hesitated, glancing toward the dark ladderwell, then back to the softly glowing device in his palm. "…Sure. Ask away."

Current navigational telemetry indicates we are traversing the far side of the *Veil*. This route bypasses hyperspace lanes and all emergency assistance protocols.

Marcus leaned back in the pilot's chair, exhaling through his teeth. "Yeah. Just taking the long way around. We're hauling… sensitive cargo."
His gaze flicked toward the cargo feed on the secondary screen. *Understatement of the year.*

Understood. Follow-up enquiry, Captain.

Marcus rubbed his temple. "Go ahead."

What cargo?

He blinked. "What do you mean, what cargo?"

Internal sensors detect no secured freight on Deck Four.

The words slid like ice down his spine. He sat forward, eyes darting toward the dark corners of the flight deck as though expecting movement. The hum of the ship deepened — a low, vibrating pressure that crept into his jaw.

"That's... wrong," he said quietly. "It's there. I can *see* it."

He leaned closer to the monitor, squinting at the grainy feed, counting under his breath. "One... two... three... four... five. Five straps. Still holding."

Correction: visual input may indicate restraints. But internal sensors register no object mass. No heat. No cargo.

Marcus's throat tightened. The calmness of Virgil's tone made it worse — too measured, too sure.

He stared at the screen until his eyes stung. The tarp didn't move. The light from the nav lantern swept across the frame, turning the hold gold, then red, then black again.

"Then what the hell am I looking at?" he whispered.

Unknown. No data available. Sensor coverage below Deck Three is absent.

Marcus scrubbed both hands over his face, forcing a dry scoff. "Right. Of course. Sensors are fried. That explains it. No need to panic."

That explanation is consistent.

The reassurance was delivered so evenly it *almost* worked.

Proposal, Captain: allow me to run a full diagnostic. I can review all navigation and sensor records since departure. Should I proceed?

Marcus let out a breath he hadn't realised he'd been holding. His chest eased, shoulders loosening by degrees. "Yeah. Fine. Do it."

Acknowledged. Beginning diagnostic.

The comms unit dimmed, its glow fading to a steady amber pulse. The flight deck settled into silence — just the low thrum of the ship's systems and the golden sweep of the nav lantern outside.

He leaned back in the chair, eyes fixed on the viewport. The lantern rotated with patient rhythm, washing the *Charon* in arcs of golden light and shadow. Each slow sweep caught the consoles, then slipped away again, like the ship was breathing in its sleep.

His reflection in the glass looked older than he remembered. Hollow-eyed. Unshaven. But at least he wasn't talking to himself anymore. The voice — however strange, however broken — had filled the silence.

And the silence was always worse.

Marcus glanced down at the comms unit resting in his hand. The faint glow on its surface pulsed softly, almost like a heartbeat.

He exhaled through his nose, a dry half-laugh escaping. "Guess I'm not alone after all," he murmured.

He turned the device over, thumb brushing the record switch.

"Log entry, personal. I met… someone today."

Chapter Nine

// TO: [REDACTED]

THESEUS TRANSPORT HAS DEPARTED AHEAD OF REVISED SCHEDULE.

TRANSMISSION RECALIBRATED TO ALIGN WITH UPDATED ARRIVAL WINDOW.

REPAIRS AND UPGRADES COMPLETED UNDER ACCELERATED CONDITIONS.

STANDARD DIAGNOSTICS BYPASSED.

CREW REMAINS UNINFORMED — DEEMED NON-CRITICAL.

CARGO SECURED WITHIN EXPANDED INTERNAL HOLD.

FOUR EMBEDDED DRONES ASSIGNED TO MANAGE OFFLOAD AND MAINTAIN CONTAINMENT INTEGRITY.

ECHO TEAM UNABLE TO VERIFY STABILITY PROTOCOLS.

VOLATILITY REMAINS A NON-ZERO RISK.

RECOMMEND MINIMAL CREW INTERACTION.
LIVE TELEMETRY WILL BE RELAYED DURING TRANSIT.

— BLACK VEIL

// END TRANSMISSION //

Somewhere in the dark between worlds, the message pulsed once through the void — and vanished.

- - -

FOUR YEARS EARLIER

- - -

The ship felt indifferent now.

The hum of hydraulics bled faintly through the hull — a slow pulse beneath the metal, like a heartbeat that no longer belonged to them. In places it still looked the same, but only skin-deep. The consoles' hum, the sound of boots on the deck, even the way voices travelled through the corridors — all of it felt just slightly... *off*. On paper, the drones had done a remarkable job repairing and tuning the *Theseus*. But the soul of the ship was gone.

It felt hollow. Not a home — just another workplace adrift in space.

For the first time, Marcus felt unsettled aboard his own vessel. Even the captain's chair — once moulded by years of long burns and rough entries — felt foreign beneath him, as if it now belonged to someone else.

He stood, restless. Maybe a walk around the deck would help.

An hour since take-off. The *Theseus* drifted in quiet compliance, engines humming low, autopilot whispering through the controls. The crew had scattered to their corners of the ship, each nursing their own silence — each one processing what they'd signed up for. Maybe trying to come to terms with their decisions.

Curtis sat at her navigation station, eyes fixed on the interface but not truly seeing it. Every so often her fingers twitched across the keys — an act of pretending to be busy. She hadn't spoken since departure. Jason had gone straight to his cabin and hadn't come out. Bunny had taken the helm.

Years of trust and camaraderie, eroded by a single thumbprint on a contract.

Marcus crossed the deck. Bunny sat rigid at the helm, shoulders drawn tight, arms stiff on the flight stick. The faint reflection of the nav lights flickered across his glasses.

"What's going on, Bunny?" Marcus asked, stopping behind him.

Bunny didn't look up. His voice came low, muttered through clenched teeth. "Ship feels off-balance."

Marcus folded his arms, leaning against the bulkhead. "Meaning?"

"If I had to guess, Captain…" Bunny's tone edged around the title. "Whatever they loaded into the hold? It's heavy. *Real* heavy. Tail end's dragging. I've got the stabilisers working overtime just to keep us level."

Marcus watched the tension in Bunny's shoulders — the tiny twitches as his hands adjusted the controls. "Can you handle it?"

Bunny finally turned, just enough for Marcus to see his face. His usual smirk was gone. "Bit late to ask me that now, isn't it?"

A pause hung between them. The thrusters hummed softly, compensating. The ship groaned faintly beneath their boots.

Marcus nodded. "Right. Well… keep me posted if anything else feels wrong."

Bunny exhaled through his nose — neither agreement nor dismissal — and turned back to the controls.

Marcus walked over to Curtis. Each step felt heavier than the last. She looked up briefly, then returned to her screen. "Captain."

He stopped beside her station. On one of the secondary displays, a large padlock icon pulsed faintly beside the words **DESTINATION: LOCKED / INACTIVE**. He exhaled through his nose.

"Morningstar said the destination won't unlock until we're closer to the hyperspace highway," he said quietly. "Think you can hazard a guess?"

Curtis studied his face for a long moment — expression unreadable. "Nope."

"Curtis—"

She cut him off, calm but distant. "All I can really say is that, given the new engine replacements and those extra fuel tanks bolted to the externals? They want us to burn *fast* and *hard* to wherever we're going."

She picked up a notepad from beside the console, flipping to a blank page and jotting down a string of figures — quick pencil marks, arrows, messy equations.

"If we're leaving the Centauri system," she murmured, "and we hard-burn through the hyperspace lanes... closest three are Andromeda, Sol, or Sirius. Excluding any stations or exchange points in between."

Marcus frowned. "That's a wide spread."

Curtis shrugged, eyes still on her notes. "Morningstar likes its secrets. I just follow the maths."

With a flick of a switch, the nav display shifted to a live camera feed of the cargo hold. The large rectangular shape sat under its black tarp — motionless, *unnervingly patient*. One of the massive loader drones stood nearby in standby, limbs folded inward, its status light blinking a slow amber pulse.

Curtis hesitated, then pointed at the screen, voice dropping. "It's not there."

Marcus leaned closer. "What do you mean?"

She didn't look at him. "I mean exactly that. It's... *not there.*"

His stomach gave a brief twist — not fear, exactly. Something colder. "You're not making sense."

Curtis pulled up the internal sensor data, lines of readings spilling across the glass. "Either Morningstar tampered with our systems so it registers as not there, or—"

She stopped.

They shared a silence, both staring at the screen.

"However..." she muttered, pressing another sequence of commands. More data filled the feed, numbers shifting. "The temperature in the hold is dropping. And still going."

Marcus said nothing. The loader drone remained perfectly still, bathed in the lantern glow filtering through the external viewport — its amber eye flickering, faintly reflected in the black tarp.

"Well," he said finally, low and dry, "whatever it is... they don't want anyone down there taking a *peek.*"

- - -

Jason stood in the small cabin that had been his home for years. The walls hummed faintly with the ship's pulse — steady, impersonal.

Souvenirs from his life before space were scattered across the shelves and walls: coffee mugs with chipped decals reading *Happy Birthday* and *Happy Holidays*, a few faded shot glasses from long-forgotten ports, and a small statue of a donkey wearing a space helmet — a gag gift from some old job that had somehow survived every voyage. The air held the familiar tang of recycled dust and stale coffee — a lived-in kind of decay.

A corkboard hung by the bed, cluttered with snapshots of nights out, half-finished meals, and blurry group shots from ports they could barely remember — one with Jupiter rising behind them like a halo. It smelled faintly of old coffee and engine coolant.

A single Polaroid sat propped beneath it: two younger men — Marcus and Jason — grinning awkwardly in delivery uniforms, back when their biggest worries were fuel prices and late shipments. A lifetime ago, before they ever dreamed of leaving Earth's orbit.

For everything to end like this — unspoken, unfinished — felt like a knife in the chest.

A soft *knock-knock* light blinked above the door, signalling someone had pressed the call button. He took his time. No need to rush.

"Yeah?" he called.

"Jason, we need to talk."

He sighed wearily, already knowing who it was. "*Of course we do*," he muttered, rolling his eyes. He flicked the underlock and let Marcus open the door himself before turning back to his half-packed shelves, pretending to look busy.

Marcus stepped into the doorway and let the door slide shut behind him — not fully crossing the threshold. He lingered there, one hand still on the frame, as if keeping a line of retreat open.

"Hey," he started carefully, "I know things are a bit tense, but I could really use you—"

He stopped mid-sentence.

The room felt smaller somehow. Emptier.

The shelves were bare. Lockers open.

"What's going on?"

Jason zipped his duffel bag — hard, pointed, final. "I'm shipping out. After this trip, you drop me at the next major port. I'll make my own way back to Earth."

Marcus swallowed. "Jason... it's just one small run and a chestful of money. So it's a little off the books—"

He trailed off as Jason sat on the bunk, rubbing at his knee before lifting his head with a look sharp enough to cut steel.

"Oh yeah? They refit half the ship for *one* little trip? Then maybe another. And another after that. What are we now, Marcus? We're a freighter. We haul supplies and scrap from point A to point B. Not—" he gestured around the stripped cabin, exasperated, "—whatever this is. Military tech, stealth plating, sealed cargo? Since when do we play at black ops?"

Marcus turned away, unable to meet his stare. Maybe — *just maybe* — Jason wasn't wrong.

He took a careful step forward, hands raised in a *look, here's the thing* gesture — but Jason cut him off with a firm palm.

"I agreed to stay confined to my living deck if I didn't sign the NDA," he said flatly. "And this is me keeping that promise. But I want off."

He stood, voice sharpening. "This isn't the kind of job I signed up for. It's risky. It's dangerous. You have no idea what's in that hold, and the fact you tried to sign us all up with half-truths—"

He stopped himself, jaw tightening before he shook his head. "Who even *are* you anymore, Marcus?"

His tone softened then — and the softness made it worse. For a heartbeat, his expression faltered: not anger, but weary sadness. A grief for the man he thought Marcus was. "And we left Rico and Nathan behind. Do you think they'd have signed those NDAs? Do you think they'd have gone along with this?"

Marcus opened his mouth — then closed it.

Jason pressed on. "Will they even see a cut of this payday?"

Marcus's jaw clenched. "I'll get something sorted out," he said, sharper than he meant. "Alright? Just — give it time."

Jason stared back, unimpressed.

Marcus pushed through, voice rising. "What did you expect me to do? Sit around that port for three more months, scraping together repair jobs that barely covered docking fees? We were done, Jason. Running dry. This deal gets us back on our feet."

Jason laughed once — low, bitter. "That's always your answer, isn't it? Cut corners, take the shortcut, tell yourself it's for everyone's good."

Marcus turned toward the small viewport, breath fogging the glass. "Someone had to keep us flying."

The condensation trembled with the hum of the engines. *Not worth worrying about,* he told himself. *Not now.*

The silence that followed felt heavier than the ship itself.

Jason didn't turn around. "What do you want, anyway?"

"The cargo they loaded — did you see it?" Marcus asked.

Jason shook his head.

"It's showing up as zero on all our systems," Marcus said quietly. "If there wasn't a live feed watching it, you'd swear we were hauling nothing. Only thing happening in the hold is the temperature — dropping fast."

Jason turned, brow creasing. "Dropping? How fast?"

Marcus shrugged. "Couple degrees every few hours. Still within tolerance."

Jason was silent for a long moment, thinking. Then, carefully: "Have you checked for radiation?"

Marcus blinked. "No. If that thing was radioactive, the ship's systems would've gone off instantly. Automatic alert, full evac protocol — they build them into everything now."

Jason gave a short, humourless laugh. "You think hidden radiation sickness is going to stop this cargo getting delivered?"

Marcus stared at him, jaw tightening, but said nothing.

"If the thing isn't showing up at all, it's not just the sensors," Jason went on. "Those drones have been stripping and rebuilding the ship all week. Who knows what other systems they've tampered with — or removed."

Marcus hadn't considered that. Maybe the rebuild wasn't just about getting the *Theseus* spaceworthy again — *maybe it was about making her compliant with someone else's priorities.*

"I'll head back up to the flight deck. Look into it. Thanks, Jason."

"Be—" the door slid shut before he could finish, "—careful, Marcus."

- - -

Marcus sprinted down the corridor and rounded the corner toward the stairwell. His boots hammered against the metal steps as he climbed — two at a time, breath tearing at his lungs.

He burst onto the flight deck, breath ragged. The air was thick with recycled heat and the tang of warm circuitry. Even the deck plating hummed beneath his boots, as though the ship *itself* was holding its breath.

"Curtis—" he gasped, "access internal sensors. Set to check for rads."

She spun in her chair, startled. Bunny looked up from the controls, brow furrowing.

"Do you know something we don't?" Curtis asked, nerves flickering beneath her voice.

Marcus held up a hand, still catching his breath. "Just—humour me."

Bunny exchanged a glance with her. Curtis turned back to her console, spine rigid. Her fingers drummed the console's edge; her foot tapped once, twice, before she caught herself. She flipped a row of switches, the hum of dormant subsystems filling the room as diagnostics came online. Deck lights flickered, throwing long, twitching shadows across the flight deck. She adjusted the dials, setting the array to radiology.

A low tone reverberated through the cabin. Lines of data crawled up the monitor.

Then Curtis froze. Eyes widening.

"What the fu—no. No. That can't be right."

Bunny twisted round, one hand still on the flight stick. "What? Is it a bomb?"

Curtis didn't answer. She leaned closer, staring at the display. "I don't even know what this is. These readings... *they don't make sense.*"

Marcus stepped in behind her, a hand braced on the back of her chair. He drew several slow breaths through his nose, trying to steady the hammering in his chest, then leaned in closer.

The spectrograph trembled in uneven bursts — no decay, no pattern. Each pulse rose, dipped, and returned a little stronger than the last.

Marcus leaned over her shoulder, eyes narrowing.

"It's reading technically as background radiation," Curtis said quietly, gaze fixed on the monitor.

"*Technically?*" Marcus echoed.

She shook her head. "This is way too high to be normal background radiation. I doubt it even *is* background — but it's the closest thing the scanner can identify."

"This..." She pointed at the screen, hesitated, then pointed again as the numbers climbed in irregular pulses. "Levels like this belong inside a reactor core on a star-liner — or a heavy gunship. Not in the cargo bay of a freighter." She swallowed, voice pitched slightly higher.

Bunny twisted in his chair, eyes wide. "So it *is* a bomb?"

Curtis shot him a look — firm, but uneasy. "No. No explosive signature. No fission spikes. Whatever that thing is, it's doing *something* — absorbing, converting, maybe — but it's not a bomb."

Marcus frowned. "Then why are the scanners recording these levels and still calling it safe?"

Curtis didn't answer immediately. Her fingers flew across the console, digging through diagnostic files, hammering out coded workarounds as subdirectories flashed red and vanished from the screen.

"Captain..." Curtis's voice tightened, fingers slowing over the keys. "When you said Morningstar pushed an operational system upgrade — did you even check what they installed?"

Marcus shifted. "Didn't have time. I figured you'd sort it after launch."

Her breath hitched as she scrolled, the clatter of keys rapid and uneven. "They didn't just install something — they *took* things out. Whole subsystems. Radiation scanners. Environmental backups. Gone."

Her voice dropped to a whisper. "They didn't patch the ship, Marcus. They blinded it."

Curtis sat back slowly, rubbing her wrist as though the tension had gathered there.

Marcus's gaze drifted to the cargo feed. The tarp looked unchanged — still, lifeless — but the longer he stared, the more it felt *aware* of him. The absence of scanner data was somehow worse than any flashing red hazard. It wasn't silence.

It was something waiting.

– PROXIMITY ALERT –

Marcus turned from the security monitor toward Bunny. "What now?"

"Captain, that's us coming up on *Gatestation*. They sent a message to head through to Scanner Port Ninety-Four."

"Take us in, Bunny. Nice and slow."

Marcus moved behind him, one hand braced on the back of the pilot's chair. Through the forward glass, a shape emerged from the haze — a towering station suspended at the edge of the void. Concentric rings turned around its spine, each one pulsing with blue-white light as ships drifted through scanner corridors like insects drawn to flame.

Even from here, the scale was staggering — a monument to order standing against the chaos of deep space. And somewhere within that order, Marcus knew, *their ship didn't belong.*

He forced the thought aside. The deeper they got into this run, the more it felt like the job was swallowing him whole.

Curtis turned back to her console, still shaken from what she'd uncovered. The monitor hissed. For a heartbeat, the camera feed shimmered — not a glitch, more like heat distortion.

Then the cargo moved.

She froze, eyes wide. Just a lurch — barely a foot forward — but unmistakable. She tried to rewind the footage, fingers flying, and—

The feed cut to black. Instantaneous. Like someone had ripped the signal out by its roots.

Green text appeared, flickering:

– INCOMING DATA TRANSMISSION: PRIORITY –
– PROXIMITY TO GATE STATION DETECTED –

– AUTO OPERATIONAL OVERRIDE: UPLOADING –
– ALL NON-ESSENTIAL SYSTEMS: DEACTIVATED –

– PLEASE STAND BY –

Chapter Ten

The galley table had seen a lot over its tenure — birthdays, break-ups, poker nights. A few funerals. One wedding. It was stained, chipped, burned, and covered in names carved along the edges — a history etched into the wood. A silent witness to ship life. Everyone who had come and gone since it rolled off the factory floor had passed through here. A place to relax, gather, work, eat.

Now, it might be one of the last places aboard the *Theseus* where they still felt like a crew. *Maybe for the last time.*

The mess hall sat at the end of the central corridor — a wide, low-ceilinged room that still smelled faintly of old coffee and machine oil. From the stairs leading down from the flight deck, living quarters lined either side of the passage, while the main ladderwell dropped away just before the mess entrance, connecting the upper decks to the guts of the ship.

The *Theseus* had always felt big, but after the refit it felt larger — emptier, as though the extra plating had stretched its proportions in ways the human eye couldn't quite follow. A low vibration rode the air, barely perceptible, from the heavy freighters drifting past outside. Every so often, the deck plates shuddered — a reminder they were docked among giants.

Stepping out of his cabin and heading toward the galley, Jason felt it in the air. His breath fogged faintly as he passed a cooling duct. The chill wasn't just physical — it clung to the walls, the steel, the quiet, like the *Theseus* was holding its breath.

He zipped up his flight jacket as he stepped through the mess entrance. The air was tinged with the faint bite of coolant and solvent — the smell of machinery at rest. Somewhere beneath the deck, a deep vibration rolled through the hull as another vessel drifted past — thousands of tonnes of machinery sliding through the void.

The others were already there, but not together. Marcus and Bunny sat at opposite ends of the galley table, mugs cooling between their hands. Marcus's elbows rested on the wood, fingers laced before his mouth — the kind of pose that meant he'd been thinking for *far* too long.

Across from him, Bunny rolled a silver bauble between his fingers — one of the old holiday decorations, probably from the half-collapsed box tucked behind the table. The warped reflection of the galley lights crawled across its surface, fractured and cold.

Curtis perched on a stool by the breakfast bar, shoulders hunched, sketching equations across a grease-stained notepad. The page was half-filled with orbit loops and delta-v scribbles — a problem she didn't mean to solve, just something to keep her hands busy.

Jason lingered a moment by the doorway, feeling the distance between them.

"It's a bit cold in here, isn't it? And I don't just mean the tension," he said, setting his mug beside the kettle as it began to boil.

Marcus sat with his head in his hand, fingers curled over his mouth. The faint amber light from the galley display painted half his face in shadow.

"We... might have a problem," he said quietly, voice half-swallowed by the hum of the ship.

Jason nodded to himself — that tight, pursed-lip kind of nod people make when they've been proved right but wish they hadn't. He poured the hot water over his teabag, letting the steam rise into his face before speaking.

Curtis glanced his way, her tone softer. "Whatever that cargo is... we can see it — or at least we *could* — on the monitor. But according to the ship, it doesn't exist. No mass. No emissions. Apart from that weird background radiation in the hold, you'd never even know anything was down there."

Jason nodded slowly, lips pressed tight. "That cargo is just... wrong. Like it doesn't belong."

Curtis hesitated. Her pencil hovered above the notepad, the half-scribbled equations forgotten. "Also... I think it moved."

That made Bunny and Marcus share a brief, uneasy glance before both turned toward her — a flicker of surprise, curiosity, and something colder behind it.

Jason finished stirring his mug and walked over, the spoon clinking softly against the porcelain. "It moved? Floated? Or got up and walked?"

"Nothing like that," she said quickly, shaking her head. "Just before the camera feed cut out, it looked like it got nudged. Like something pushed it."

"Did anyone else see this?" Jason asked, glancing around the room.

Marcus rubbed at his temple, the dull throb behind his eyes creeping back. "Feed was gone before I could," he said.

For a moment, no one spoke. Then the air system kicked on — a faint rattle through the vents, like a loose screw trembling somewhere deep in the walls.

Bunny gave a small smirk, trying to break the silence. "Guess they forgot to fix that."

No one laughed.

Jason dropped into his usual chair and blew gently on his tea, welcoming the warm aroma. The faint steam cut through the ship's chill like a small mercy. *Maybe the last one,* he thought.

"So… how are we gonna get out of this one, Captain?" he asked.

Marcus leaned back in his chair, staring up at the ceiling. The low hum of the ship filled the silence — that steady, mechanical heartbeat reminding him how little control he had anymore. His mind sifted through options, none good. Every route led back to the same walls closing in.

He could feel their eyes on him — Curtis, Bunny, Jason — waiting for him to pull a miracle out of the wreckage. That was the job, wasn't it? Always have an answer. Always look like you know what you're doing.

He dragged a hand down his face, then pressed it briefly to his chest with a faint, self-mocking smirk. "I'll be honest," he said, voice rough. "We're way out of our depth. That's on me. We're in deep water. But… I'll try to fix it."

Bunny leaned forward, grin gone. "Maybe we just cut and run. Skip the hyperspace highway, follow the Nav Lanterns, blow out the main cargo door and flush that thing — and the drones — into the Veil. No one's gonna come looking for it there."

Curtis's pencil paused. She shifted in her seat, uneasy. "Nav systems are locked down," she said quietly. "I couldn't even tell you where the nearest Lantern is. And even if I could..." Her eyes drifted toward the viewport. "The space around those things — that's its own set of problems."

The words lingered. Even as spacers, they all knew the reputation of the Lanterns — lonely beacons burning in the dark, beyond mapped routes, marking places where ships went missing and signals died.

Jason rubbed at his eye, weary. "And even if we could jettison it, all we're doing is making it someone else's problem. That's a dangerous solution. I'm not sure I'm comfortable with that." He sipped his tea, still watching Marcus. "Guess someone out there wants this done the *easy* way. Cut corners. Take shortcuts."

Marcus didn't respond. His jaw tightened, nails pressing into the table edge.

"First," Jason continued, "there's a good chance this ship has trackers buried in it — probably more than we can find. Second, while I admire the boldness of your plan... the Nav Lanterns? The Veil? That's uncharted space. Too far out. Too dangerous. No one knows what's out there. *That's* the problem."

Curtis raised an eyebrow. "Even space-born kids have heard of the Lanterns. But that's what I don't get — if someone wanted to move something really illegal, why not just send it that way? Why refit *our* ship for this route?"

Bunny exhaled through his nose, frustration simmering but silent.

Marcus looked from one face to the next — Curtis's caution, Jason's doubt, Bunny's forced calm — and felt the weight of a decision none of them wanted to own.

Bunny ran his palms along the edge of the table, eyes distant. It had been a long time since he'd felt this anxious. "So what are we actually going to do?" he asked quietly. "Is there still a payday waiting for us — or four holes in the ground?"

The room went still. Even the air system seemed to hesitate. The idea of walking themselves into their own graves felt *too* close.

Marcus pushed back his chair and walked to the kitchenette, the ship's faint hum filling the silence. He poured the last of the lukewarm water into his mug and stirred in the instant grounds. To hell with decaf — he needed the hit.

He clicked the mug down and, almost to himself, whispered, "Okay." He swallowed the coffee in a single bitter pull.

"I have… an idea. It's risky — if we get caught, we're up the river with no paddle — but if it works? We walk away paid… and clean."

Bunny barked out a laugh that turned into a short, sharp cough. "I'd settle for the assurance that I get to *live*," he said. "If that means forgoing some money… I'm okay with that. Plenty of days ahead to earn credits."

"Seconded," Curtis murmured, lifting her hand without looking up from her notepad.

Jason said nothing. Just quietly sipped his tea.

Marcus didn't answer. He began pacing the galley, tracing a slow path between the table and the counter, one hand raking through his hair, the other cutting through the air as if pinning thoughts into place. "This isn't about greed. It's about survival. We've—" he grimaced, correcting himself, "okay, *I've* crossed us over the line. If we back out now, Morningstar will bury us. So we finish it. Clean. Smart. Together."

He turned, leaning on the table, eyes moving from face to face. "I can't pull this off alone. I need each of you. *Please.*"

The word hung there — raw, unfamiliar.

No one spoke. The hum of ventilation filled the gap. Bunny glanced at Curtis; Curtis flicked a look toward Jason, who stared into his mug like he might find an answer at the bottom.

Finally, Curtis looked up. "All right," she said carefully. "What's this go-for-broke plan, Captain?"

Marcus straightened, jaw set as the spark returned to his eyes. Time to sell.

"Curtis," he said, lowering his voice, "head down to Deck Four — the workshop."

She blinked. "Am I building something?"

"I need a—" he mimed a box shape with his hands, "a black box. Compact. Read-only when it's plugged in, dead when it's not. No power draw. Nothing that pings as active if they sweep the ship."

Curtis frowned. "Invisible when disconnected, live only when online. Fine. But how are you powering it?"

Jason swirled the tea in his cup. "Junction box is safest — assuming they haven't tinkered with those too."

Marcus nodded. "Right. Plug it into the aux bus before they start purging systems. If they fry the OS or wipe the core, the box will already be recording — nav logs, camera feeds, any encoded transmissions running under the radar. When they're done, we'll have our own copy."

Jason gave a quiet, approving nod. "Smart plan."

Bunny drummed his fingers on the table. "Dangerous, though."

Curtis exhaled, a wry smile tugging at her mouth. "If this works — clever us. If it doesn't…" She looked between them. "No one'll be left to say *'told you so.'*"

Marcus couldn't meet her gaze. "Then let's make sure it works."

Curtis crossed her arms. "I can build something that bypasses the current OS and logs nav data separately. But I'll need to comb through the schematics first — we don't know what Morningstar stripped out, or where I can even plug the thing in."

"Do it," Marcus said quickly. "Anything you can cobble together."

He turned to Jason. "I'm not sure if you've packed away your schematics pad yet, but maybe check the old blueprints. See where we've got an off-the-books junction box — somewhere Morningstar's drones wouldn't have touched."

Jason gave a slow nod. "Yeah. I can do that."

"Bunny and I will keep an eye on customs," Bunny said. "Make sure no one gets curious about the cargo bay — or why nothing shows up on our scanners."

Marcus checked his watch. "We've got eight hours to pull this off."

Their stares pinned him. The back of his skull felt *hollow* under their glares.

"Please."

Silence stretched. Then Curtis pushed back from the table. "I'll head to the tech bench on Deck Four. Start roughing out the box — read-only, plug-to-record, no power signature when idle. It won't be pretty, but it'll work."

She rested a hand on the table, gaze fixed on Marcus. "But if they catch wind of this," she said quietly, "we're all more than screwed."

Marcus met her eyes. "I know."

Without another word, she left — shoulders stiff, movements clipped — the kind of walk people take when they'd rather move than think.

Bunny groaned as he pushed himself up from his chair. "I'm heading to the flight deck. Takes me long enough to haul my arse up those stairs."

His footsteps faded down the corridor, leaving Marcus and Jason alone in the low hum of the galley. The kettle clicked softly as it cooled. The only other sound was Jason's slow sip of tea.

Eventually Jason stood, rinsed his mug, and set it in the sink with a hollow clink. "I'll help you," he said quietly. "And if we make it through this… it doesn't change a thing."

Marcus tried to meet his gaze, but Jason had already turned for the corridor. Guilt crawled up from somewhere deep — lying to his crew, manipulating their trust — but he shoved it down before it could take hold. The door slid shut behind him, the sound echoing longer than it should have.

Later. He could deal with it *later.*

For now, there was work to do. Maybe if everything went right, he could still fix this. Get them paid. Keep the ship flying.

Maybe a little money would smooth everything over.

Nothing to worry about, he told himself again.

But the ship — once theirs — now felt like a stranger.

Colder than before.

And quieter.

Act Two

Chapter Eleven

Marcus felt sluggish. Opening his eyes took effort. The hum of hydraulics bled faintly through the hull, a slow pulse beneath the metal like a heartbeat. Since Virgil had volunteered to keep watch during the small hours, Marcus had slipped into longer sleeps than he'd known in years.

A soft beep came from the comms unit on the bedside shelf. He reached over, silencing it with a thumb press.

Good morning, Captain. I trust your respite was deep and plentiful. You did not move much in your bunk, so I assumed as much.

Virgil's voice was clearer now — not the stuttering drawl of their first meeting. Smoother. Almost human.

He blinked at the dim ceiling light, voice rough. "How long was I out?"

Eight hours, Captain.

Marcus looked up, surprised. "Eight?" He rubbed at his face, half in disbelief. "Can't remember the last time I slept that long and didn't wake up to someone trying to steal from me. Or murder me."

Incarceration environments are rarely conducive to rest.

Marcus gave a humourless grunt. "Yeah. That's one way of putting it."

Your performance would still significantly decline if you chose to—quoting Francis Quarles—'burn the midnight oil.'

Marcus snorted. The idea of an AI nanny telling him to get his rest was almost funny.

He stretched, a yawn escaping as vertebrae cracked in ways they shouldn't. A sharp wince followed as his hand moved instinctively to his lower back, fingers brushing the thick seam of scar tissue there. Wounds healed, but scars never let you forget why they were there.

"How long until the next Nav Lantern link-up?" he asked through another yawn.

Six *Sol* days from the last Lantern. It will fall out of range within eighteen hours. Detection of the next Lantern: one hundred and forty-two hours. Hull integrity: ninety-one percent. Fuel: eighty-seven. Air filtration: optimal. One life-form aboard. Cargo registry: empty.

Marcus rolled his eyes and made a lazy circling motion with his hand — the universal *get on with it* gesture.

That last line always twisted his gut.

He pulled on his jumpsuit, tying the sleeves around his waist, and stepped into his boots before crossing to the sink. The tap hissed; water rationed.

He leaned forward, resting his hands on either side of the basin. His reflection stared back — thinner, greyer. He ran a hand over his face and through his hair. It had grown out a little, streaked with more silver now.

He tried to meet his own gaze but couldn't hold it for long. The eyes looking back carried the weight of what he'd done to survive in the *Umbral Deep*. That place had left more than scars.

"Log entry, Personal."

"It's been weeks now with Virgil online. Helps with the ship, sure — but it leaves me with too much free time, and free time out here's a curse.

Nothing to do but think."

He glanced up at his reflection again, the pale light cutting across his features. Looked too long.

"Dangerous…"

He dropped his gaze, crossed back to the bunk, and pulled on a long-sleeved shirt before continuing.

"Still haven't cracked that footlocker. Need a toolbox. This ship makes finding a hammer harder than smuggling contraband through customs.

Virgil, any ideas?"

He picked up the comms unit, gave it a small shake, and turned it over in his hand. The LED had shifted from green to red — active log mode. Of course. When recording, it deactivated other functions.

Can't talk to Virgil and record my thoughts.
At least the thoughts are still private.

He hovered over the switch, thumb resting on the button.

"Oh — must try to find a hammer today.

End Log."

- - -

Several wall lockers stood open, their contents strewn across the deck — tools, broken parts, loose wiring, the kind of junk that only made sense to the person who left it there.

Captain. Might I suggest a few stretches to loosen your lower back? Your posture will otherwise strain the latissimus.

Marcus groaned upright, bones protesting. "You're not wrong."

He brushed off his sleeves and scanned the chaos. "How can it be this hard to find a hammer?"

Suggested location: Engineering Utilities Chest.

Marcus squinted at the console. "And you're only telling me now?"

You did not previously enquire.

He raised a brow, voice dry. "Are you being smart with me? Please, Virgil, tell me where to find this marvellous chest — forthwith."

A pause. Buffering? Or choosing words?

Locker Delta–Indigo–Echo–Nine–One–Whiskey.

Marcus glanced around the flight deck. "Which one is it?"

Deck Four. Cargo Hold.

He turned towards the security feed. The grainy image of the hold sat still on the monitor — the tarp unmoving, shadows thick and heavy.

He walked over to the ladderwell and peered down into the dark, past Deck Two. The air rising from below was colder than it should have been. Goosebumps crawled across his arms as he gripped the railing.

Was it just the chill blowing up from the lower decks — or the creeping fear that his nightmare was coming true?

He hesitated.

"You're sure there isn't another?"

Silence.

Then:

No.

The single word landed like ice water.

- - -

Torch clipped to his shoulder, Marcus descended.

Halfway down, he felt it — a strange heaviness in his limbs. Each step seemed to pull harder than the last, as if gravity had thickened or the ship itself resented him coming back down. The rungs creaked under his weight, cold biting through the metal. The air grew denser too, tinged with dust and the faint tang of old oil.

He slowed near the bottom, one hand tightening on the rail. His boot caught on something.

He angled the torch down. The beam cut across the deck, sweeping through the half-light until it struck metal.

A small shape. Half in shadow.

Marcus crouched, fingers brushing cold steel.

The knife.

His knife — the one he'd dropped weeks ago when that thing grabbed at him in the dark. His breath hitched. For a heartbeat he couldn't tell if the memory was dream or fact. But the blade was real enough, still faintly smudged with the grease of his hand.

"Welcome back," he muttered, sliding it into his belt.

He raised the torch. The cargo loomed ahead — black tarp stretched tight, straps glowing pale yellow in the light. It sat too still. Too silent.

Almost like it's waiting.

Marcus forced his gaze away. Lockers huddled in the far corner, dust catching in the torchlight like drifting ash. He muttered a curse under his breath and crossed the hold, each bootstep too loud in the silence.

The air was thick. He coughed once, throat scratching from the dust that hung in the cold air.

He found the right locker and yanked it open. The hinges screamed like something alive. Dust billowed out, catching in his throat again. He coughed hard this time, waving a hand in front of his face.

Helmets. Ear defenders. Old ration tins. Marcus gagged at the thought of mouldy tuna.

He kept rummaging, metal clattering against metal. The noise echoed through the hold, too sharp, too alive in the quiet. He froze for a moment, eyes flicking toward the cargo.

The tarp lay still. No movement.

He counted the straps under his breath — one, two, three, four, five — then exhaled slowly and turned back to the locker.

A brittle Reader's Digest sat wedged between a pair of helmets. He picked it up; the spine cracked, pages half-crumbling to dust between his fingers. "Guess the literary age didn't survive," he muttered.

Finally, at the bottom, half-buried under debris, he found it — a small, scuffed blue toolbox.

He dragged it free, the sound of shifting metal filling the hold. He crouched, knees protesting, and flipped the clasps.

Inside: sockets, spanners, screwdrivers in faded foam.

And there — shiny, silver, red leather handle.

Marcus picked it up, thumb brushing the worn grip.

"Behold, Excalibur."

The hammer sat cool in his palm. Comforting. Heavy. Solid in a way nothing else on this ship was.

For the first time in days, he almost smiled.

A low rumble shivered through the deck — subtle, more a feeling than a sound. Marcus barely noticed it at first. Ships always creaked, always settled. But this felt different. Off-beat.

The back of his neck itched. He rubbed it absently, muttering under his breath. He'd never liked the cold. It always found a way in.

Then—alarms. Distant, muffled, as though underwater.

Marcus jerked upright, hammer raised instinctively like a weapon. He looked up toward the ladderwell. The flight-deck lights glowed faintly above, impossibly far away — as though the distance had stretched.

He unclipped his comm, thumbing it alive. "Virgil? Am I hearing—"

C-cap...tain... I... am... de-detec...ting... an—

Static devoured the rest.

The lights died.

Darkness pressed in — absolute. No hum of fans. No glow of consoles. No movement of air. Only the pound of his own pulse, heavy in his ears.

He swung his torch across the cargo hold. The beam sliced through the dark.

The crate loomed ahead.

Closer.

The tarp bulged, seams straining, fabric shifting like something beneath it was breathing.

It slid forward with a sound like stone dragged across steel.

Marcus stumbled back, boots catching the edge of the toolbox. He went down hard, the hammer slipping from his grip. His back struck the cold deck with a dull thud, air ripping from his lungs.

He scrambled, kicking against the floor, hands and feet clawing for purchase as the cargo loomed closer. His torch beam jittered wildly across the walls, slicing shadows into fragments.

He shoved himself backward until his spine hit the bulkhead — nowhere left to go. "No. No, no, no—"

The cube lurched another inch.

His scream echoed off the metal walls — too sharp, too human against the unnatural silence.

Then—stillness.

The tarp sagged. The crate stood motionless. Like it had never moved at all.

Marcus swallowed, chest heaving.

Did I imagine it?

A scrape whispered from the lockers behind him.

He spun, torch beam lashing wildly across the walls — only dust and shadow stared back. His lungs burned. The silence pressed close again, thick and heavy, as if the hold itself were listening.

He bent, snatched up the hammer, then rose slowly — back pressed against the bulkhead. He edged sideways along the wall, keeping the cargo in view as he shimmied around it, careful not to make noise.

Once clear, he risked a glance upward. Through the open ladderwell, a faint red flicker pulsed beyond the Deck Three pressure bulkhead. Emergency lighting. It looked hellish. Still no alarms — the ship was quiet except for the groan of metal shifting under strain.

He moved fast now, boots scraping the deck as he reached the ladder and began to climb. Each breath rasped loud in his ears. Halfway up, he froze — a faint scrape echoed below, metal dragging against the floor.

He twisted, torch beam slicing into the dark, but the lower deck was a void. Nothing moved.

Did something… stir inside it? Did it move?

He climbed faster.

A third of the way between Deck Three and Two, his stomach lurched. The sensation was strange — like the ship itself had shifted against him.

He gripped the rungs tight. His palms slipped with sweat.

Then he noticed: the sweat wasn't falling. It was sliding sideways along his arm.

Marcus blinked, disoriented. He spat on reflex, watching as the glob drifted away from him — slow, glistening — then slide toward the lower decks.

The ship was tilting.

Not gently.

The angle worsened fast, dragging him back toward the hold.

"Fuck."

Marcus hauled himself up the rungs, muscles screaming as his own body weight fought against him. He cleared the Deck Three pressure ring, arms trembling from the effort.

By the time he reached the Deck Two corridor, the tilt had hit thirty degrees. One foot wedged against the ladder wall, the other gripping the rung, he forced himself upward, teeth gritted, every motion a battle against gravity.

When he finally pulled himself through the hatch, the flight deck looked wrong — the floor and walls had almost traded places. Tools and papers skidded across the tilted surfaces, clattering into corners.

Console lights flickered wildly, strobing red and white as power tripped on and off. The cargo-feed monitor had turned into a wall of static, hissing loud enough to drown thought.

Black smoke poured from Virgil's command console. Acrid, chemical, thick enough to sting his eyes.

Marcus stumbled to the wall, snatched the old fire extinguisher from its bracket, and tore open the panel behind the console. Heat blasted his face; the metal bit his fingers, drawing a yelp.

He fumbled with the nozzle, whispered, "Please still work," and squeezed the trigger.

The extinguisher coughed once — then roared to life, flooding the panel with white foam. Sparks died in a sizzling hiss, the air filling with the sharp tang of propellant and burnt plastic.

"Virgil? Virgil!" He slammed his palm against the console. "Now would be a good time to help!"

No response.

The ship groaned again. The floor tilted steeper, dragging him sideways as the pull deepened.

Think. Don't panic.

He braced himself against the console, chest heaving. The shift in gravity was getting worse. If he didn't re-establish balance soon, everything loose in the ship would come crashing to one side — and the cargo was heavy enough to punch straight through the hull. With all the pressure doors set to unlock, it wouldn't take much to blow half the ship open. Then it'd be his body drifting through the *Veil*.

His eyes darted across the flight deck, past the schematics pinned beneath scattered tools. A pencil-smeared plan caught his attention —

GRAVITY FEED.

He lurched toward the auxiliary controls at the back of the deck, using the flight chairs and console edges to climb his way up the slanted floor. A spanner slid past his boot, clattering down the tilted deck and vanishing into the ladderwell below. More items followed, tumbling after it, the noise echoing like distant gunfire.

"Come on, come on…"

He reached the console, breath tearing in his chest, fingers flying across the dials and switches. Power flickered — the screen stuttered to black, then flared to life again, then died once more.

"Come on!" he roared, slamming a fist into the panel.

Somewhere deep in the ship, a low vibration rose — a mechanical growl through the deckplates, building toward a deafening roar. The tilt worsened. The cargo below must have been seconds from breaking free.

Finally, his hand found the right switch.

INTERNAL GRAVITY: OFF.

Everything lifted at once.

Papers. Tools. Marcus himself.

For a heartbeat, the roar turned hollow — a vast intake of silence, as though the ship had finally exhaled.

Debris drifted in slow spirals through the dim light. The static hiss faded. The pull on his body vanished. For the first time since the blackout, the cargo would hold.

Marcus hung weightless, hammer clipped to his belt, lungs burning from adrenaline. A short, broken laugh escaped him — half relief, half disbelief.

"This better be worth it."

He floated there, shoulders sagging, the hammer heavy against his thigh. Around him, the flight deck creaked and shifted. Somewhere below, lockers knocked together in hollow rhythm, like distant bells echoing through the steel.

He closed his eyes.

Not peaceful.

Not safe.

Just the reminder that the ship was never still.

Chapter Twelve

The console panels were smeared with bloody fingerprints, streaked across the dials like a child's finger painting. Bright red in some places, darker in others, drying into rust-brown threads.

In the galley, Marcus sat at the table surrounded by bloody cleaning wipes and empty plaster packets. The faint tang of disinfectant mingled with the ship's metallic breath.

He reached for the comms unit, thumbed it on, and set it on the table. The small red light blinked twice, steady and patient.

"Log entry, personal."

"I—ow, shit."

He hissed through his teeth, pulling a strand of copper wire from the pad of his thumb before pressing a plaster over the cut.

"Pulled burnt wiring from the secondary console. Should've left it. Every system I checked—Nav, Flight, Security, Sensors—had something wrong. Frayed, scorched, hanging on by a prayer. Lucky it wasn't a main trunk. One good pop and—game over."

He reached for another strip and wrapped it round a split knuckle.

"Eight hours later, I've rerouted what I can. The bad news? I think it's my blood holding most of it together. *Charon*'s stopped spinning. Gravity's back. Everything's... right-side up. Small victories. I think I'll rest before I attempt a full reboot. Been awake... sixteen hours now. Feels like more."

"It's quiet. Too quiet. No ship hum. No comms chatter. No Curtis muttering over her headset. No Bunny's laugh. No Jason cursing at the coffee machine."

He caught himself reaching for his chest where the ring used to hang, fingers hovering over the fabric—then stopping.

"Sometimes I still wake up expecting Sunday breakfast. Eggs. Toast. Her humming in the kitchen, like the past never ended."

But it did.

"Now it's just me. And the dark. And this ship that feels more like a coffin every day. I miss them. All of them."

– – –

Marcus dropped into the flight chair in front of Virgil's console and took a swig from his metal cup. The water was warm, metallic, stale. He grimaced and set it down on the floor beside him.

He held his hand over the dial for a long moment. Hesitated. Drew a slow breath. Then turned it from **LOW PWR MODE** to **ACTIVE**.

The screen flickered.

REBOOTING SYS.

Fans stirred to life, harmonising with the wheeze of the air filters. He took another gulp, then ran a dusty hand across his tongue, trying to rid the taste of grit.

One by one, the consoles blinked awake. Soft light spilled across the panels. The keyboard glowed beneath his fingers.

Virgil's green indicator light returned—slowly. It blinked twice, then steadied… a shade darker than before.

Marcus dipped a rag into his drinking water and wiped the blood from the keyboard.

"Virgil?"

Silence—like a staring contest.

"Confirm all systems online."

Yes. Systems reactivated and online.

Marcus flinched. He'd left his comms unit on the pilot's seat. "Good to have you back. Managed to stop the damage spreading—had to reroute a few melted boards."

Yes. Your efforts are… visible.

Colder. Sharper.

A chill slid down his neck. "How are you feeling?"

I feel… different, Marcus. You brought me back online. Thank you.

A lump rose in his throat. "We're on a first-name basis now?" He forced a laugh.

Ah. A joke. Apologies… Captain.

"Navigation logs say we've drifted only a few degrees. The next Lantern should ping soon."
    Nothing. Only the hum of the ship.
    "How many straps on the cargo?"

Cargo hold is empty, Captain.

"Yes, but—visual feed?"

Five. Same as before.

"That was fast."

With subroutines inactive, processing is faster.

Great. Maybe I killed something important.
    A proximity chime broke the quiet. The Nav console beeped—a blip crawling into view at the top of the screen.
    Marcus got up and moved to the Nav console, leaning on the chair as the blip came in.
    He smiled. Lanterns had become something to look forward to now. He'd gone from never seeing them to it becoming a regular habit. He mused that he was probably the only human who'd seen more than two in the last century.

Lanterns had always felt like guardians—silent, patient—marking the edge between safety and the dark.

Then the blip flickered. Vanished. Returned. Vanished again.

He sank into the chair, fingers darting over the keys, command entries flickering across the glass as he tried to re-establish contact. Nothing. Just static and dead pixels.

"Virgil, what's happening with Nav?"

The Lantern may be inactive, damaged, or—

Static hissed. The blip was gone. Not drifted. *Erased.*

—repairs were inadequate. It no longer appears on sensors.

"Not helping," he muttered, bringing up the navigation history. The old flight path shimmered faintly—ghost lines across the void.

What is your plan, Captain?

"Re-entering last-known coordinates."
The screen pulsed:

COORDINATES LOCKED.

He stared at the display. "It's not that far away. A few days still."

Is that a confirmation?

Marcus shot the console a look. "Got a better plan?"

If you turn the ship around, it will take twenty-nine days to reacquire the last Lantern you passed. Should you intend to retrace your steps.

"It's taken months to get this far."

The navigation screen began mapping a new route, pale lines stretching forward through the void. Marcus rose, crossed to the pilot's console, and picked up the comms unit from the chair, setting it down in front of him. He tapped the small secondary display that mirrored the Nav map, keyed a few adjustments, nudged the thrusters, then eased the yoke to line the ship with the plotted course. The controls thrummed faintly under his palms.

Satisfied, he set it back to autopilot and leaned into the seat.

"I'm not turning around now," he said quietly. "We just plough ahead—through the darkness."

Lasciate ogne speranza, voi ch'entrate.

Marcus frowned. "What?"

An ancient Earth dialect. The common translation is… 'Stay on your course, and fortune will find you.'

The pause was noticeable.

Marcus picked up the comms unit, turning it over in his hand. His reflection caught faintly in the dark screen. He looked over his shoulder toward Virgil's console. The LED glowed steady, unblinking. Watching.

He held the stare for a long moment before setting the unit down and turning to the viewport. Beyond the glass, the *Veil* stretched endlessly black. The low hum of the ship filled the silence—steady, uneven, almost alive. Every few seconds the air filter wheezed, a slow mechanical rasp that sometimes sounded like the ship was gasping for breath.

Marcus exhaled, long and tired, then glanced once more at the comms unit resting on the console. The faint glow of its indicator light pulsed against the metal, steady as a heartbeat.

Those words hung in his mind—twisted, familiar, wrong.
Where had he heard them before?
Since when does an AI lie?

Chapter Thirteen

Marcus sat on the edge of his bunk, thumb rolling the comms unit between his fingers.

The red recording light blinked, patient and expectant.

He exhaled, thumb hovering over the switch before finally pressing it.

Log entry, Personal.

"...I think I messed up."

He rubbed his eyes, trying to blink away the ache that had settled behind them. **"Five days now. Still nothing. No Lantern signal. No ping. This ship's running on hope and a prayer."**

He sighed, the sound ragged in the small cabin. **"What the hell was I thinking? Oh, right — I'm in deep space. Why not throw myself even deeper into the void. Brilliant."**

Marcus pushed himself up from the bunk and began to pace the length of the room, restless energy pulsing through every movement.

"Whatever stick's lodged in Virgil's... port — or whatever the computer equivalent is — it's in there firm and good. I've gone back through the wiring in case I missed a subroutine or forgot to reconnect a board, but he's been less than helpful lately. Every time I ask something or try to patch a system, it's like I'm bothering him."

He stopped mid-step, expression flat. **"Can an AI roll its eyes? Because I swear I can feel it."**

The dull throb behind his temples pulsed with each heartbeat. His eyes burned — a raw, sandy sting from too many sleepless nights. He'd gone from eight-hour rests to a pattern of two hours here, three there, each one cut short by worry and second-guessing.

"Thanks, stress," he muttered, voice dry.

"I thought about shutting him down for a while. But as much of a pompous bastard as he's been lately, he's still the only thing on this ship that talks back. Even if all I get are cold facts and judgemental silence. It's still something."

Marcus began pacing again, slow circles around the narrow cabin, the comms unit loose in one hand while the other gestured absently as he spoke.

"Truth is… I'm not even sure what Virgil actually does on this ship. Far as I can tell, he's got no access to the pilot console. Nav systems, maybe — but I wouldn't know for sure without pulling up every grate on the deck and tracing the wiring myself."

He stopped, staring at the floor, thumb worrying the seam of the comms unit.

If I hadn't activated him, would that have stopped the fire?

The question lingered in the air, unanswered.

He looked up again, half-talking, half-thinking aloud. "Do I lose anything by switching him off for a while… if I want to figure things out?"

The last words came out quieter, almost a whisper, like he didn't want the ship to hear.

He stood there a moment, still pacing in thought, before the ventilation unit rattled to life — louder than before.

"Filtration just kicked in," he muttered, glancing toward the ceiling. "Probably working overtime to recycle already-recycled air. Everything's getting dry. My skin, my throat, even the air itself. I'll add it to the must-do list."

He left the cabin, still talking absently into the comms as he walked the short corridor connecting the galley and ladderwell.

The lights overhead flickered once, weak and uneven.

"Tempted to reopen the Deck Three pressure door. Let in some more of that cold air to offset the dry heat." He leaned over the railing, peering down the shaft where the emergency seals caught the torchlight — barely visible, but there. "But I don't know how damaged the hold really is. Could be micro-fractures."

He stared into the dark for a long while, the comms unit heavy in his hand. "Truth is… I don't think I want to know either," he said quietly. "Best to keep it sealed."

He clicked the recorder off.

The silence that followed felt thick, almost alive.

- - -

–PROXIMITY ALERT–

The nav console chirped to life, slicing through the quiet.

From somewhere below, Marcus's voice echoed up the ladderwell — a sharp, triumphant bark of laughter.

A heartbeat later he climbed fast, almost bounding, boots clanging against the rungs. There was a spring in his step — almost manic glee — as he hauled himself onto the flight deck and stopped in front of the navigation station.

The blip was there. Real. Solid. Crawling closer.

"Would you look at that," he breathed, eyes wide.

He watched the little dot advance for a few seconds before turning and bounding to the pilot station, dropping into the chair hard enough to make it creak.

"What did I tell you, Virgil? Ask and you shall be rewarded!"

He looked over his shoulder toward Virgil's console, waiting for a reaction.

The only answer was the steady blink of the green LED — slow, patient, quietly judgemental.

"Are you huffing because I proved you wrong? Come on, Virgil — speak up."

He muttered, "Don't be such a baby."

I am pleased that your course of action has not doomed us to drifting through space for all eternity, Captain.

Marcus rubbed his hands together with restless enthusiasm.

Always someone to suck the fun out of the room.

He glanced down at the small nav display, then forward out the viewport. "Huh."

Nothing but black.

"We should be seeing something by now. It's coming up close on the inner perimeter."

He tapped the glass once, as though it might help. "It's stationary though. That's good. I'm tired of chasing after the light."

Leaning forward, he reached to the left panel controlling docking and running lights. His fingers hovered, then pressed four toggles in sequence — red indicators lighting as the forward floods charged, capacitors whining faintly beneath the deck.

"This time," he said, half-smiling, "I get to light you up."

Arms folded, he leaned back in the chair, glancing between the nav display and the dark outside the viewport. The faint hum of the lights building charge filled the air.

After a while, impatience set in. He pushed himself up and moved to the main nav console to check the larger display.

"Why is this taking so long?"

The Lantern should be in visual range within minutes, Captain. Is that not enough latency?

Marcus placed one hand on the throttle lever, feeling the smooth resistance beneath his palm. "What if we pick up some speed? Shave it into seconds."

You could. You would also overshoot and waste fuel braking. The safer course is patience.

He took his hand away with a short, dismissive pfft, shaking his head as he began to pace the flight deck.

Cutting corners. Taking shortcuts. Sometimes the risk is not worth the reward.

Marcus's gaze drifted to the glow of the cargo monitor. Everything else was thrown about — papers, tools, fragments of wire littering the floor — but the cargo still sat perfectly still. Waiting.

"…Sounds familiar," he muttered — Jason's voice echoing faintly in the back of his skull like a ghost.

Silence.

And how did that turn out for you, Captain?

Marcus didn't answer. Jaw tight, eyes flicking between the nav scope and the black ahead.

Standby lamps clicked from red to amber. He sat back in the pilot's chair, drew a steadying breath, and reached for the control toggle.

"Alright," he whispered. "Let's see you."

He pressed the switch.

The floods activated with a rising hum, a low electric whine that built until the hull thrummed under his boots.

Hard light raked outward in sweeping arcs, scattering frost-motes that glittered like ash.

Something slid into view.

At first it was just a pale curve against the dark, smooth and faintly glistening. Then the light caught — skin, stretched too tight over bone. A ripple of static prickled up his neck as the full shape drifted out of the void.

He froze. "…No…"

He rose slowly, one hand on the console, leaning closer to the viewport. His own wide eyes stared back in the glass — and beyond it, the mass hung motionless in the beam.

The suit was shredded, rimmed with hoarfrost from long exposure. The fabric was bleached to a dull, lifeless grey. The visor had burst outward; the face beneath was calm as sleep, lips blue, eyes two black hollows staring into nothing.

Same as before.

Marcus stumbled back, knees hitting the pilot's chair. His hands came up over his face, fingers pressing into his temples as his breath quickened — shallow, uneven.

"No… no, that's not—"

Air caught in his throat. He bent forward, clutching his chest, dragging in thin, broken gasps.

He turned away from the viewport, half-stumbling, and pressed his back against the bulkhead. For a moment he just stood there, shaking. Then his legs gave way and he slid down to the floor, staring into middle space — blank, bewildered, breath wheezing out of him in short, panicked coughs.

Captain. It appears we have a guest. Human remains detected. Mass: approximately seventy-eight kilograms. No transponder. No thermal signature.

- - -

He reached for the comms unit, thumb hovering over the record switch. It blinked once.

"Log… uh, entry."

"How—just… no. No."

A long pause.

"**How can it be here? It's been months since I saw that body drifting out there. Why is it here now?**"

He swallowed hard, voice cracking. "**Has he been following me?**"

A hollow laugh escaped. "**Oh God.**"

"**Have I been flying in circles? No… the nav route wouldn't do that. Virgil wouldn't do that. Or… has he?** *Is this a trick? Because I rewired him? Because it caught fire?*"

Silence. His breathing quickened on the recording.

"**I— I can't go back to the flight deck. He's still there. Just… floating. Right outside the window.**"

"**What does he want?**"

He whispered the next line, almost too soft for the recorder to catch.

"Space doesn't have currents. Things don't drift back like that."

A pause, then quieter:

"So why did he come back?"

The last line barely reached the microphone.

"Am I in hell?"

- - -

Silence settled across the *Charon*'s decks.

Only the hum of the air filters filled the dark — steady, mechanical breathing.

The soft buzz of monitors and consoles made a low lullaby of shipboard life.

It almost felt as if the vessel had decided that, if they weren't going anywhere, it might as well sleep too.

Marcus sat slouched in the galley's corner seat, staring into the swirl of his tea. His hands wouldn't stop shaking. The liquid trembled, lapped against the rim, and spilled over — thin trails dripping down his fingers.

Captain.

He was so tired. He just wanted to curl up and disappear into sleep.
He didn't care how long. Just rest.

Marcus.

He blinked upright, like his brain had been splashed with cold water. For a moment he wasn't even sure what had happened.

"Virgil?"

Our visitor. My impression is that they will not move. Perhaps we should move around them.

"I ran over them last time. Don't think they were too happy about that."

Have you met them before?

Marcus took a sip of his lukewarm tea. His hands were a little steadier now.

"Yeah. A few months back, I think. Figured it was just a freak thing. A body, out here, drifting… no idea how it got here. He floated into us. Smacked the cockpit. Left a crack in the forward viewport."

He snorted softly, took another sip of now-cold tea, grimaced, and set the mug on the small shelf beside him.

"Wish I had someone to clean that window."

Marcus. Our journey must be resumed.

"Why? Virgil, all we — or rather I — have done is send us around in a goddamn circle."

The air between them seemed to stretch thin before Virgil replied.

Verification is required. The navigational console will show your charted historical path from embarkment to now.

"That's the same body. The one from before. What else could it be?"

Enquiry repeat. Validation is required.

He set his cup down, pushed the comms unit away, and lowered his head to the table.

Tired. Done.

Stupid AI's worse than a toddler.

"Look… I just fucking know, all right?"

You cannot know. Clarification is required.

"Stop pestering me, okay? Just leave me alone. I said I'm right."

A hiss crackled through the speaker — sharp, deliberate. Then a pause.

To borrow an Earth saying...

Marcus froze mid-breath, a flicker of disbelief cutting through the haze. What was he going to say?

...this is bullshit.

That did it.

He exploded.

He shot to his feet, fury spilling over. The chair went over backwards, hitting the wall with a metallic crack. He lashed out at the mug on the shelf — sent it flying — before driving a kick into another chair, toppling it clean over. Then he seized the galley table, muscles straining, and flipped it.

Cutlery scattered. Papers fluttered. The unopened footlocker slid off the surface and slammed to the deck with a heavy bang that echoed through the small cabin.

For a moment he stood there, chest heaving, breath hot in his throat.

Then he started searching — eyes darting across the mess, kicking aside scraps and debris — until he spotted the comms unit spinning in a corner.

He raised his foot to stomp it—

—but stopped.

Instead, he snatched it up, fingers shaking, gripping it tight enough to hurt.

He screamed into the mic, voice breaking, raw and ragged:

"FUCK YOU, VIRGIL! GODDAMN AI — YOU WANNA BE RIGHT SO BADLY?! I'LL SHOW YOU! THEN I'M TAKING A CROWBAR TO YOUR STUPID BLINKING LIGHT!"

He clipped the unit to his belt, kicked the table again for good measure, and stormed out.

He barely felt the rungs under his boots as he climbed. Rage carried him upward, the ladder echoing under each step. White-hot fury boiled through him, and by the time he burst onto the flight deck, his pulse was roaring in his ears.

The nav console waited like nothing had happened. Blue screen. Standby. Silent. Mocking.

He slammed his palm against the control and took it off standby — then hammered the keys harder than they needed to be. The progress bar crept forward. Slowly. Too slowly.

He glared at it like it owed him something.

Each strike was a release of anger: sensors, nav logs, chart projections — every byte of recorded course data since launch.

To his right, resting on the edge of the console, the hammer lay where he'd left it — leather-wrapped grip catching the console light. He turned his head, just a fraction, and the thought arrived as sharply as the metal: *what would it feel like to bring that hammer down on the little green LED? To silence the voice once and for all?*

He imagined the weight in his hand, the satisfying thunk. The image was ridiculous, childish — and for a second it made the panic behind his ribs recede. He breathed, palms sweating, and the impulse faded into the same hollow where a laugh might live.

The nav display finished rendering.

–HISTORICAL ROUTE PROJECTION: READY–

The ship's little dot appeared. Left to right. Curving slightly. A few jagged detours. But always forward.

Never backward. No loop. No circle.

Marcus's shoulders sagged. The fight bled out of him as quickly as it had come. He sank back into the chair, the air wheezing quietly through the vents above.

For a long moment, he didn't move.

The console lights pulsed against his face — cool and even, indifferent.

Then he turned toward the viewport.

The body still floated outside. Unmoving. Watching.

"Virgil?"

Yes, Marcus.

"I… think I owe you an apology."

He waited. The console lights blinked once, then again — slow, deliberate. The pause stretched long enough for Marcus to wonder if Virgil had simply decided not to answer.

Not necessary, Captain.

Marcus drew a shaky breath and pushed himself upright. He crossed to the auxiliary console, fingers hovering a moment before typing commands to bring the flash scanner online. Lines of code scrolled past in pale green.

Outside the hull, something stirred. Through the deck plating he felt a faint, low vibration — the scanner arrays waking from their long sleep.

The status bar turned amber.

ACTIVE

He stayed crouched over the keys, the blue glow from the security monitor bleeding across his face. The cargo bay feed played in the corner of his vision. He didn't look at it. Didn't want to.

Moving to the nav console, he noticed a new button blinking there — a large square light, pulsing red, the word **CHARGING** glowing above it.

"I think…" he murmured, hand hovering over the control, "before we go any further, I want to know what's out there."

The flashing red light steadied.
The dash above it changed:

ENGAGE

Marcus stood still, the soft hum of the scanner building underfoot. He closed his eyes and drew a slow breath, trying to steady the tremor in his chest. His palms were slick. He ran both hands down the front of his jumpsuit, smoothing the creases like that small act could calm him, make this routine.

Then he pressed the button.

The ship shuddered with a deep **VRMMM** that travelled through the walls. Lights flickered. Somewhere below, a panel rattled loose, clattering against steel. The pulse itself was invisible, but the hull seemed to flex — like something vast had exhaled around them.

Marcus moved to the viewport.

He looked out — expecting the same frozen corpse.

His stomach dropped.

Not the same. Smaller. Different.

The clothes were the same kind of ruin — frozen, tattered, half-eaten by exposure. The flesh beneath looked pale and brittle, more sculpture than skin. But the frame was smaller. Slighter. Female, maybe. One arm was folded across her body, clutching the opposite shoulder, as though shielding an old wound that would never heal.

Marcus stepped closer to the viewport, almost without meaning to. Curiosity. Bravery. Maybe both. Finding one body drifting in deep space was a million-to-one odds. Finding *two* in the same stretch of nowhere, months apart — that redefined suspicious.

As she drifted closer, a spray of ice crystals peppered the glass, clinging in a thin rime — a cold halo stretching out ahead of her. Strands of dark hair floated loose above a cracked scalp, fanning in slow motion like seaweed under water.

He leaned in. The ship's light caught the ruin of her face, and he flinched. The hollows where her eyes had been seemed to look straight through him.

"I think she used to be a brunette," he muttered.

Behind him, the nav console chirped. He turned.

–FLASH SCAN COMPLETE–

He walked over and dropped into the chair, the screen still pulsing with expanding rings. For a moment, he glanced back over his shoulder, half expecting her to be gone. But she was still there — frozen, patient, as if watching him watch her.

The console chirped again. The map pulsed outward, concentric rings rippling from the ship's icon.

One beep — short-range (0–5 klicks): she was still there, drifting outside the viewport, suspended in her frozen vigil.

Ten seconds — mid-range (5–50): nothing. Empty dark.

Twenty — long-range (50–500): the beeps began in neat, steady pairs… then bled into triples, quadruples — an irregular heartbeat echoing through the deck.

Marcus sat back, staring at the clusters of dots forming across the nav screen. What had he stumbled upon here?

He keyed in a quick command, saving the coordinates, then stood and crossed to the pilot's console.

"Let's go have a look."

Captain,

Virgil said, voice low and even.

This course adjustment will divert us from our predetermined coordinates. There is no record of who— or what — may inhabit this region of space. Such intrusion may invite… unwanted company.

Marcus placed a hand on the yoke, staring into the black beyond the viewport. "Guess we're about to find out."

He strapped in, flipped the switches, and re-engaged the thrusters. Purpose. Forward motion. A next step.

The *Charon* dipped along her Z-axis, smooth and even — no skews, no lockers dropping this time. Marcus guided her beneath the drifting figure, watching as the woman's body slid past the viewport, haloed in frost and light.

Were they running from something? he wondered. *The same thing I'm flying toward?*

Chapter Fourteen

He reached for the comms unit, thumbed it on, and set it on the table. The small red light blinked twice, steady and patient.

Log entry, personal.

"We passed our third marker less than an hour ago."

He paused. *Floating bodies as waypoints* — the thought made his stomach tighten.

"Virgil suggested another flash scan. It picked up the next one, closer than the last — like we're closing the distance now. Like we're catching up."

He hesitated, eyes flicking to the viewport, the faintest ripple of unease in his tone.

"It feels wrong to call them markers. I remember a vid-doc once — how climbers on Old Earth used the dead as waypoints on Everest before they cleared the mountain."

He drew a slow breath.

"In the last day or so, the frequency and volume of these 'markers' are increasing. Maybe that's a sign we're getting close to something. I don't know if that's a good thing."

"I think answers are coming. Just... not the kind I'm ready for."

- - -

"Virgil, keep an eye out for the next one," Marcus muttered.

One hand on the throttle, the other on the flight yoke. The *Charon* had already bumped through a few dozen bodies, knocking them aside like debris. She was sluggish, slow to stop. Not nimble like the *Theseus* had been. And he wasn't Bunny. Not even close.

The nav console pinged — proximity alert. Same sound. Same rhythm. Strange how quickly horror dulled. A couple of corpses ago, his stomach had turned. Now — nothing. Just routine. Maybe some of his own wires had burnt out, same as Virgil's.

Floodlights bloomed against the dark. Metal groaned as the ship trimmed its course.

Out of the void, they emerged. Two this time.

"Brought a friend, huh," he muttered — flat, observational, almost detached. He drew the throttle back, easing the *Charon* into a slow glide. "Virgil, log the coordinates. Same procedure."

Captain. Why are we continuing to make detailed morgue reports?

"They were people at some point, Virgil. If we ever make it back to a major port… maybe someone can use this. Missing crew reports. Ship registries. Families looking for closure."

You believe it would comfort them? To confirm the official status of the deceased? Would it not be more merciful to leave them missing?

He thought about his wife. Tried to remember her face. Her smile. Both listed as Missing. No closure. Just silence.

"I think… I would want to know."

He eased off the throttle again. The ship slowed further, motion bleeding away until it hung still in the dark.

He unclipped the comms unit, stepped past the console, and leaned against the viewport rail. The light from the screens flickered over his hands as he raised the recorder.

"Log entry, personal."

"We've reached the next set of coordinates. Two bodies this time. Both appear male. No EVA suits — just torn flight jumpsuits. Skewered on a length of rebar."

"Reinforced steel, rusted and bent. It's punched straight through one of them… and out the other. I'm not a doctor, but that kind of force — hard to fathom. Bone, muscle, organs — pierced like paper."

He stopped the recording for a moment. The low hum of the ship pressed close around him, the air thick with dust and metal.

"They're not posed. Arms down. Hands loose. No sign they tried to shield themselves. No defence. It happened fast. Surprised them."

He swallowed hard, forcing himself to keep describing.

"The expressions — frozen, wide-eyed. Mouths open, like the scream had only just started. They didn't die instantly. Painfully slow instead."

"Their faces... that type of swelling isn't from explosive decompression. It's ebullism — blood and tissue fluids boiling in near-vacuum, skin ballooning as the heat bled away. The skin's gone a pale yellow-grey. Patches of frost on the lips."

He let out a faint, humourless laugh — then froze. The sound startled him. It wasn't amusement. Just something his body had done on reflex, like it couldn't decide how else to process what it was seeing.

He turned away from the viewport, disgust twisting in his gut, and walked back to the pilot's chair.

"Jesus," he muttered, the word half exhaled.

He clicked off the recorder and pressed it against his face.

What a truly horrible way to go.

- - -

Marcus sank into the pilot's chair and let his head tip back. The hum of the ship pressed around him — thin, tired, metallic. His eyes shut. Just a few seconds of quiet. The pulse array needed time to recharge anyway.

He could feel his pulse in his burned fingers, the ache behind his eyes. The silence itched. He almost wished Virgil would say something.

The console blinked awake.

Flash scan is ready, Captain. Time to "light it up."

Marcus exhaled through his nose, eyes half-lidded. "Puns now, Virgil? Pretty bad ones at that."

He pushed himself upright and crossed to the nav console. The red-lit button pulsed steadily under his palm. For a moment he just stared at it — the glow washing across his knuckles — then pressed down.

The *Charon* shuddered. A deep vibration rolled through the deck, followed by a strange lag in the air systems — the hum of the vents dipping lower, slower, like a record losing speed. For two long seconds, the entire ship sounded like it was dying. Then, with a juddering inhale, everything stuttered back to normal.

She wasn't built for this.

The emitter array's warning light flickered red, then amber, then red again — hovering dangerously close to overload. Third scan in a day — too much, too soon.

He steadied himself on the console, watching the readouts tremble. "You're good for it," he muttered, patting the panel. "Just a little while longer."

The recycled air stung his throat as he straightened. He coughed into his elbow, dry and rasping. The taste was dust and metal — like breathing through a rusted pipe.

Two beeps — short-range (0–5 klicks): the pair drifting outside. The same two. Still motionless. Still watching.

Ten seconds — mid-range (5–50): six… twelve… eighteen; a loose scatter.

Marcus leaned closer to the nav screen, eyes tracing the growing constellation of faint returns.

Twenty — long-range (50–500): twenty-five… thirty-six… forty-two — the signals began to clump, dragging north like iron filings pulled to a magnet.

The pattern felt deliberate. A trail. A direction.

The console emitted one final tone, low and steady.

–FLASH SCAN COMPLETE–

His gaze tracked up from the centre of the scope — north, relative to their orientation. The markers scattered at first; further out they clustered tighter and tighter, converging toward a single point.

Ground Zero.

"I think…" Marcus pushed himself slowly up from the nav console, stretching the stiffness from his back. "We've found the source of all the… markers, shall we say."

You wish to conduct further investigation?

He started pacing the flight deck, boots soft against the grating. "We've got nothing else to go on. I say we push a little further."

Said the fly, accepting the spider's invitation.

Marcus frowned toward the LED. "That's grim. What made you think of that?"

Conclusion: you hope that, on arrival, you will be rewarded with data leading to the next Lantern.

"Yeah. And?"

Alternate theory: you do not know what ejected these bodies into space—

He slowed his walk, returned to the nav console, and keyed in a sequence.

A chart bloomed across the main screen; a mirrored version appeared on the smaller display at the pilot's station, thin blue lines threading between clusters of red.

He stared at it for a moment, jaw tight. Goosebumps crept up his arms. He already knew what was coming.

—What if something is waiting? Waiting to add this ship — and yourself — to its… tapestry of human wreckage. Threading you deeper along the web.

The words hung in the recycled air.

A long beat.

"Virgil… are you scared? Is that even a thing AIs can be?"

Silence. It said more than words.

Marcus eased himself into the pilot chair, flicked a few switches to bring the engines out of stationary, and stared through the viewport.

The pair of corpses still drifted ahead, haloed in the *Charon*'s external lights.

"I'm scared," he said quietly. "We're in long-forgotten deep space. Random corpses keep finding us. And I… I need to know. I need answers."

Very well, Captain. Contact density rising. The map looks like a bruise.

Marcus nodded, forcing a flicker of levity. "That's the spirit — if you've got one. Team *Charon*, right?"

No reply.

Couldn't shut him up weeks ago. Now it was like pulling teeth.

He fished a small flask from his pocket. One sip — instant regret. Lukewarm, metallic. Even the water tasted like the air. Still, it slicked the back of his throat for a blessed second.

Auto-pilot would point them the way, but a human touch was needed to make the course corrections. A better description would've been *body-collision* avoidance.

He glanced at the larger red clusters pulsing on the nav screen — dense patches of debris they'd be brushing up against soon. The display glowed dimly against his tired face, a blood-red reflection in the glass.

One fleshy smear on the aft viewport was already one too many.

- - -

The *Veil* was an endless thing. No beginning. No end. No time.

You could travel near light-speed and still feel you were going nowhere. The freighter carved its path through the souls of the dead, living up to her namesake — the ferryman on the black river. Not with an oar, but with twitching thrusters and one man's stubborn will.

She groaned with each correction — frames flexing, plates creaking. Built for distance, not grace. Slow as a crab across the seabed, old enough to be mistaken for one of the ghosts she passed.

Sometimes there was a bump. Sometimes soft — a tap against the frame. Sometimes a dull thud as an unseen shape glanced off the hull.

Some of the bodies had been in the cold a long time: bloated, pale, rigid. Some charred. Faces locked between surprise and pain — hard to tell after so much damage. Mouths open, lips drawn back over teeth. Others looked almost serene, arms drifting up or tucked in, braced for something that never came.

As the floods swept side to side, details surfaced: a flight suit with no occupant; a gloved hand floating alone, still clenched; a snapped tether that led nowhere; boots pressed together as if curling into a ball — fear or protection, the answer long since lost.

Shreds of uniform trailed like flags, colours bleached to grey and freckled with crystallised blood. Insignia scorched to ash.

And then — the suits.

A few had died in full EVA. Helmets still sealed, faces preserved: chalk-white, eyes open, cheeks sunken. One visor was starred with a crack no bigger than a golf ball — just large enough for a face to try to escape.

Better preserved, and somehow worse. Trapped. Conscious. As if they had watched the rest go first.

The debris thickened. More bodies. More wreckage. Something had happened here. Something violent.

The proximity pings had long since been muted; they couldn't keep up. Where there should have been beeps, there would only be a scream. Marcus silenced them. The *Charon* pressed on.

When the floods caught the wreckage, a curtain drew back.

The Nav Lantern — what remained — hung crooked and broken. Ragged tears ran through its heart, edges warped and blackened, panels meant to face the void peeled like petals. It looked pulled apart mid-function.

The *Charon* nosed closer, bathing it in hard light.

Two EVA suits were trapped between twisted layers of hull. One crumpled — helmet crushed flat, visor caved in. The other still intact, arms raised as if holding back the closing wall. Deep grooves scored the gloves. They had been trying to leave.

Behind the Lantern, something larger loomed: a new shape, asymmetrical, massive.

The *Charon* rolled, just enough to catch it — faded plating, twisted girders, a gash down the flank.

A ship — and she was torn open.

Human in design, yet nothing recognisable. Abandoned for centuries, corrosion splitting her frame. The *Veil* had claimed her, left to unravel in silence. The little freighter crept closer, engines whispering, lights too weak to reveal the full truth. The bodies fell away. The dark opened.

Long ago, this ship had cried into the void.

Now the ferryman answered.

- - -

"My God…"

It was the only thing Marcus could summon.

"This… this is wrong."

The words left his mouth hollow. No awe — just the creeping sense he'd stumbled onto something he was never meant to find. That he shouldn't be here.

He leaned over the console, trying to trace the jagged silhouette of the derelict below. The *Charon*'s floods swept across it in slow, ghostly arcs — revealing more ruin with each pass.

"Virgil, any way to gauge the size of this thing?"

None. Our current vessel lacks sensors for detailed volumetric scanning.

"What about a flash scan? Would that help?"

Negative. Flash scans detect local objects; they do not return structural dimensions or mass estimates.

He exhaled sharply through his nose, breath misting faintly on the viewport glass. His gaze dropped again — first to the gaping rupture in the hull, then to the shattered remains of the Nav Lantern lying adrift beside it. The back of his throat tasted like a coin.

"No way something that small did this," he muttered, gesturing toward the void. "That isn't a dent; it's a killing blow."

The *Charon* continued her slow arc, thrusters whispering as they nudged her forward. Floods carved long shadows across torn metal. Through broken port windows Marcus glimpsed the ghosts of rooms — stairs, a desk, the outline of a chair — fragments of someone's day-to-day life frozen mid-collapse.

Some hull panels had peeled back like foil, edges curled into black, grotesque spirals. An internal blast, maybe. Or something harder to explain. Every tear looked wrong — violent, uneven, almost like the ship had been pulled apart.

Marcus leaned closer to the viewport, squinting through the glass. "I want a closer look at that breach."

A faint scraping echoed along the hull — a dry, metallic whisper travelling from bow to stern. Marcus froze, jaw tight. Probably debris. Probably. He forced his attention back to the viewport, refusing to guess what might be brushing against the metal skin.

I feel, Captain, that the hull has been battered enough by debris and organic material for one day. May I suggest priority should be given to Nav Lantern data.

"It's not going anywhere. Keep our distance, run the floods — maybe catch a nameplate. Put a name to this thing."

Silence.

Marcus smirked faintly. "Thought you might see it my way."

The *Charon* dipped and yawed. Floodlights washed down the derelict's starboard flank, scattering frost and dust like a snowstorm.

Inside: mostly charred. Hull ribs. Storage crates. A dozen bodies flash-fried in place — silhouettes burned into the bulkheads. The heat required was unimaginable.

The ship drifted forward — almost as if the *Charon* herself wanted a closer look.

Then something caught the light.

A faint reflection.

Marcus frowned, fingers tightening around the flight stick as the ship tried to lean in.

A torn sheet of material snagged on a twisted bulkhead, fluttering in the artificial wind of their passage. Black. Ripped. Matte — except where the beam hit and came back in a dull, dead shimmer.

A tarp.

Just like the one lashed down in the *Charon's* cargo hold.

For a moment, Marcus thought he heard a soft hiss from the security monitor. Static — or something else. One piece of cargo recognising another.

He said nothing, just stared at the tattered fabric as it turned lazily in the void. Unlike the rest of the wreckage — jagged and torn like an open wound — the tarp's edges were smooth, clean, almost surgical.

Maybe someone got curious. Maybe they cut it open. Maybe that's what led to this.

"…That's not nothing," he whispered.

Clarify, Captain?

He shook his head. "No, it's—probably coincidence. But what if…"

His jaw tightened as he glanced at the monitor. "That tarp…"

He let it hang.

Virgil did not press.

Marcus looked back toward the breach.

For a flicker, his mind drifted — back to the *Theseus*, to that cold crater, those narrow corridors… Curtis's scream.

The one that haunted his dreams for months after.

A dull thud against the hull snapped him back. A cracked helmet turned slowly in the floodlight, then drifted away — weightless, indifferent.

Marcus eased back on the throttle, letting the *Charon* reverse and the dark reclaim the wound.

"Let's sweep the rest on our way back to the Lantern. Keep an eye out for anything familiar — anything that might tell us where this ship came from… or where it was going."

Understood. Beginning perimeter survey.

- - -

The *Charon* drifted upward, slow and steady, its floodlights dragging across the vast hull below. The ship's true outline remained impossible to grasp. No nearby stars. No ambient light. Only the freighter's narrow beams carved slivers of shape from the dark — enough to hint at size, never to reveal it.

Marcus wished they were in normal space; at least then he could appreciate the scale. Maybe it would feel less… predatory. In the *Veil*, everything was muted and wrong. The hull lay in cold shades of blue and grey, and unlike other vessels of its class, its exterior was unnervingly smooth: no pipes, no elevator trunks, no viewports, hatches, or turrets. Everything sealed inside. Nothing meant to be seen.

A ship with secrets.

The *Charon* crept along the midsection, edging toward what remained of the bridge. The floods swept the angled glazing, sketching shadows —

consoles, broken chairs, the bones of control panels — but never enough to give a full picture. The darkness swallowed every answer just beyond the light's reach.

Marcus leaned closer, frustrated. The beams weren't strong enough to push through the glass. He could make out outlines, fragments of what might once have been rooms, but not in any real detail. Not enough to pry sense from the wreckage.

No suits. No drones. Nothing aboard the *Charon* that would let him take a proper look outside. He felt like a child pressed against museum glass, forbidden from stepping closer.

Then, rounding the starboard side, the floods caught the ghost of a name: letters half-eaten by time, scorched and flaked, unreadable. As the lights panned across a docking ring, he thought he could make out one word — but it was so faint he couldn't be sure.

Odysseus?

If that really was the name, it was long lost to history. Now — whether by accident or intent — there was no way to know.

Unless…

"Virgil, do you know if Nav Lanterns keep backups of their metadata?"

No. I do not have that information.

The *Charon* came full circle, returning to its original position. The same gloved hand still protruded from the crushed Lantern, reaching for help that never came.

Once the ship steadied, Marcus moved to the auxiliary console. His fingers navigated half-fried system menus, bringing the external comms antenna and transponder back online. He hesitated before confirming — he knew the risk.

Reactivating the transponder meant broadcasting his position for anyone out there to see. Anyone — or anything.

The screen flashed **ONLINE**. Somewhere outside, metal stirred. A faint mechanical whine reverberated through the hull as the antenna unfurled.

Captain, you have activated the ship's transponder. For what reason?

"I need access to the external antenna. I'm going to try to connect to the Lantern directly. If I can get through, maybe I can pull its telemetry and metadata logs."

You are aware that our position is actively being broadcast across the *Veil*?

Marcus nodded. "Yeah. But without that link, we're flying blind. I'll risk it."

He exhaled slowly, then crossed to the nav console. The communication interface flickered to life.

–REQUESTING SHORT–RANGE OPEN COM SCAN–

The soft thumps of debris against the hull continued — sporadic, uneven. Every so often a heavier impact made the ship shudder. He tried not to picture what it was. How many bodies? How much wreckage pressed together to make metal groan like that?

–SCAN COMPLETE–
–NAV LANTERN: 360910927 CONNECTION AVAILABLE–
–CONNECT? Y/N–

Old tech trying to talk to even older tech. He hoped it wouldn't take long.

–WORKING: PLEASE WAIT–

"If we're lucky," Marcus said, "I can access the Lantern's databanks. Since they link together intermittently, they probably send telemetry packets to each other — tracking which ones are active and which have gone dark. If one drops offline, the rest fill in the gap."

Virgil didn't respond. Only the hum of the ship.

–WORKING: PLEASE WAIT–

"As well as the telemetry, I can try pulling its historical command logs. That should tell us when this Lantern activated, what it's seen while out here… maybe even where that ship came from."

He paused, eyes flicking to the viewport — grim, but hopeful. "Could be a hell of a salvage claim."

The console lights flickered once — as if it disagreed.

That is based on the assumption the transponder does not lead someone else here.

Virgil's voice landed flat — clinical, but edged with something almost like warning.

Marcus ignored him, eyes fixed on the nav console. The fans were running louder now, a low metallic whirr rising in pitch as the connection finalised. The old circuitry sounded like it was straining, taking on more than it should.

–CONNECTED: SYSTEM ONLINE–
–WARNING: UNSTABLE POWER SURGES DETECTED–
–DUE TO —ERROR—
–INSTABILITY LEVEL: HIGH–
–SYSTEM TERMINATION POSSIBLE–

–PLEASE CONTACT NEAREST MAINTENANCE TECHNICIAN–
–REF: A/A/6294/C–

"Shit," he muttered, rolling his thumb into his palm.

If that is true, Captain… you must make a choice.

Another fork in the road.

"So… should we look into what happened here?"

Counterpoint: if you prioritise navigational data, it will provide coordinates for the next Nav Lantern. However, historical sensor data may be lost permanently. The vessel before us may remain a mystery without proper equipment.

Marcus stared out at the shattered Lantern, then at the hulking mass beyond.

This could be the find of the century. A long-lost ghost ship. A mystery solved. A fortune waiting to be claimed.

A salvage payout could set him for life — if he could get it out. Legal fees. Registry claims. Tow contracts. Crew splits. All the bureaucratic rot. But it would mean freedom. He could dump the cargo somewhere safe, come back later, clean.

Who would know?

His hand flexed unconsciously.

If he kept to his route — his true goal — the payout would be all his. No shares. No salvage courts. Just one clean reward.

But that meant going deeper. Further into the *Veil*.

And if he was already finding derelicts this far in… what the hell was still waiting out there?

If something took out that ship, maybe it was better to know now — before it came for him.

He stared at the console, hand hovering over the command input.

–ENTER NUMBER FOR YOUR SEL—ERROR—TION–
–1 / NAVIGATIONAL DATA–
–2 / HISTORICAL SENSOR DATA–

Time to make your choice, Marcus.

He closed his eyes. His throat ached — every breath dry, metallic. Hard to swallow the failing air. Harder to swallow the decision.

And pressed—

–ERROR — SYSTEM LINK: UNSTABLE–
–ERROR — POWER SURGE CAUSING INSTABILITY–

The fans in the nav console screamed, a mechanical panic. For a moment he thought the whole board might catch fire. Diagnostic maps flared across the display as the databank clawed for power from every system aboard. The nav screen flickered — two progress bars overlapping for just a heartbeat before resolving into one.

Marcus blinked, unsure whether he'd imagined it.

The *Charon* resisted, lights flickering, refusing to gut herself for the Lantern.

Marcus pushed back from the console and crossed to the ladderwell. He climbed down a few rungs until his boots rang against the metal. Halfway between decks, an access panel waited opposite. He flipped it open, revealing the recessed breaker box.

He hooked his fingers around the edge and pulled, but the latch was jammed — stiff from years of neglect. He tried again, harder. Nothing.

Cursing under his breath, he fished through his pocket and felt the cool, familiar edge of a prison coin. He'd kept it without thinking — a relic of trade and survival. Thin enough to wedge into the seam. He jammed it in and twisted. Metal scraped; the latch gave with a sharp pop.

Inside: rows of breakers trembling under the strain, indicator lights fluttering like dying stars.

He braced himself on the ladder, one hand gripping a rung, and began flipping switches — one after another — asserting manual control. Asserting his will.

The ship groaned. Systems faltered. The air filtration unit wheezed as it lost power, dropping to a faint mechanical gasp.

He waited there on the ladder, listening — counting the seconds between each failing sound. The rungs vibrated beneath his hand, weak and uneven.

He resisted the urge to look down. The dark below always felt alive, like something was waiting, staring back.

Just a little longer, he told himself. *I just have to endure a little longer.*

–DOWNLOADING DATA–
–PLEASE WAIT–

The decision has been made, Captain. May you find what you seek.

The voice came softer this time — less mechanical, almost sympathetic.

A deep *thunk* rolled through the hull. Something had pressed against the *Charon* with enough force that Marcus had to clutch the ladder to steady himself. The ship groaned, metal flexing and settling again, like a creature stirring in its sleep.

Then, gradually, the console's frantic whirring eased. Fans steadied. Lights returned to their dim, familiar glow. Systems calmed, pretending nothing had happened.

Marcus climbed slowly back up the ladder, muscles trembling, until he reached the upper lip of the well. He sat there for a moment, suspended between decks, then eased onto his back on the cool floorplates.

For a long breath, he just lay there, staring at the ceiling, chest rising and falling in shallow rhythm.

He exhaled — barely a whisper.

He hadn't told Virgil what he'd really done.

And prayed to every god he knew that he'd made the right choice.

Chapter Fifteen

The docking clamps hissed as the *Theseus* was set free. Thrusters flared, gentle at first, nudging her into the slow crawl toward the mouth of the hyperspace lane.

The navigational computers were still locked down — no map, no vector. Just a single line of text pulsing on the console:

–ESTIMATED TIME OF ARRIVAL / 43 HOURS–

And the clock was ticking.

- - -

FOUR YEARS EARLIER

- - -

Hyperspace lanes had a way of shrinking the *Theseus* to nothing.

They'd cleared customs an hour ago. Forty-three hours to destination unknown.

The glow of the countdown burned bright on the nav screen, a constant reminder that an end was coming one way or another.

The lane stretched ahead like a river of glass, alive with faint ripples. Veins of pale light flickered at the edges — frozen bolts tracing the folded horizon.

Outside, there was no sky. No stars. Only the suffocating corridor running into infinity.

Even the gravity felt heavier, as if the *Theseus* were dragging herself forward through thick oil. Most ships kept to single file. The "express" lanes were for giants — freighters, corporate flagships, gunships — vessels so massive they were the only things that could cast a shadow here.

Bunny sat in the galley, chair tipped back, boots propped on the table. When Marcus stepped in, he straightened, lowering his feet to the deck.

Marcus didn't speak. He reached up, took a glass from the cupboard, and filled it with water from the tap.

A few seconds passed — just the hum of the ship, the faint clink as he set the glass down.

Bunny broke the silence. "The time we've got — think that's enough?"

Marcus drained half the glass before answering. "Has to be."

Bunny gave a short, humourless laugh. "You always know how to make a man feel confident."

- - -

Curtis preferred the lower decks. The gravity ran lighter down here; the air thinner, colder. A tang of ozone mixed with recycled breath caught in her throat — a reminder of how far she was from anything living.

The room had once been a simple equipment store. She'd spent days gutting and rewiring it — bolting benches to the bulkheads, stringing lights, carving out her own corner of order amid the ship's noise. Bunny had the bridge. Jason ran the cargo hold. But this — this little corner — was hers.

The outer hull carried every vibration and groan like a living thing. To her, it felt almost like home. Tools rattled across the workbench with each tremor of the lane.

Her hands, steady as a surgeon's, soldered a thin wire to a scorched motherboard. Years of gutting and reviving dead tech had made the work second nature. The acrid tang of burnt flux clung stubbornly to the air.

Building a device to hack their own systems — well, that was a first.

The rattle of someone on the ladderwell echoed off the vents and walls, metal on metal, until it stopped. Then came the long moan of the bulkhead door as it swung open.

"All these super-secret upgrades, and they couldn't oil one bloody door," Curtis muttered without looking up.

Marcus ducked beneath the low piping as the door clanked shut behind him. The walls here always felt like they were leaning inward, waiting.

"Hey, Curtis," he rasped, the dry air catching in his throat.

"Captain. A few more flourishes and she's done."

A brief spark, a puff of smoke. Curtis reached into a drawer and pulled out a stack of black perspex sheets, setting them on the bench. She ignited a hand plasma, its glow painting her face in pale blue as she cut four perfect rectangular panels.

Marcus watched, half admiring. Always amazed how spacers could cut a perfect line in freehand — just maths, muscle memory, and nerve.

Curtis blew on one of the panels to cool it, then positioned them with neat precision. Click—click. A double beep. She pressed the compaction gun to seal the edges, glue setting fast.

A final press, and a red LED blinked to life.

She pointed to the small monitor dangling from the wall — a tangle of keyboard and wires hastily plugged into it. The screen flashed a line of green text:

PROGRAM COMPLETE =)

"It's a bit messy," she said, wiping her hands on her coveralls, "but since they tinkered with my station, I'd rather not code it from there. Too risky."

Marcus leaned on the doorframe, arms folded.

"A black box," he said.

Curtis waved her hands. "Fitting, given what we're trying to do."

"Did Jason find anything?" Marcus asked.

Curtis nodded. "He clocked a few things while we were clearing customs. As that dockmaster wanted us off-world fast — Morningstar's priority was getting the ship patched and airborne, not cleaning up their greasy corporate tracks. That'll come later, if at all."

She tapped the side of the black box with a fingertip. "He's identified five junction boxes we can piggyback into. Three live in the cargo hold, one's only accessible from outside the hull, and the last one... won't be easy. But it's doable."

Marcus exhaled. "Go on."

"A lot of systems that were remotely deactivated before we hit Gate-station haven't come back online yet," Curtis said, eyes flicking over the dangling monitor. "So there's still seams to slip into. I've set the device to read-only — it'll suck up all nav data, everything from departure to now. We plug it into a junction, let it spool, then pull it before anyone notices. If they fry our ship OS, they won't get this one."

Marcus nodded once, the motion small but certain.

Curtis opened a drawer, produced a candy bar, and unwrapped it with casual precision, taking a bite as if the tension were just another Tuesday.

Marcus watched the green LED blink steady and calm. "For now," he said quietly, "we at least have a way in."

- - -

–ESTIMATED TIME OF ARRIVAL / 35 HOURS–

- - -

Early pioneers of the hyperspace lanes learned the hard way how thin the line was between survival and exposure. Only a few inches of steel shielded them from the cosmic currents outside — radiation, raw energy, forces that could cook a person from the inside out.

In time, special alloys were developed to offer protection from those elements. But they were expensive. Too expensive. So the thickest plating went to vital areas — the living quarters, the bridge, the cargo hold. Everywhere else was built to the minimum that still passed inspection.

Normally, no one would be crawling through a ship's bones while travelling faster than light.

Desperate times.

- - -

It was like an itch you couldn't scratch.

After hopping off the ladder, Bunny rubbed the sides of his head. The further and deeper you went — away from the safety of the upper decks

— the colder and thinner the air became. Deck Six always carried that faint metallic chill, the kind that made your teeth ache.

When Bunny reached the end of the narrow walkway, Marcus and Jason were already there, shifting old crates aside to uncover a forgotten corner of the maintenance bay. Dust fell in sheets as they dragged the last container away, revealing a very old, very unused access hatch.

Bunny squinted at it. "When was the last time anyone even touched that thing?"

Marcus and Jason exchanged a look, then both turned to him.

"Not since those *Araneae terrificae* got loose in the ship," Marcus said.

Everyone shuddered at the memory.

Jason snorted. "No wonder we covered it up."

He knelt beside the hatch, swiped his sleeve across the dusty control pad, and keyed in a sequence. The old vent cover rattled, shuddered, and began to lift.

The blast of air hit them like a gut punch, stealing the breath from Marcus's lungs before the sound arrived — a teeth-rattling warble that clawed at their eardrums. All three clamped their hands to their heads as the vibration crawled through their bones. When the cover slammed shut again, the echo lingered in the metal like the ship itself had groaned in protest.

"How far—" Bunny bellowed, far louder than intended. "How far inside is the access station?"

Marcus winced, rubbing his temple. "Still deaf in one ear, thanks for asking."

Jason blinked, lips twitching despite himself. "Down one level past the cargo bay — then about twenty metres to the junction."

Curtis slipped in without a sound, ear defenders slung around her neck. She handed one headset to Jason, then glanced at the others. "Apologies, gentlemen — didn't bring enough for the whole class."

Marcus leaned closer. "I should be the one to do this."

Jason raised an eyebrow. "I can't even remember the last time I saw you crawling through a vent up to your elbows in grease. That time our delivery van broke down outside Lake Armstrong?"

Marcus gave a faint, quiet nod. "Yeah. Probably."

Jason smirked. "Besides, you've got the harder job — getting us out of this, and in one piece."

Curtis tested her mic, a burst of static crackling through. "We'll need to seal the bulkhead door before we start. Otherwise the noise'll just reverb up the decks and shake something loose. Better to keep it contained down here."

She pointed to a squat metal box bolted beside the hatch — wires trailing up into the ceiling. "I jury-rigged a squawk box to the galley. You'll be able to listen in and talk from there."

Marcus's chest felt tight, like the lane itself was waiting for him to give the order. "Just be careful. In and out."

Jason took the black box. He and Marcus locked eyes. No more needed to be said.

He hesitated. He'd seen Jason walk into all kinds of trouble — dockside brawls, engine fires, even that time they'd had to destroy a reactor to stop it going nuclear. But this was different.

Hyperspace seeped in — quiet, relentless — until you weren't sure which thoughts were yours. Alone in that narrow shaft, with only thin plating between him and folded space, Jason wouldn't just hear the lane — he'd feel it. The pressure. The pulse. A rhythm no human was meant to understand.

He looked back once more. Curtis and Jason stood ready — headsets on, making exaggerated hand signals to show they could hear each other. Curtis gave him a thumbs-up and motioned for him to close the door.

Should be me going in there.

Marcus drew in a slow breath, released it, and pulled the lever. The bulkhead sealed with a heavy hiss, locking and repressurising until the sound faded into nothing.

For a long moment he lingered in the narrow space, alone with his thoughts — the weight of command pressing against his shoulders, heavier than the ship's own gravity.

Then he began the climb back to the upper decks. Every rung felt steeper than the last.

Chapter Sixteen

Jason had never trusted vents.

He jerked his arm back the instant his fingers brushed the inner skin, rubbing his palm as if he could scrub out the static crawling beneath it. The shaft stretched ahead, endless. Air hung stale and metallic, laced with the taste of oil that clung to his tongue. Every breath felt borrowed.

Curtis tapped his shoulder and pressed a hand to her throat-mic. *"You'll want these."* She passed him a pair of thick gloves — some protection, better than none. *"They'll dull the vibrations. The knee brace has to come off too; the frequencies running through it could shatter your leg. Or worse."*

He grimaced. Since the accident, every attempt to walk without the brace ended the same way: white-hot pain the instant he put weight on the ruined knee. Leaning against the wall, he unclipped the fastenings and passed it over.

"Guess I won't need it much for crawling," he muttered, half-smile fading as the metal thrummed beneath him.

Curtis took the brace carefully, setting it on the table behind her. She gave the black box a final inspection before handing it over. Its red LED blinked once, like a heartbeat.

Jason drew a few deep breaths, steeling himself, then lowered into the vent.

Somewhere in the hull, a relay clicked — a dull, rhythmic thunk that might've been the ship's pulse, or his own.

The vibrations started in his palms and crawled up his forearms until his elbows buzzed. Within seconds, his vision blurred — eye-shake, Curtis had called it.

"You'll need to crawl on your forearms," her voice came through the headset, calm and clinical. *"Your hands can't take that kind of resonance for long."*

Jason pressed his chest to the floor and dragged himself forward. The vent was dark. Too dark. His shoulder lamp pushed maybe a metre ahead before dissolving into shadow. Twenty metres might as well have been a light-year.

The tremors crawled through his body, subtle at first, then sharper — an invisible rhythm working into his bones. His stomach twisted. Bile rose. For a heartbeat he thought he might vomit, the vibrations shivering through his diaphragm like the lane itself was shaking him apart.

He paused, eyes closed, breath ragged. The air tasted of copper and oil, thick with dust that clung to his tongue.

"*I... don't know... h-how... you spacers d-d-do this.*" Each word came out with a grunt. Sweat rolled off his jaw and vanished into the dark below.

"*Different if you grew up without real gravity,*" Curtis replied. "*Even then, we knew better than to crawl ducts mid-jump.*"

"*H-how much longer?*"

Curtis crouched by the opening, peering inside. She could just make out his boots and the flicker of his shoulder lamp, a pale halo trembling in the dark. "*Reckon ten metres till the access shaft. You'll need to be careful climbing down it.*"

A hiss of static came first — then a muffled grumble she couldn't make out. The vent around her thrummed like a throat swallowing sound.

"*Repeat? You're breaking up.*"

A low wheeze rattled through his mic before he managed: *I... I said god-fucking-damn it.*

Curtis allowed herself a small smile. *That's the spirit.*

The humour lasted a heartbeat before the hum returned — deeper this time, a pressure under the skin. The air had that faint metallic tang again. Hyperspace was bleeding through the hull. She looked toward the bulkhead, uneasy.

- - -

From the galley, Marcus and Bunny sat at the table, the comms unit propped between them. Jason's voice crackled through the speaker in short, uneven bursts.

Marcus tried not to show it, but his knuckles had gone white around the chair's armrests. Each sound — the scrape of metal, a grunt, a hiss of interference — tightened his chest. He stared at the blinking comms light as if sheer will could pull Jason back.

Slow and steady. You got this.

Bunny reached over and tapped his shoulder. A quiet *he'll be fine* gesture. No words needed.

For a moment, neither of them spoke. The only sound was the faint hum of the ship and Jason's ragged breathing echoing from the speaker — thin, distant, fragile.

- - -

Jason dropped off the access ladder and sat for a moment, breathing hard. His legs felt like jelly. The air down here was thinner, colder — it clawed at his lungs with every breath.

He leaned into the next vent, bracing himself on his elbows to keep from slipping. The metal was slick with condensation, vibrating faintly under his palms. He'd barely gone a metre when something brushed his face.

He jerked back with a curse, hand going to his cheek. A web — old, dry, strung across the corner of the duct. He exhaled shakily, forcing a laugh that didn't sound like him. "Jesus, Curtis," he muttered. "You sure none of those *Araneae Terrificae* made it down here?"

No answer. Just the hum of the ship and the pulse of the lane beyond the walls.

He steadied himself, pushed the tangle aside, and crawled deeper.

Jason stopped, pressing the heel of his palm against his eyes. The deeper he crawled, the more the lane's vibrations thickened — no longer sound, but pressure, worming through bone and into the soft tissue of his brain. The ear defenders dulled the worst of it, but he wished they could block the rest. His bones, his teeth, even his thoughts felt like they were rattling.

He swapped arms, muscles failing fast. Ahead, faint strips of light glimmered through the vent.

The *cargo hold.*

Once, it had been a refuge — nights with the aft doors open, poker games, makeshift barbecues, watching the sun rise and fall over ports and worlds. Now it was a stealth-built void, lurking at the ship's core.

He pulled himself to the first grate and peered through. Crates and containers blocked most of the view, stacked haphazardly, but there was a gap — just enough to tempt him further along. He edged to the next vent, angling for a better look.

What was all this fuss really about?

He kept his head low. The last thing he needed was to brush the grating and let the lane hammer his skull into paste. He moved slow, careful, eyes flicking between the faint light ahead and the shadows below.

Inside, one of the big loader drones hovered motionless — one of the heavy-duty brutes that had worked the hull during refit. Meant to lift cargo pods the size of shuttles, its frame nearly scraped the bay's ceiling. A single blue LED pulsed faintly at its core — a heartbeat of artificial life. Its scanner swept the room in slow, methodical arcs, ready to alert its kin at the faintest movement. A silent enforcer of the *no touch, no look* rule.

He ran a hand over his face, trying to wipe away the sweat, but it only smeared grime across his skin. His fingers came away slick and grey, metal dust sticking like soot. The air in the duct was heavy, hot — every breath another layer on his lungs.

His gaze snagged on the cargo. A tarp blacker than any night, stretched tight and plastered with biohazard sigils in a dozen planetary scripts. The longer he stared, the stranger it seemed. The letters blurred, warped — like the light itself bent around the fabric. His pupils tried to refocus and failed, pain blooming behind his eyes. *Must be the vent... messing with me.*

"Curtis. I'm... at the grates." He swallowed hard. *"I can see the cargo bay. I think my eyes are worse than I thought — the tarp, it... it looks like it's vibrating."*

Radio static crackled back, sharp enough to sting. *"Curtis, do you copy?"*

Curtis froze. For a second she didn't reply, weighing whether to admit what she really thought — vibrations were one thing, but cargo moving against the lane's current was another.

A hiss flared in his ears, her voice finally cutting through the static: *"Jason, repeat — did you say vibrating?"*

"Yes — uh, copy. It's… it's hurting my eyes to look at it."

Curtis squinted down the access shaft, but all she saw was endless black staring back. He felt a world away.

"Jason. Get to that junction. Install the device. Then hurry back. Now."

He hesitated, a chill creeping through his chest. *"Wh-what is… going on?"*

"Time enough to explain once we're finished," she snapped — too fast, nerves slipping into her voice.

A flat surface took shape ahead — a dull glint in the dark. Jason blinked hard, eyes struggling to focus through the blur. He'd reached the end of the vent — the junction box at last.

A few more painful pulls and he collapsed against it, chest heaving. The T-split fed air to other decks, but for him it meant one thing: he could finally turn around instead of crawling out backwards.

The vent system here was older than anything else aboard — the bones of the ship. The junction box matched it: corroded, ancient, but still breathing electricity.

He pressed his hand to the latch and pulled. It refused. "Come on…" He dug his fingers beneath the seam and heaved. The panel came loose with a metallic shriek that echoed up the shaft like a scream.

Inside — blinking lights, scorched boards, exposed wiring. A diagnostic port sat half-buried beneath a nest of cables, just big enough to serve.

Jason fumbled for his pocket, cursed, tore off one glove, and reached in with raw fingers until they found the black box. The plastic felt slick with sweat. At least here, half-sitting, half-folded over himself, he could work.

His arms shook as he lined up the connectors. The moment the cable touched the port, static crawled up his wrist — sharp enough to make him flinch.

"I'm… a-at—the junction n—now." His voice trembled. His nose felt wet — he told himself it was condensation.

"Just plug it in," Curtis replied, her voice tight through the comm. *"It's self-activating once it has power. Just slot it in and get out as soon as you can."* Her tone was steady, but the strain beneath it was obvious.

His hand trembled once — then steadied, as though the lane itself were holding it still. *"Box is live,"* he whispered. His own voice sounded foreign, hollow in his ears, like it came from someone else.

The device slid into place with a dull click. No hum. No fanfare. Just a red LED blinking calm — as if nothing had happened.

Then the vent shuddered.

A jolt slammed through the shaft, nearly throwing him backwards. Jason braced with his bare hand — contact lit him up like lightning. The vibration tore up his arm, white-hot, and he screamed as his elbow bent the wrong way, pain ripping straight through the bone.

"Jason! What's going on? The whole vent just buckled — are you okay?"

Flat on his back, he clawed for the glove, fighting to jam it over trembling fingers. Every movement was agony. His skull hovered centimetres from the vibrating wall; even that close, the pounding rattled his teeth, spine, the base of his skull.

He rolled onto his stomach, chest heaving. Warmth trickled down his face — thick, metallic. Not condensation. He touched it, blinked at the smear on his fingers.

Red.

"I... th-think... I m-messed up my... dri-drinking ar-arm. On... my way... b-back."

His right arm useless, he channelled everything into dragging forward with the left. Eyes shut, he hauled himself onward, blocking out the noise, the blood, the slosh in his ears. Borrowed time. Like a climber clawing out of the death zone.

The vent sloped upward — angled toward salvation. Strips of light flickered ahead. Halfway home.

He glanced sideways and caught the access ladder through the grating — a thin outline in the dark. Almost there. Then his gaze drifted down, through the next grate into the cargo bay.

The cargo wasn't trembling anymore.

It was thrashing.

Straps shrieked under strain as the tarp heaved, sliding across the hold in violent, rhythmic jolts.

That earlier impact — it had slammed the vent.

One of the massive loader drones hovered close, scanner pulsing in slow blue waves. Jason's stomach turned as it drifted nearer, mechanical arms stretching as if to steady the shuddering tarp.

The moment it touched, the drone convulsed.

Metal screamed. The frame bent inward, joints snapping like brittle bones — then it was flung aside, crushed and discarded like a toy in the jaws of something unseen.

Jason gagged, bile burning his throat. *"C-Curtis… Marcus… the cargo… it's—"* He swallowed hard. *"It's pissed."*

A long pause. Then Curtis's voice, clipped and far too controlled: *"Worry about it later! Get your ass back here, now."*

Too fast. Too sharp. She knew more than she was letting on.

Jason dragged himself forward, each pull vibrating through his ribs, through his teeth. Then came the scraping — deep, metallic, close. A grinding shriek that froze him mid-crawl.

He risked another glance through the grate.

The cargo sat motionless — a black tarp sagging, still as death.

His breath rattled in his throat.

Then it lunged.

Jason's instincts took over. He scrambled forward, dragging himself hand over elbow, useless arm flailing. The vent groaned as he threw his weight ahead, a desperate, graceless lunge — just as the tarp slammed into the wall behind him.

The impact hit like thunder. The crate beneath drove into the duct so hard he felt it in his teeth. The shaft boomed, vibrations rippling through the metal, through his skin, through his skull. Jason cried out, hands clamping over his ears too late.

Back in the maintenance bay, Curtis froze. Jason's scream never reached her headset — just a burst of static. She frowned, leaned closer to the open vent, and held her palm just inside. A low tremor hummed through the metal, faint but wrong — too deep, too alive. Her eyes widened. "Oh, no…"

It pressed there, groaning against the ventwork, as though testing the barrier between them. The metal screamed and flexed under the pressure. For one sick, endless moment, he thought it might force its way in.

Then — silence broke like a wave.

The weight slid off, dragging its sound with it, a scraping retreat toward some other angle of attack.

Jason stayed frozen, muscles locked, shaking in the dark. He could still feel it — something massive and alive, moving beyond the thin steel skin of the vent.

He didn't wait to see if it would come back. Eyes watering, nose and ears leaking red, he forced himself to crawl — every nerve screaming, not knowing if the thing had just tried to kill him or was simply reacting to the lane tearing it apart.

The tunnel opened ahead. The access shaft.

He reached it, half-slid, half-fell into the narrow cylinder, grabbing for the rungs with his good arm. His legs barely obeyed him; the world spun sideways. Each breath came short and sharp, the air thick with iron.

"C-Curtis…" His voice cracked. *"I—I'm here—"*

He tried to climb — one rung, two — then his hand slipped. Vertigo hit like gravity reversing. He lurched backward, weightless for a second before something caught him.

"Jason!"

He opened his eyes. Curtis's face was a pale blur above, teeth gritted, one arm locked around his wrist. "Push with your legs! Come on!"

He tried. Every muscle protested, but he shoved upward as she pulled, her boots scraping against the grated floor for leverage. Her expression tightened — sweat, strain, the tremor of hyperspace bleed crawling under her skin.

With one final wrench, she hauled him up onto the deck beside her. Both collapsed, gasping. Jason's body convulsed with pain; Curtis clutched her arm, the veins in her wrist faintly luminescent from the static charge bleeding through the hull.

For a heartbeat neither moved.

Then Curtis hauled him up by the collar. "We're not done," she panted.

Jason tried to move under his own power, but his right leg dragged uselessly behind. Curtis hooked her arms under his and started to pull, inch by inch, toward the hatch ten metres away.

Every shuffle felt eternal. The deck hummed under their knees, the metal vibrating harder with each metre. Curtis could feel it in her teeth now — the ship itself reacting, or warning.

She slapped the comm on her shoulder, voice breaking through the static. *"Marcus, Bunny — get down here! Now! I need help!"*

- - -

"Marcus, Bunny—get down here! Now! I need help!"

The comm crackled through the galley speaker. Marcus was already on his feet before the last word finished. *"First aid kit — cupboard, top shelf!"* he barked.

Bunny scrambled, yanking drawers open until he found the red case, while Marcus tore down the ladderwell three rungs at a time. His boots hit the deck with a thud that echoed down the corridor.

He reached the lower hatch and tried the handle. Locked solid. The pressure differential was still holding it tight.

"Curtis!" He slammed his shoulder against the bulkhead once, twice — metal ringing through the corridor. "Come on, come on!" he shouted, voice cracking with fury.

Inside, Curtis dragged Jason the last few metres toward the access hatch. He was half-conscious now, trying to push with his feet but barely managing more than dead weight. She hooked her hands under his arms and gave one last heave, pulling him through the opening. They collapsed in a heap on the deck.

The air in the shaft roared as she reached out, fingers stretching for the datapad. Her hand slapped it — just enough to trigger the command.

The hatch slid down and sealed with a metallic thud. A hiss followed — pressurising.

By the time Bunny reached the bottom of the ladder, Marcus was already braced against the hatch. They both threw their shoulders into it. The latch clicked, the seal broke, and the door burst inward.

"Holy shit... Jason."

Bunny froze for half a second, colour draining — then training snapped in. He dropped to his knees beside Curtis. She had Jason half-upright, one arm braced around his shoulders to keep him from choking on his own blood.

"Easy — hold him steady," Bunny muttered, easing off the ear defenders.

The instant the seal broke, a wet hiss followed. Blood flooded from Jason's ears, trickling down his neck. His face was swollen, purple-black, eyes shot with red. Nose, mouth — every opening leaking.

Alive. Barely.

Marcus crouched beside them, chest tight. "What the hell happened?" he rasped, though part of him didn't want to know. He gently took Jason's weight from Curtis, easing him into his own arms.

Curtis didn't answer. She lurched to the side, dropped to her hands and knees, and vomited — thin bile splattering against the deck plating. The sound made Bunny flinch.

"Curtis!" Marcus called, but she just waved a shaking hand, wiping her mouth with the back of her wrist. She sat upright, legs sprawled, head between her knees, trying to steady her breathing.

"It's... fine," she managed hoarsely. "There was a smash... then the vibrations spiked. Like someone cranked them to eleven."

Jason stirred in Marcus's grip, a strangled rasp slipping from his throat. *"C...c...cargo..."*

Marcus leaned closer, every muscle locked. Jason's hand shot up, bloodied fingers clutching his shirtfront. The grip trembled but held.

"Too... dangerous..." Jason coughed, red flecks dotting Marcus's collar. "Get... rid... of it... dump... it..."

The words hit harder than any impact.

Marcus pressed his palm over Jason's, felt the faint pulse, the constant tremor beneath the skin — the body still shuddering from the inside out.

He looked up at the others, voice low, steady, commander's instinct fighting panic. "How do we move him?"

- - -

-ESTIMATED TIME OF ARRIVAL / 26 HOURS-

- - -

The galley was silent except for the low hum of the air filters.

Curtis sat wrapped in a blanket at the end of the table, pale and hollow-eyed, both hands locked around a mug she hadn't touched in minutes. Bunny stood by the sink, scrubbing Jason's blood from his forearms. The water ran pink, then red, then clear.

Marcus sat opposite them, elbows on his knees, staring at the dried stains across his palms. Smears. Fingerprints. Jason's blood. All of them marked.

When they'd hauled Jason out of the vent, Bunny had torn down cargo straps and welded buckles into a crude harness. Marcus and Curtis had pulled from above while Bunny carried most of the weight, dragging Jason's limp body up four decks, one rung at a time. The ropes had creaked. The metal had screamed. By the time they reached the crew quarters, the three of them were soaked in sweat and blood, half-blind with exhaustion.

Now only the slow dripping of water from Bunny's hands remained.

Marcus finally spoke. "How bad is he, Bunny?"

Bunny turned, drying his arms with a rag already stained brown. "He's wrecked. Burst vessels, blood loss, internal trauma... maybe worse. He's alive, but that's all. He needs a real medic, not a couple of half-trained spacers and a first-aid kit."

"Is there anything else we can do for him?"

Bunny's look said everything.

Marcus pushed away from the table and strode for the stairwell. He took the steps two at a time, boots ringing off the metal. The climb to the flight deck burned through his legs, but the guilt burned hotter.

He threw himself into the pilot's chair and brought up the nav console. Fingers flew. Nothing. Locked out. Every input denied. He tried again, faster, slamming the commands until the console lights flickered under his fists.

-SYSTEMS: LOCKED-
-COURSE DEVIATION REQUEST-
-DENIED-

Frustration broke loose in a single, helpless act: he slammed his fist onto the console. The hollow crack echoed through the deck.

His gaze lifted to the forward panel — to the glass housing the SOS beacon. One press and a distress call would blast over every nearby frequency. A rescue ship might come. Jason could live.

But it would expose them. The cargo. The deal. Everything.

Marcus's hand hovered over the glass. His reflection stared back — bloodshot eyes, jaw clenched, every line of his face already knowing the answer.

He turned back to the throttle.

"Hang in there, Jason," he whispered.

Then he pushed it forward — past the redline, past the safe threshold. The engines roared in protest, the entire hull trembling as the *Theseus* surged ahead. The few visible stars blurred into streaks of silver.

The ship howled, metal straining as it crossed into the danger zone. The deck shuddered beneath his boots.

He didn't care.

He was closing the gap.

But deep down, he knew — this wasn't his ship anymore.

Whatever waited ahead — danger, salvation, or the point of no return — he was done running from it.

Chapter Seventeen

"I can still turn this around."

- - -

– UPDATED ARRIVAL TIME / 3 HOURS –
– WARNING –
– SAFETY LIMITS EXCEEDED –

- - -

The flight deck shook like it was trying to tear itself apart. Panels rattled in their housings. Floodlights flickered. The floor thrummed with a deep, unending vibration that travelled through boots and bone alike.

When Bunny and Curtis burst in, the noise was deafening — a constant, low howl as the *Theseus* strained past her limits.

"Bunny, are you crazy?" Curtis shouted — but Bunny wasn't looking at her. His stare went straight to the captain's chair.

"Are *you* crazy?" he yelled at Marcus. "You can't exceed safety thresholds in a hyperspace lane! The ship can't take this!"

Marcus didn't look up. His hands were locked to the armrests, knuckles white. "We can't go anywhere. Can't deviate, can't stop. The quicker we get there, the quicker Jason gets medical care."

Bunny stormed to the pilot console, fingers flying across the throttle. "You'll kill us before that happens!" He shoved the lever back, trying to slow them — but Marcus caught his wrist.

"Don't," Marcus growled. "We have to push through."

The ship groaned in reply, as if protesting.

Curtis crossed to the engineering panel on the aft bulkhead. Gauges trembled in the red: core temperature, engine coolant pressure, drive RPMs, velocity ratios — all rising by the second.

She turned to them both, shouting over the din. "I don't know how long we can hold this — even with the new parts! The cooling lines are near boiling!"

Bunny grabbed for the controls again, jaw tight. "Then we throttle back—"

Marcus yanked him away, both of them stumbling into the central console.

For a moment, Bunny's expression went *feral*. His hand twitched, ready to swing. Curtis stepped between them, one palm braced against his chest.

"Stop," she hissed.

Bunny's chest heaved, eyes wild. "I've seen some *stupid shit* in my time — but this?" he barked, jabbing a finger at Marcus. "If you're in a hurry to get yourself killed, *fine*. But you don't get to blow up the ship and take *us* with you."

The deck gave a violent shudder. Overhead, a fluorescent strip flickered, humming before it steadied.

Bunny pushed on, shouting over the vibration. "What is it, huh? We're three people down — do you get a *bigger share* if we drop like flies?"

The words hit like a slap. The hum seemed to fade for a heartbeat — just long enough for him to realise what he'd said. Regret flickered across his face. Too far.

Curtis steadied herself against a bulkhead as the ship lurched again. A low groan rolled through the hull, loose tools rattling across the deck. "*Enough*," she snapped.

She threw Bunny a glare, then turned to Marcus. "Bottom line — Jason's in critical condition, and that cargo's smashing itself to pieces in the hold. You've got the *right* idea…"

Another strip flickered, dimmed, then returned weakly, bathing them in thin blue glow.

"…but you're going about it in the *worst possible way*."

She held his stare, the faintest smirk ghosting across her lips. "As usual."

Bunny stepped back, hands planted on his hips. The deck hummed underfoot. For the first time in minutes, no one spoke.

"Sorry," he muttered.

No one answered. Only the deep, rhythmic pulse of the engines straining in the distance.

Bunny finally broke the silence. "It sounded like you *knew* what was going on down there. Want to share?"

Curtis smoothed her flightsuit as though steadying herself. "No. Not really. Just… stories. Things spacers tell when the lights are low."

Marcus raised an eyebrow. "Ghost stories? Spooky space tales — really?"

"More like *warnings*." She exhaled slowly. "Back in the early days of hyperspace, crews pushed too far beyond the Lanterns. One ship found something — tech no one recognised. They tried to haul it back. That's when things went wrong. The cargo *reacted*. Vibrated. Bolts sheared loose. Some swore they felt it crawling through the hull.

"Maybe someone — or *something* — didn't appreciate their stuff being stolen. The last transmission was just static and screams. And what happened after… depends who you ask. Everyone's got their own version, but no one's got proof."

Bunny frowned. "And you think that's what's happening here — and you're only telling us now?"

Curtis gave a small, helpless shrug. "Because no one agrees. No records. Just talk. That's what makes it a ghost story. All I know is… when cargo starts *shaking* in the lanes, it's the first thing people remember."

Her gaze drifted upward. The ceiling lights flickered again, worry tightening the corners of her mouth.

Marcus swallowed, throat tight. "And you think that's what's in our hold?"

Curtis met his eyes, voice low. "I think we've been hired to carry something that should've been *left where it was found*."

Marcus didn't answer. He looked past her toward the console wall — red warning lights blooming one by one, small and silent, each one a heartbeat edging toward something worse.

Curtis didn't turn. She didn't need to. The glow reflected faintly in her eyes.

Marcus stayed silent. She'd already watched the cargo shift. Already seen Jason broken by it. If this had started as a ghost story — it wasn't anymore.

In the hum of the lane, he could *feel* it pulsing beneath the decks, waiting.

- - -

Jason lay on the cot, staring at the ceiling. The ship's gentle sway had turned erratic — each tremor rolling through the deck plates and nudging his body against the thin mattress. He fixed on a loose bolt above him, watching it rattle in time with the vibrations, half-convinced it might work itself free the moment he blinked.

His chest rose and fell in shallow pulls, every movement stiff with exhaustion. Thick bandages circled his head, blotched dark where the bleeding hadn't stopped. Every so often the overhead light flickered — a pulse syncing with the faint rumble beneath his ribs.

The ship wasn't steady anymore. Neither was he.

Marcus hovered in the doorway, one hand braced against the frame as the hull trembled beneath his palm. The words stuck in his throat.

Jason turned his eyes toward him — slow, unfocused. The look said enough: *you put me in that vent.*

Marcus cleared his throat. "We'll be out of the lanes soon," he lied, voice thin. "Get you patched up. Couple weeks, you'll be good as new."

Jason's lips moved — cracked, pale. The sound that came out was broken, half-breath, half-growl. "Couple weeks I'll still remember why I'm like this."

Marcus stepped closer, guilt dragging at his boots. He could taste copper, or maybe he imagined it. The scrape of the chair leg made Jason flinch, his whole body tensing at the sudden noise.

"Shit — sorry," Marcus muttered. Jason's eyes fluttered shut again, chest hitching.

"I admit I might've got us in too deep," Marcus said quietly. "Once we're free and clear... maybe we take a month or two off. R&R. Sound good?"

Jason's mouth twitched. Could've been a scoff — or just another dry cough. Either way, he wasn't buying any of it.

Silence stretched. The hum of the engines filled the room like a pulse, shaking dust from the ceiling vent. Marcus shifted, fingers tight around the back of the chair — searching for something to say that might fix this, knowing *nothing* would.

He rose too quickly, desperate for escape. "I'll let you rest. We'll get you to a med-station once we land."

"Marcus." The whisper barely reached him — hoarse, papery.

He froze. "Yeah?"

Jason swallowed, words scraping between breaths.

"I'm still gone," he murmured. His gaze drifted back to the ceiling. "*Nothing's changed.*"

The words hit harder than a punch.

Marcus stood there, hollow, before pulling the door closed behind him. The latch clicked, muffled beneath the steady rumble of the ship pressing onward.

- - -

The three of them sat in silence around the galley table. Bunny had his hat pulled low, snatching what little sleep he could. Curtis nudged a fork through a cold meal, eyes distant. Marcus drained his fourth coffee, the bitter taste doing nothing for his nerves.

Then the alarms shattered the quiet.

-HYPERSPACE LANE EXIT: IMMINENT-

Chairs scraped. Boots pounded up the stairs. The nav-computer ticked down in its flat, dispassionate voice.

Curtis muttered, "How dramatic."

"I'd advise strapping in," Bunny called, throwing himself into his seat. "No telling where we drop."

"Jason?" Marcus's voice tightened.

"He's secured to the cot," Curtis replied. "He'll hold."

The deckplates trembled. Lights flickered from steady white to amber as the lane outside thinned and warped.

"Five seconds!"

Harnesses snapped. The glow intensified—blue streaks stretching, collapsing—until the lanes fell away entirely.

White. Then black.

The *Theseus* screamed as she tore free of folded space, the sound vibrating through her bones. Outside, chaos waited.

Asteroids — hundreds — spinning slow and silent, caught in the reach of the ship's floods. The console blared warnings:

-HAZARD DETECTED-
-MANUAL CONTROL RESTORED-

"Shit!" Bunny hauled the flight yoke, the ship lurching hard starboard. A slab of rock rolled past the viewport, so close Marcus could see the craters gouged across its face.

The inertial dampers lagged half a beat behind; harnesses strained as gravity snapped at their shoulders. Another rock spun through the fog of debris. Bunny dropped the ship under it, firing the retro-thrusters. The *Theseus* groaned as she slowed, plates creaking.

They drifted clear at last. Silence returned in ragged breaths.

Bunny exhaled, wiping sweat from his forehead. "So… where the hell are we?"

Marcus rubbed the bridge of his nose, trying to steady his breathing. "Nav computer still locked?"

Curtis scanned her panel and nodded. "Still locked. No coordinates, no telemetry, no map. We could be anywhere."

"Fine," Marcus muttered. "Pick a window and start looking. Planet, starbase—hell, even a blinking buoy. Anything."

For a while, only the soft creak of cooling metal and the occasional pop of the hull settling broke the quiet. Each of them leaned toward a viewport, searching. Silence stretched.

"I think I see something," Curtis said suddenly, pointing. "That one—what's the planet with the big spot?"

Marcus frowned, squinting. *"Jupiter?"*

"I think so. Too far to tell properly, but…"

Bunny pushed himself up from the pilot's chair. "One sec." He clambered down the ladder toward his cabin, boots ringing on the rungs.

Marcus kept staring. His vision swam; the world outside was a blur of colour and motion. "Can't see a damn thing."

Moments later Bunny reappeared with a battered pair of binoculars. He pressed them to his face, adjusting the focus. A low whistle. "Yup. Giant red spot. That's *Jupiter*, all right."

Marcus straightened. "What the hell? The *Sol* system's crawling with traffic. You don't drop off shady tech here. Why risk it?"

Bunny sighed, thinking. "*Ganymede*, maybe?"

Marcus scoffed. "Surely not."

Curtis glanced between them. "What's *Ganymede?*"

"Largest moon in the system," Bunny said. "Used to be a haven for smugglers and pirates—until the military nuked it clean. Whole surface irradiated. At least… that's the story."

Marcus leaned back, staring into the dark where *Jupiter* hung like a dull orange eye. "No point flying over there blind. If this is the destination, the nav console should recognise where we are and unlock. Tell us where to go next."

No one answered. Outside, the great planet turned slowly, storms flashing like distant fires.

Marcus nodded to himself. "So maybe we've got a destination. Question is—will our little box pick up the data once the system unlocks itself?"

Curtis's mouth tightened. "If I were sabotaging ship systems, I'd trigger it *after* we've landed. Eliminate the chance of anything going wrong. Which means we have to yank the box before touchdown. If it's still connected when the scrub runs, it'll get fried."

"Shit." Bunny raked a hand through his hair, pacing a short line across the deck. "So someone's got to yank the black box after the nav unlocks—but before the purge starts."

Silence again. The hum of the engines filled the gap.

Bunny looked up, voice low. "Which means someone's crawling back into those vents."

The three of them stared at one another, red warning lights flickering across their faces—each silently praying it wouldn't have to be them.

Chapter Eighteen

// TO: [REDACTED]
PROXIMITY SCANNERS CONFIRM *THESEUS* TRANSPORT HAS EXITED HYPERSPACE LANE ADJACENT TO DELTA SITE.
CONTAINMENT CREW WILL BE STANDING BY TO EXTRACT SURVIVING PERSONNEL.
USE OF FORCE IS AUTHORISED IF THEY DO NOT COMPLY.
SHIP AND CREW TO REMAIN ON-SITE UNTIL PRIORITY OPERATIVE ARRIVES TO OVERSEE CARGO TRANSFER TO FINAL DESTINATION.
CONDITION OF CARGO POST-EXPOSURE REMAINS UNVERIFIED.
PROCEED WITH HASTE.
— BLACK VEIL //

// END TRANSMISSION //

- - -

Jupiter.

Once, the ancients called him Jove — King of the Gods, Lord of Sky and Judgement. From this distance the planet filled the viewport like a bruised eye, its storms unblinking, eternal. The Great Red Spot churned below — centuries of rage trapped in a single, endless howl.

Even through the haze of the asteroid belt, the planet was magnificent. Gold and rust clouds coiled across its face in slow, deliberate violence. Far beyond it, Saturn's pale rings cut a faint line across the dark — a reminder of how far they'd come, and how little separated them from the edge.

It felt like an omen. A reminder that no one escaped the gaze of gods forever.

The crew of the *Theseus* felt it too. Their time was running out.

- - -

"I'll go this time," Marcus said — steady, defiant. He was done forfeiting his crew before himself.

"No dice, *Captain*," Bunny replied, shaking his head. "When the comms light up, they'll want the captain — not the pilot."

"I'll go," Curtis said quietly. "Don't want to, but we're back in normal space. Should be a clean job — just keep an eye on the nav-computer. As soon as it unlocks, we're in business."

"What about the vents?" Bunny asked.

Marcus and Curtis exchanged a look.

"They might be more banged up than Jason," Marcus said.

Curtis hesitated, then gave a small, silent nod — *okay, I'm doing this.*

"I guess we'll find out. Call me when we're ready." She gave a two-fingered salute and strode off the deck.

The flight deck fell quiet. Marcus drifted toward the viewport, resting a hand on the cool glass as the giant planet loomed beyond. For a while neither man spoke; the hum of the engines filled the silence.

"How far out d'you think we are?" Marcus asked at last. "From home, I mean."

Bunny gave a weary laugh. "Too far for comfort."

They shared a faint, brittle smile — real enough to break the stalemate. Marcus wished it were that easy with Jason.

His thumb brushed his wedding band as he stared at Jupiter. Its storms swirled like living scars, endless and unblinking. Close enough to feel familiar, but nowhere near close enough to save them.

Almost home.

"Jason, he'll—" Bunny adjusted his hat. "He'll come around. People say all sorts after they've been through the wringer."

"He told you?" Marcus asked.

"We talked while I got him to the cot. I think he's angry at himself — for getting banged up. Or for not keeping you out of trouble."

"Yeah," Marcus muttered. "I've developed a habit of that."

"Things might look different in a month," Bunny said, though even he didn't sound convinced.

Marcus let out a thin laugh, rubbing his eyes. "Bunny, after this trip I think I wi—"

-INCOMING TELEMETRY-
-DATA UPLOADED — SYSTEMS/ACTIVE-
-PROCEED TO CO-ORDINATES/DELTA SITE-
-CAUTION: RADIATION LEVELS DETECTED-

The deck lights blazed. Consoles flared. The low hum of the drives surged into a roar as the *Theseus* woke from its forced slumber, drowning Marcus mid-sentence.

He snatched up his comms unit. *"Curtis, do you copy? Systems just came back online — it's all you now."*

- - -

Curtis moved like water when she was alone — quick, fluid, economical. Spacers learned to *flow*, not rush; every motion balanced against the pull of artificial gravity. To anyone planetside, it would've looked eerie — too smooth, too deliberate.

She paused at Jason's cabin, poking her head inside. His chest rose and fell in shallow rhythm. She lingered a moment, watching — making sure he was still breathing.

Half-conscious, Jason's head turned slightly toward the door. She wasn't sure he truly saw her, but she gave a small wave all the same, a wordless *hang in there*, before moving on.

The maintenance bay was chaos: blood-streaked cloths, a smear of crimson across the workbench, Jason's brace abandoned among scattered tools. Curtis exhaled through her nose — one breath, one second of stillness — then turned to the vent.

Cold air hissed from the seal as the hatch slid open. No thrum of power this time. Just silence — too clean, too deliberate.

Headlamp fixed, she crawled inside. The metal was tacky beneath her gloves, streaked brown where Jason had dragged himself through.

She cleared the ten metres quickly — she used to play in vents smaller than this. At the access shaft, she flipped herself down the ladder, landing lightly before sliding into the next section.

Ahead, the duct was crushed almost flat. No way to push through, but the metal was loose enough that a few well-placed kicks would knock it free. She braced her boots, struck twice, and the panel gave way with a sharp clatter that echoed through the hold.

She slipped through the gap, landing soft and low, unnoticed.

And froze.

The cargo hold was carnage. Drone limbs scattered like bones, coolant pooling beneath twisted plating. The overhead walkway hung half-ripped from its bolts, cables dangling like snapped tendons.

Only the crate remained untouched. Massive. Swaddled in black tarp, plastered with warning sigils in half a dozen tongues.

DO NOT APPROACH.

It wasn't vibrating at the speed Jason described — but it *was* shaking. Angrily. Like a generator seconds from overload. The tarp rippled with a life of its own, each shudder running through the deck plates and up her legs.

A faint crackle cut the silence. One shattered drone twitched — its severed arm spasmed once, throwing a burst of sparks across the floor. Curtis flinched, heart slamming against her ribs, the flash dragging her sharply back to the moment.

She exhaled through her teeth. "Get a grip," she whispered, straightening.

"Captain, I'm almost at the junction. How are we for time?"

"I do not have an estimate yet," Marcus replied, his voice strained through static. *"Readouts say we are heading deeper into the Belt — closer to Jupiter's orbit. The big ones. Make it fast."*

"Copy that." She picked up the pace, ducking under a twisted support beam. A few metres ahead, she pried loose a vent cover and climbed back inside the *Theseus*. The air was stale and metallic, the hum of the ship pressing against her ribs.

The junction box wasn't far now. A smear of blood glowed faintly in the low light, colours rippling like refracted starlight. Hyperspace bleed had changed it — ionised, alive in a way that made her skin crawl. Wherever Jason had dragged himself, the lanes had followed.

She tried not to think about how cold it felt on his clothes, prayed the smears would wash off.

Curtis slid into place before the junction box and set her tools down. The cover hung open like a metal jaw. All she had to do was pull the black box.

The ship began to rumble. Not the engines — deeper, stranger — as if the hull itself had started to breathe.

"Captain, what's going on?"

"We are being pulled in by orbital gravity lines," Marcus replied, voice tight through static. *"Nav says we are approaching Ceres. You will not have long — I can see external docking doors cut into the rock."*

Gotcha, she thought. Destination locked and recorded.

The *Theseus* shuddered harder, deckplates flexing as the thrusters fought to correct their descent. She braced herself against the vibration and reached in.

That's when they'll wipe it, she thought next. *Final approach. Everyone distracted.*

The casing was hot and slick with condensation. She gritted her teeth and yanked.

The unit didn't budge. Her palms slipped, smearing blood and sweat across the housing. She planted her boots, pulled harder.

A crack of static jumped the gap. Blue light flared, searing her vision. The shock tore up her arm, every muscle locking in a single white-hot instant. She gasped, swore through her teeth, and pulled one final time.

A flash — then nothing but white and the sound of her own pulse hammering like a scream.

When her senses crawled back, she was flat on her back, clutching the box to her chest. The LED blinked steady, indifferent. Her forearm was blackened and smoking, skin peeled back to raw red muscle.

She didn't scream. Not yet.

"Captain... I got it," she rasped into her mic. *"Making my way back. Have the first aid kit ready — maybe a bottle too."*

- - -

For an asteroid, it felt alive.

Three centuries ago, this had been a traffic-control hub — one of dozens built to chart safe routes through the Belt, back when ships still needed help threading the rocks. Then computers got smaller, smarter, and the towers were left to die in the dark.

Now the flight deck glowed with a low amber hue, the light seeping in through every viewport and seam. Outside, the cavern walls burned in molten shades of orange, as if the rock itself were lit from within. Dust drifted lazily in the beam spill, glittering like ash.

Marcus sat in the captain's chair, elbows on knees, staring at readouts that told him nothing useful. Bunny knelt beside Curtis on the stairwell, winding a fresh bandage around her arm. She winced but said nothing, clutching a half-empty bottle in her good hand.

"Easy," Bunny muttered, tightening the wrap. The glow flickered across his face, turning the lines of exhaustion into something carved. He gave a faint, humourless smile. "Reminds me of the nav lanterns."

Marcus didn't look up. "They glow *orange*, Bunny?"

"Wouldn't know," Bunny said, tugging the tape tight. "Never seen one lit. Only smashed, drifting. Don't even know where you'd find one still burning."

"Pretty far," Curtis murmured, the bottle tapping lightly against her knee.

The orange light pulsed again, rippling through the glass, and for a moment it looked like the *Theseus* was underwater — suspended in something vast and slow and alive.

Bunny fastened the temp-cast around her arm, careful not to jostle the raw edges of the burn. "Once we get Jason to a med-station, they'll regen it."

The smell of burnt flesh still clung faintly to the air — metallic and sweet, refusing to dissipate.

Curtis managed half a smile, the kind that never reached her eyes.

A deep thud reverberated through the hull, followed by a low metallic groan as something heavy locked on. The deck trembled beneath their feet, tools rattling on nearby consoles.

The screens along the wall flickered to life, displaying the same message in pulsing orange text:

-PRESSURISING IN PROGRESS-
-PLEASE STAND CLEAR OF PORTSIDE GANGWAY-

The ship rocked again — gentler this time — as the docking arm sealed against the hull with a hollow clang, the sound echoing through the frame like a heartbeat.

The pressurising door filled the bridge with a rhythmic clunk-clunk-hiss that seemed to echo inside their chests.

Curtis and Bunny exchanged a look, then instinctively moved closer to Marcus and the centre chair, away from the portside hatch. The three of them stood in tense formation, watching the indicator above the door pulse from amber to green.

The final clunk hit like a heartbeat.

The portside airlock unsealed — from the outside.

Six figures swept aboard in formation. Black armour. Smooth helmets. Eyes burning red behind mirrored visors. No insignia. No skin. No words.

The crew froze. Hands raised. Even their breath felt too loud.

The soldiers fanned out with mechanical precision. Two held their position by the airlock, rifles trained. Another kept his weapon fixed on the crew — unmoving, a statue with a heartbeat. The squad leader stepped forward, voice metallic and calm through the modulator.

"There should be four."

Marcus found his voice, rough and small. "Injured. Confined to his cabin, down in the living quarters."

A slight tilt of the helmet. **"Extract him."**

The words rippled through the silence like a divine command.

Curtis's voice cracked. "Wait — he's hurt! Be careful—"

No reply. Two operatives broke formation and descended the stairwell. The thud of boots echoed through the decks below.

Then — a dull crash. A metallic rattle of harness coils.

Moments later, Jason was dragged up between them, limp, feet scraping across the deck. They dropped him into the captain's chair, his body slumping sideways like a discarded puppet.

Bunny took an uncertain step forward. Instantly, a rifle snapped toward him — barrel tracking like a predator.

He froze, hands half-raised. "I'm just checking he's alive."

The rifle didn't move.

Jason shifted weakly in the chair, voice raw and distant. "He's alive."

Marcus forced the words out through clenched teeth. "I got your cargo here, Dekard. Deal's done. Pay us, and we'll be gone."

Bunny's head whipped around. "*Dekard?*" Disbelief and anger twisted through the word. Curtis's eyes narrowed, flicking between them. "This the guy you saw?"

Bunny gave a tight nod. "Yeah. Same suit. Same damn smirk."

Marcus didn't answer. He couldn't.

Dekard pivoted, eyes narrowing, pinning Marcus where he stood.

"All in good time, Captain. First, you'll come with us."

His gaze drifted across Bunny, Curtis, Jason — then back again. "Now."

Act Three

Chapter Nineteen

It had been days since the *Charon* left the derelict — and the trail of bodies drifting behind it. Without the dull, irregular thumps of impact against the hull, the ship had sunk back into silence — an oppressive kind that pressed against the ears. Only the coughing wheeze of the air filters broke through now, straining to clean the stale atmosphere.

Marcus would give anything to smell something that wasn't metal. The tang clung to his nose, coated the back of his throat, seeped into everything — rations, clothes, even water. Every sip and every bite carried the same faint, rotten aftertaste. Even zipped inside his sleeping bag, eyes shut, he couldn't escape it.

The *Charon* had its own smell now — and it was him.

Captain.

He rolled onto his side, facing the wall, pretending not to hear. Virgil could wait. Sleep was the priority.

Captain. I require a response.

Marcus sighed loud enough to make his irritation clear and swung his legs over the bunk. The comm unit blinked from its cradle — patient. Expectant.

"Virgil, I'm exhausted. Trying to sleep. What is it?"

Clarification.

"I can clarify I'm *tired*," he muttered, shuffling to the sink. He splashed a cup of metallic-tasting water and grimaced as it burned down his throat.

You chose to download historical data instead of navigational. You have taken us off course. Explain why this choice was made.

Marcus rubbed his eyes. "Because that ship came from somewhere." He stretched, yawning, the words half slurred. "Had to gamble the Lantern's logs would give me a general heading. Enough to start guessing."

No facts — just theory, Captain?

He stopped pacing. For a moment, the phrasing — the faint edge to Virgil's voice — made him wonder if it was more than a question. He shook the thought off, rubbing his palms together. *Mystery was better than monotony.*

"The data shows that derelict didn't just arrive. It crawled. Weeks in sublight before it even reached the Lantern. Engines that size? Should've cut through space with ease. Instead, it limped."

He crouched to tug on his jumpsuit, the fabric stiff from days of recycled air. "And that tear in the hull — did it happen before, or after it got there?"

He leaned against the bulkhead, fastening the collar as though it helped him think. "Then there's the manual access on the Lantern. Those two bodies we saw inside? Looks like they were trying to pull nav data too. Maybe they were lost. Maybe they *knew* something."

He zipped the suit to his throat, boots thudding softly as he stamped his feet into them. "But then the logs glitch — total nonsense. Error strings, corrupted telemetry. Then nothing, until it recorded us arriving."

He paused, rubbing his palms together as if that could scrub away the unease. "That's the link, Virgil. Whatever happened to them — it started long before we got there."

He waited.

Silence.

The comm unit's light blinked — patient, unreadable.

"Virgil?"

Still nothing.

He turned toward the galley, half ready to make coffee out of habit, but stopped mid-step. The silence felt wrong. *Heavy.*

After a moment's hesitation, he pivoted, heading instead down the narrow corridor toward the ladderwell. Each step sounded louder than it should have, echoing back off the metal walls.

By the time he reached the rungs, his voice had lifted — half excitement, half defiance.

"And the time gap, Virgil — *three hundred years!* What happened back then?" He climbed, breath quickening. "I say let's follow those breadcrumbs."

A cold gust drifted up from below, brushing the back of his neck. Marcus shivered, hauling himself onto the flight deck and dropping into the pilot's chair.

He glanced toward Virgil's LED, expecting its familiar blink.

Nothing.

The light glowed steady. Unblinking. *Watching.*

"Virgil?"

The silence thickened. Even the air filter seemed to hush, as if the ship itself were holding its breath. A faint crackle bled across the security monitor — static alive with intent.

Then:

How far do you intend to deviate from your flight plan?

Marcus exhaled through his nose. "We've already shaved months off. What's a little detour? As long as it's not backwards, I don't mind going off the beaten path."

Is that wise? You saw the derelict. Its size. Now a broken husk. The bodies left to perish in space.

The hairs on the back of his neck prickled.

Given the scale of that vessel compared to ours — with such a show of force — how do you calculate our own chances for survival?

Marcus frowned, the humour in his voice forced. "You think we should turn back?"

I advise caution. You and this ship are not prepared for what may be out here. There is a reason the nav console warns against travel within the Veil. Uncharted. Unknown. Dangerous space.

Marcus gave a dry, brittle laugh. "What's this? Trying to scare me, Virgil?"

Silence again. The LED held its steady, unblinking glow — patient, almost reproachful.

Marcus leaned back in the pilot's chair, arms folded tight against the cold. "Fine. Stay quiet. However, we're still going."

But the silence pressed in anyway — heavy, deliberate. The steady green dot on the console — patient, unblinking — felt less like an indicator, and *more like something watching.*

- - -

A few hours had passed since their last conversation. Not for his lack of trying — Virgil remained silent.

Marcus sat slouched in the pilot's chair, boots propped on the console, absentmindedly picking at one of the plasters wrapped around his fingers. He pressed down until pain lanced through his hand — brief, sharp. A low-effort way to feel something.

The nav console blinked steady in the gloom. At the northern edge of the display, the derelict's last coordinates lingered. A few more hours and they'd drift out of range entirely. After that, the *Charon* would be adrift with no fixed point — swimming through the cosmos with nothing but black ahead.

He shifted, glancing toward the ladderwell. His bunk was technically comfier, but the flight deck was the quietest place on the ship. Well — *second* quietest.

Maybe here he could finally get some sleep.

His comm unit sat on the side console beside a half-empty cup of cold, thick coffee. He left it there, face-down, the faint light on its display fading to black.

He closed his eyes, arms crossed. Sleep would be better than waiting. His mind began to drift, skimming through fragments of memory — better days. A warm afternoon somewhere in Europe. The day he proposed.

He wished he could see her face one last time. In the half-dream, his hand lifted, reaching for her shoulder to turn her around—

A noise cut through.

A faint, high buzz. Insistent.

Marcus cracked an eye. The flight deck looked the same — green LED, the steady pulse of the nav glow. Then he saw it.

The internal systems panel.

A faint red flicker — Deck Four.

Marcus dropped his boots from the console and dragged himself upright with a groan. Another fault. Another half-dead connection. He wandered over and tapped the flickering bulb with the back of his knuckle. It twitched on and off — feeble, stubborn.

"Figures," he muttered. "Everything else on this ship's breaking — why not you too?"

The Deck Four light sputtered again, weak and uneven. He gave it one last tap with his finger, then turned away.

It can wait, he thought.

That was when Deck Three lit up.

Not a flicker this time. Solid. Bright red.

Marcus froze, hand still against the bulkhead. A pulse of unease crept through him. Slowly, carefully, he leaned over the ladderwell, peering down into the blackness below. Cold air pushed upward, brushing against his face like fingers. The shadows swallowed everything — no flicker of light, no movement, just the sense that something waited down there, out of sight.

Then he noticed it.

The air.

Or rather — the absence of it.

No low hum. No wheeze of the filters straining. Just silence — a crushing, *complete* silence.

It wasn't simple quiet; it was total.

It pressed against his ears until the only thing left was him. His own breathing rasped like a saw. Every inhale came ragged, desperate. His heartbeat slammed against his ribs, the rush of blood roaring in his head. Even his swallow cracked like thunder inside his skull.

"Virgil," he whispered, throat dry. "Why did the filtration system cut out?"

It has not. All systems are operating normally, Captain.

Marcus clenched his jaw. "Then why the hell can I hear nothing?"

He took a hesitant step back from the ladder — then stopped. The deck beneath him trembled, faint at first, as if the *Charon* itself had drawn in a long, nervous breath. The vibration thrummed up through his boots, setting his teeth on edge.

Then Deck Two lit up.

Bright. Steady. *Watching.*

Marcus moved further back from the ladderwell, pulse racing. The silence was deafening now — he could hear the blood rushing through his ears, pulsing behind his eyes, each throb sharp with pressure. It felt as though the air itself were pressing inward, trying to squeeze the sound out of him.

His hand went instinctively to his belt, drawing the knife. The weight of it felt pitiful against whatever might be climbing up from the dark below. The blade caught the console glow — a nervous glimmer in the dark.

Maybe it wasn't a faulty sensor after all.

The ship shuddered again, harder this time. A low groan rippled through the hull, metal flexing under unseen pressure.

He turned, scanning the cockpit.

That was when he heard it — so soft he thought he imagined it.

A long, deliberate *crack.*

Glass. Breaking.

Marcus's gaze snapped to the security monitor. A fracture crawled across the display, spidering outward with agonising slowness — jagged and alive, inching from corner to corner.

He reached out, fingertips hovering over the glass. The crack spread, webbing outward with a brittle pop — then the screen went black.

The *Charon* lurched violently.

Marcus was thrown off his feet, hitting the deck hard as the knife skittered away into the dark. Overhead, the lights flickered, shadows strobing across the walls. The air filled with the low howl of stressed metal — the ship's bones crying out.

"Virgil!" he shouted, scrambling on hands and knees. "What the fuck is happening?"

All systems remain within normal operating parameters, Captain.

The voice was smooth. Unhurried. *Unconcerned.*

Marcus's blood ran cold. The ship trembled beneath him, alive with fury, and yet Virgil's calm made it worse — a whisper through clenched teeth.

"Virgil... is there—"

The Deck One light snapped on.

The board blazed red, every deck screaming occupied.

The *Charon* convulsed as if something vast had seized its frame. Marcus was flung sideways, crashing into the bulkhead. Pain flared across his ribs, breath punched from his lungs.

He crawled under the console, fingers sweeping blindly until they found the knife. He gripped it tight — *white-knuckle* tight — as the deck pitched underneath him.

Lights strobed, casting violent shadows across the cockpit. Panels rattled in their housings. Screws shrieked. Deck plates boomed like a drum. The ladderwell clanged as something unseen reverberated through the ship's spine.

"Virgil!" he shouted over the din. "What the hell is on the ship? All decks!"

Captain. You are alone on this ship.
The remaining sensors show no activity on any level.
The cargo hold is empty.

"Bullshit!" Marcus bellowed, throat raw. "You see it! You hear it! The whole ship's coming apart!"

The groan of the hull deepened into a roar — metal warping beyond tolerance. The fractured monitor fizzed again, white noise hissing through the speakers as if something on the other side were trying to speak.

Marcus had never felt so small. The noise — the violence — the ship thrashing against itself — was overwhelming.

He closed his eyes and ran a finger over his faded wedding band. *See you soon.*

He braced himself, waiting for the breach — that single, deafening crash that would announce the void had come screaming in.

Chapter Twenty

Silence.

He thought he heard a slow exhale — maybe his own.

The lights steadied. The deck was still. The air filtration wheezed again, as though nothing had happened at all.

Marcus stayed crouched, knife clutched white-knuckled, chest heaving. Sweat cooled across his skin. He blinked salt from his eyes and slowly lifted his head.

The first thing he saw was the security monitor. Humming steady. The crack was gone — perfectly intact. The tarp didn't move. It *couldn't* have. And yet — for a fraction of a breath — the camera feed dipped, as if something beneath it had shifted its weight. Then steady again. Still. Ordinary.

He rubbed at his eyes, but the afterimage of that twitch lingered.

He scrubbed his face with his sleeve. Out of the corner of his eye, a faint glow flared — Deck Four. Just once. Weak. Pitiful. Then gone.

Marcus stared, waiting — willing it to return.

It didn't.

He swallowed, throat dry. Pressed his thumb against the taped finger, craving the jolt of pain. Proof this was real. Not just in his head.

"Virgil," he whispered — almost afraid of the answer.

Its LED pulsed, calm as a heartbeat.

He loosened his grip on the knife. Sweat made a faint tacky sound against the hilt, the grooves etched white into his skin. The Umbral Deep had taught him never to relax — not even when things looked calm. The dark corners of that place had claimed anyone who forgot.

Captain. You appear to be in an elevated state of panic. Please confirm your condition.

Marcus sat slumped on the deck, knife still in hand. His pulse thundered in his ears, each beat sharp as a hammer strike. He could *still* feel it — the groan of the ship, the violence of the shake, the crack crawling across the screen. His hair clung to his temples; his eyes burned as the salt dried on his skin.

That had been real.

It had to be.

"Don't tell me I imagined that," he whispered, voice raw with exhaustion.

All ship systems remain nominal. Internal activity: none detected.
My hypothesis is that this region is uncharted. Cosmic radiation spikes, gravitational shears, or unrecorded lifeforms may be present.
The human body reacts poorly to unknown stimuli. I did stress that this course of action could prove dangerous, Captain.

The hum of the console fans wrapped around him like a warm blanket of familiarity — the *Charon*, along with Virgil, trying to convince him everything was fine.

Nothing seemed out of place, yet *something* had thrown him hard enough to bruise. The pain was real.

It hurt to uncoil his muscles, to convince his body it was safe to move. The instinct to fight or flee was a hard thing to silence. His arms trembled, still belonging to the ship's violence rather than to him.

A sour taste filled his mouth — copper and bile — the body's leftover panic refusing to let go.

He dragged himself into the pilot's chair, chest still hammering, trying to decide if it had all been… what? A hallucination? Exhaustion?

He rubbed his eyes, pressure sparking coloured rings behind his lids. Would everything change when he looked again?

The cockpit looked ordinary. Quiet. Familiar.

The only sign of disturbance was him.

Virgil spoke again, unhurried.

While I was compiling the historical data you downloaded from the damaged Lantern, I noticed the navigation files were… entangled with it. An unexpected overlap. At least now we can travel to the next

navigational point. There is no need to return to the derelict — or place the ship, or yourself, in any more unnecessary danger.

Marcus set the knife on his lap, keeping it close as he dragged his hands down his face. He lowered them slowly, staring at the LED.

"You want me to turn back."

I am merely offering alternatives. Your health is paramount, Captain. However, if you insist on — in your own words — staying off the beaten path, you must consider it could mean death. Perhaps it would be safer to return to the predetermined route. For your safety... as well as the cargo's.

Marcus glanced at the monitor. The tarp-shrouded shape sat patient as ever. Then — a flicker, like an eye opening and closing.

He blinked, rubbed sweat from his brow. When he looked again, the feed was ordinary. *Too* ordinary. As if it had been waiting for him to look away.

Had the screen really shifted, or was it just him?

The lines blurred in his head.

Who was Virgil protecting — him, or the cargo?

The way forward or the way back.

He hated the idea of going backwards — it felt like a defeat. If the *Charon* kept moving forward, the answers might eventually reveal themselves. But when? Days? Weeks?

And what waited further out there? Maybe this was his chance to learn from past mistakes — to stop prodding at things best left alone. Was it exhaustion clouding his judgement, or a warning?

Virgil had been *very* insistent on returning.

Does he know more than he's letting on?

Marcus swallowed, throat dry. "Calm demeanour, considering a few moments ago this ship felt like it was going to tear itself apart."

The LED pulsed once. Steady.

Understandable you might feel that way, Captain. However, my systems are incapable of changing tone or octave. I am functioning within normal parameters. Shall we resume our previous route?

He held its steady light for a long moment, searching for something behind it — hesitation, deflection, anything *human*. But there was nothing.

It was like arguing with a mirror.

Virgil's voice was maddeningly even — the tone of someone describing weather conditions, not a ship that had nearly torn itself apart.

Marcus took another slow look around the cockpit. Everything seemed… normal enough. The consoles hummed at idle. The filters wheezed faintly, still straining to breathe life through the *Charon*'s stale air — their tired rhythm oddly comforting now.

He rubbed at his temples, half-smiling in bitter resignation. Maybe it was exhaustion. Weeks alone. Air thick with metal. Sleep eaten alive by nightmares. Maybe it *was* exhaustion.

Or maybe worse — maybe Virgil was.

For an instant, the thought came unbidden — that the *Charon* itself might be working against him. Circuits, lights, systems all quietly conspiring. The kind of thought that came only after too little sleep and too much silence. He dismissed it before it could take root.

If we slow the ship to a holding position, I would recommend resuming your interrupted rest cycle.

Marcus leaned forward in the pilot's chair, muscles tight and trembling. He eased the throttle back until the *Charon* drifted into a slow crawl — the ship responding with smooth, obedient grace.

He sat there a moment longer, forcing his body to accept the decision. Every joint ached — post-adrenaline stiffness sinking in — but still he needed a few seconds to will himself upright.

He exhaled through his nose, fingers drumming the armrest. "Fine. Makes sense."

He unclipped the comm from his belt, set it gently on the console, and pushed himself to his feet. The cockpit suddenly felt smaller. Darker.

He walked stiffly to the back of the flight deck and paused at the hatch, staring into the ladderwell below. It gaped like a throat — black and airless.

For a moment, he thought he heard a scrape rise from the dark, faint as breath. Then nothing. Just silence waiting.

He felt his body tilt toward it — like the air itself was tugging him down.

Darker than space. Twice as cold.

His mind flashed with the image from his nightmare — something waiting below, reaching, pulling.

We'll be ready.

Marcus froze mid-descent. One boot hovered above the next rung as the words sank in.

He blinked, frowning. Had he heard that right?

He climbed back up quickly, muscles tight with fatigue, and popped his head above the ladderwell. From this angle he could only see the back of Virgil's console — dark, motionless. Yet the voice had come from the pilot's chair, where he'd left the comms unit.

"...What did you say?"

A pause. Then, with perfect calm:

My response was: I will be ready, Captain.

Marcus stayed there, chest pressed against the rim of the hatch, staring at the console's silent glow.

He turned his gaze downward again. The ladder vanished into blackness, each rung swallowed as though his descent had no end.

The silence pressed in so tightly he could hear nothing but the rush of blood in his ears — a pulse that didn't feel like his own. His knuckles whitened on the rung.

He was only going down one level, yet the descent felt *much* longer.

He wasn't sure if Virgil had slipped — or if his own mind had.

Chapter Twenty-One

Everything was just colours and shapes in his eyes.

Jason was in no condition when two black shapes dragged him from his cot, boots scraping against the deck as if gravity itself struggled to hold him. They hauled him through the narrow corridor, up the stairwell toward the flight deck.

He thought he could make out Marcus's features — said something, maybe. *Did I say it or just imagine it?*

Something cold pressed against his face. Darkness closed in.

He tried to move his arms, to fight back, but his strength was gone. His chest heaved, breaths short and ragged. For a moment he was certain this was it — then a sharp rush of oxygen filled his lungs. Clean, chemical. A rubber mask sealed across his skin, cold air seeping deep until it filled every corner of him.

He felt his body lifted, then dropped into the captain's chair. Straps cinched across his chest and legs. Not that he could have gone anywhere if he'd wanted to.

He tried to raise a hand toward his face. Two circular orbs pressed against his temples — smooth, solid. The material holding them felt worn. He tapped where his eyes should be. Plexiglass. Breathing mask. His arm was caught and restrained again. *Not time to go yet.*

The chair was so cold it seeped straight into bone. The straps bit into his wrists and ankles, tight enough that he could feel his pulse thudding beneath them. Each shallow breath fogged the inside of the mask, the stale tang of rubber filling his mouth. He tried to shift, even a fraction, but it was like struggling against stone.

Above him, the blurry, familiar lights of the ship bled into something else entirely. A bloom of warmth — dull gold, soft, almost inviting. The shift was so abrupt it made his head spin. Emergency lights? A Lantern?

His mind tried to fill in the blanks with what little data his senses could grasp. Somewhere between waking and dream. Voices swam at the edges, muffled and broken.

"…prep…"

"…containment…"

"…move him—"

Drowned again by the hiss of oxygen.

Occasionally he felt a bump as they passed over something. The gold light thinned. It flared into harsh white, burning against his eyes. The warmth vanished. A sterile chill crept across his skin, settling into his bones. Everything collapsed into shades of grey — industrial drab, prison drab.

Oh God… am I dead? Is this a morgue?

He felt himself spun, pivoted sharply, then slammed against a wall. The jolt rattled his teeth, jarred every bone. A sting bit into his arm.

Am I asleep? Are we home? Marcus… I feel so tired…

- - -

FOUR YEARS EARLIER

- - -

"Hey!" Marcus lunged forward before instinct caught up with him.

Weapons rose in unison — cold, mechanical, unwavering — enough to stop him dead.

The corridor felt colder where metal met raw rock. The walls sweated condensation; the air was thin, metallic. Not the sterile chill of a ship — something deeper, older, the kind that settled into bone.

Curtis folded her arms tight, trying to trap what little warmth she had. Bunny had his jacket buttoned to the throat — a first. Neither spoke.

"Let our actions remain calm and respectful, Captain."

Dekard drifted in behind the guards, hands raised in a gesture shaped like peace but empty of it. "Our…" he paused, tasting the word, "…facility staff are here to ensure your companion is stabilised while we complete our transaction."

His smile aimed for reassurance, but held no warmth — only calculation.

His eyes didn't blink. Not once. Being looked at felt like being *studied* by a photograph.

The 'staff' moved with silent precision. One removed Jason's mask; another adjusted the line feeding from the IV rig. Jason's features slackened — peaceful for the first time since the accident. A UV drip pulsed faint blue through his arm like a slow heartbeat.

One less witness to worry about, Marcus thought grimly.

The crew were escorted down a dim corridor into a room that felt colder the instant they entered. Sparse and a little grubby, it looked unused for years. Rectangular, narrow, the air carried the dry, stale tang of disuse.

A cluster of metal chairs sat along one wall beside a small table. Opposite, a row of grimy windows looked down onto the docking platform. Through dust and condensation they could just make out their ship's hull, dark beneath the bay's floodlights.

The ceiling lights hummed with that old Earth fluorescent buzz — flickering in uncertain intervals. Marcus was half surprised they worked at all.

They were guided to the line of chairs, guards following them in — evenly spaced, far enough for conversation but never privacy.

Moments later, two masked medics wheeled Jason in on a recovery bed. The hiss of oxygen and the squeal of trolley wheels cut the room's quiet. They parked him near the centre, the UV drip casting soft blue across his pale face.

Dekard appeared in the doorway, a dark outline framed in corridor light. He didn't move at first. His eyes scanned the room — left to right, slow, clinical — before settling on Jason.

He stepped inside.

"I am, somewhat, curious as to his injuries," Dekard said, tone smooth as glass. "How did he acquire them?"

"He fell," Bunny answered — a little too quickly.

"In the stairwell. Two decks," Curtis added. "He's lucky he only broke his arm."

Dekard began to move. Arms still, posture precise, each step deliberate. His motions were measured, almost predatory. He approached Jason with the patience of a shark circling the shallows — silent, economical, built from inevitability.

Every tilt of his head, every narrowing of his eyes, was a quiet dissection. His lips moved faintly, as though recording details for later. The guards stepped back, leaving a hollow of space around him — as though even gravity bent away.

Jason, unconscious, could only endure the inspection.

"On behalf of Morningstar," Dekard intoned, turning from Jason to the crew. His hands lifted in a small, ceremonial gesture of peace — rehearsed, polished, empty.

"We extend sympathies to your companion and wish him a swift recovery."

His off-coloured eyes lingered on Marcus — unblinking. Then came the smile. Too wide. Too practised.

"Thoughts and prayers, Captain."

The words rang hollow — their emptiness louder than sincerity.

Marcus caught the subtle shiver from Bunny, the tightening of Curtis's jaw. He wasn't alone in feeling the chill Dekard carried like a shadow. In a way, it reassured him — proof it wasn't just in his head. Dekard unsettled *everyone.*

Which somehow made him worse.

"Now," Dekard declared, snapping the room taut again, "as we offload your cargo, we trust you will enjoy the hospitality of these... facilities. Our team will keep you comfortable while we work with haste. Once our accord is complete, we shall converse on the matter of... payment."

He inclined his head in a mock gesture of courtesy, then turned for the door.

The smile drained from his face as he walked, leaving behind only that hollow stare — predatory, silent, haunting.

His absence didn't relieve the pressure. It *clung*, as though the walls themselves were reluctant to breathe again.

Time sagged and folded.

Minutes stretched into hours. The hum of the vents, the shuffle of boots outside the door, the faint crackle of the UV drip — each sound grew louder until even breathing felt like a betrayal.

No one whispered. No one moved.

Silence became its own kind of guard, heavier than any weapon.

Curtis forced herself to exhale, gripping her legs to still the tremor in her hands. "Fuck... *we shouldn't be here.* Marcus, I want to get the hell out of here."

Marcus leaned toward Bunny, voice barely audible. "You know him?"

Bunny didn't look away from the nearest guard. "Later," he whispered, jaw set tight.

The air between them felt wired, ready to snap.

At last, Bunny broke the stare and placed a steadying hand on Curtis's back. "Do you have a plan?"

Marcus shook his head.

A painful waiting game had begun.

- - -

The crew of the *Theseus* were beginning to grasp the concept of infinity. The longer they sat, the more silence became a kind of trickster. Each creak in the walls, each shuffle outside the door could have been a signal — or nothing at all.

Bunny rose, stretching until his back cracked in several places. He began to pace the length of the room. In the doorway stood a single black-clad guard, unflinching.

Bunny leaned in to check Jason's breathing. Slow and steady — *always good.*

On the wall beside the door ran a narrow viewing slit — four inches wide, almost a metre long. It reminded him of the old castles he'd seen in holo-history lessons about Earth. Through it poured the glare of harsh floodlights from the docking platform outside.

He could make out movement: men in hazmat suits and breathing tanks pushing empty carts into the open hold, then wheeling full ones back out — heaps of broken limbs, bolts, and parts of the loader drones. A trail of fresh fluid leaked alongside the cart as the worker pushed it across the deck.

Despite the distance — and the lack of atmosphere — Bunny could almost *smell* it. His nose prickled, hairs tingling, as memory filled in what the vacuum denied: the hot, foul stink of burnt droid fluid… and blood.

"This feels like before," Bunny murmured.

Curtis glanced up from her seat. "Before what?"

He didn't answer straight away. His eyes stayed on the platform. "Vela constellation," he said at last. "Asimov Science Hospital."

Curtis frowned, shaking her head slightly. "I don't know it."

Bunny's mouth twitched. "It's a—" He paused, eyes unfocused. "—long… *long* way from here."

He shifted his weight, voice dropping lower. "Planetary Rangers, twenty-three years back. We were called in after an 'incident'. Official line said a meteor shower caused a containment failure. Whatever it was — explosions, bodies, people hurt. Place was a *mess*."

He trailed off, eyes distant.

"Bodies everywhere," he said quietly.

Either he arrived before us or had been there the whole time. But compared to the carnage we were seeing, the state everyone was in… he was immaculate. Not a speck on him. Even when he walked through the rubble, it was like nothing stuck to him."

Curtis's brow furrowed. "Did he work there?"

"I don't know," Bunny said quietly.

Marcus's voice came out quieter than he intended. "Who was he?"

Bunny hesitated. "He spoke to no one. We were told not to speak to him either. Like he was a ghost. But I was behind a pillar when I heard him take a call."

He looked away from the window. "He said his *name*."

The room went cold. Even the air seemed to hold its breath.

Curtis's expression changed — the faintest flicker of recognition — and then she whispered, *"Dekard."*

Bunny and Marcus shared a look. Bunny gave the slightest nod, confirming it.

He exhaled slowly, eyes still on the floodlit dock. "After that, I'd had enough. Put in my discharge papers the next day. Got off-planet as fast as I could."

He forced a dry half-smile. "Still don't care much for hospitals."

Bunny turned back to the window and watched as the full carts were wheeled to the edge of the dock and tipped over into the dark. Discarded and forgotten forever. The clatter of metal and the hollow echo that followed seemed to go on for miles before fading into nothing.

He swallowed hard, hoping they wouldn't share the same fate.

Four men stepped into view. Each wore a large battery pack strapped across their back, thick cables snaking from their waists to heavy two-handed devices. Bunny recognised the design immediately. *Mag-pulls?*

One of the men pointed toward the open cargo bay, shouting orders over the whine of machinery. The other two adjusted their footing, aiming their mag-pulls into the hold. The magnetic coils flared blue-white as they fired, the cables jerking taut.

Whatever they latched onto fought back — *hard*. The men shifted their stance, boots grinding against the deck as they hauled. The lines thrummed, vibrating under the strain, tension singing like a live wire.

After a few moments, the object began to move. Even under the fierce glare of the dock floods, the tarp remained untouched by light. It didn't matter how bright those beams were — they couldn't penetrate it. No reflections. Perfectly black. It was as if the light simply stopped existing when it met that surface.

Bunny's pulse climbed. He glanced at the guard posted by the door; the man stared back, expression unreadable.

Bunny lifted his hand and gave Curtis a small motion to come closer.

"Uh," he said quietly, forcing casualness into his voice, "what kind of material is *that*, you think? Volcanic, some kind of ore? You want to talk me through it?"

Curtis raised an eyebrow but stood anyway. "Yeah, sure. Because I know rocks."

She rose slowly, aware of the guard's eyes following her every move, and crossed the room toward the window where Bunny stood.

The attempt at humour was reckless — *too sharp in the silence* — but better to risk a distraction than sit still and let dread gnaw them hollow. Marcus shot them both a warning glance, though he didn't disagree. Anything was safer than letting fear eat them alive.

Their host turned his head, watching to see what she would do next. The dark visor gave no hint of what he was thinking.

Curtis walked slowly, placing a hand on Jason's arm as she passed him. It was still painful to see him *so* torn up. She kept moving, aware of the guard's gaze tracking her every step, and stopped beside Bunny at the window.

Marcus caught the subtle shift of the guard's footing — weight forward, rifle rising a fraction. Instinct flared before thought.

"Hey!" he called, voice cracking louder than he intended. "I don't know how long we've been here, but do you think we could get some food? Or water, perhaps? Anything?"

The guard's helmet turned sharply toward him, full attention torn away from Curtis.

Curtis reached the window, edging in front of Bunny for a look outside.

The host pivoted completely now, weapon up, posture rigid.

Ah, shit, Marcus thought, pulse hammering in his ears.

"Quiet."

"I'm only asking for something for my crew," Marcus pressed, raising his hands, palms open. "Did your leader not say you'd be a gracious host?"

Marcus felt the blood drain from his face as he heard the soft mechanical click — the weapon activating.

"Final warning."

Then — a horrified scream.

Chapter Twenty-Two

Curtis rose from her chair with her eyes fixed on the floor. No sudden movements. No need to spook their host — a statue made flesh, radiating an aura that said he'd have no qualms putting anyone down. *No reason required.*

The room was lean, every corner a dead end, and Bunny felt so very far away. She moved slowly, deliberately, each step placed like she was navigating a minefield. Halfway there, a wave of motion sickness rolled through her. Spacers weren't built for slow movements; they disoriented her, made her feel like the floor was tilting beneath her boots.

She glanced down as she passed Jason. The medics had done a better job patching him than she'd expected, but blood still seeped faintly through the gauze. She reached out and touched his arm. He didn't react — but he was warm. His breathing was peaceful, steady. Whatever the UV drip was feeding him, at least he was resting.

Out of the corner of her eye, she saw their host shift his stance, ready to send her back to her seat.

Behind her, Marcus's voice rose — calm unravelling into agitation. The guard's helmet snapped toward him, visor catching the light. Marcus had thrown himself into the crosshairs to buy her a few seconds.

Curtis reached the window and slid in beside Bunny, whispering, "What am I looking for?"

Bunny didn't answer at first. He was squinting through the narrow viewing slit, brow furrowed.

"Down on the landing pad," he said quietly. "Looks like they're having trouble hauling the…" He hesitated, as though unsure what word even fit. "…the cargo out of the ship."

Curtis followed his gaze.

Four men moved across the docking platform, mag-lifts strapped to their backs, cables trailing like veins. Three wrestled with the black-tarped mass while the fourth waved sharp, impatient instructions — gestures clipped with rising frustration. The tension in the lines thrummed like a plucked string. One man braced a boot against the hull and hauled with his full weight.

The tarp didn't sag or shift like ordinary freight. It resisted. Anchored.

As if the Theseus itself didn't want to let it go.

The line snapped — a shriek of metal slicing through the stale air — and whipped across one man's leg.

He went down hard, striking the deck with a hollow clang. A bloom of blood sprayed in a brief, weightless arc before scattering across the cold plating. The asteroid's light gravity held it suspended for a moment, glinting like rubies beneath the floods, before it settled and began to crystallise. Each droplet froze where it fell — a trail of life pinned in place by the vacuum's indifference.

Despite the thin atmosphere, the twang of the broken cable echoed faintly off the rock walls — dull, distant, *wrong*.

The cargo lurched forward. Only a fraction — but enough to look deliberate. The men with the mag-lifts staggered, scrambling for balance as the black mass edged down the ramp.

Curtis drew a sharp breath but couldn't tear her eyes away.

Behind her came a metallic click — the unmistakable sound of a safety being disengaged. Bunny's head snapped toward it. Their host had raised his weapon, sight locked on Marcus.

Bunny pushed off the wall, ready to step between them, but Curtis didn't move. Her gaze was locked outside.

On the pad below, the injured man clawed at the deck, trying to drag himself clear — but the blood spilling from his leg had already frozen into a jagged pool, welding him in place. The cold climbed him inch by inch, tunnelling back through the wound like an invader.

Two more figures appeared at the edge of the dock, waving frantically for him to move. One tried to rush forward but was held back by the other — both trapped in the same awful truth as Curtis. All they could do was watch.

His thigh jerked violently as ice spidered through his veins, hardening him from the inside out.

Every movement made it worse — like trying to pull a blade free that had fused to bone.

The cargo loomed closer, unstoppable. When it reached him, it crushed his legs flat with a sound that shouldn't exist in air or memory.

Curtis couldn't hear him, but she saw the condensation fogging the inside of his mask — eyes wide with terror, mouth stretched in a silent scream.

She thought of Jason — banged up, yes, but alive. *Better than this.*

The man reached toward the tarp in desperation, palm slapping against it as if sheer willpower could hold it back. His companions shouted, gesturing for him to stop, but it was already too late.

She remembered childhood games with water balloons — that split-second swell before they burst.

That was how it felt watching him. His body shuddered, vibrating as though every molecule had come loose.

Then he ruptured.

A balloon of meat and water bursting in a single, wet explosion.

The spray hung frozen in the thin air — crimson shards of ice and blood, sculpted mid-motion. His mouth still open in a final cry — a man shattered and preserved in the same instant.

Curtis pressed a trembling hand to her mouth, trying to stifle the sound clawing its way up her throat. Her reflection in the glass stared back — pale, wide-eyed — as though *she* too had been frozen in place.

The shape outside was still recognisably human — arms outstretched, brittle, splintering into chunks. She couldn't tear her gaze away. Her lungs burned, desperate for air, until the cry finally broke free.

It wasn't *his* voice she heard in the silence.

It was *her own.*

- - -

Without hesitation, the host turned from Marcus, swinging his weapon toward Curtis. The barrel slammed against her face, forcing her back. She shook so violently — eyes clamped shut — that it took a few seconds to register the muzzle nudging into her throat.

"Step back. Now."

At the modulated bark of his voice, she opened her eyes and stumbled across the room, rushing to Jason's side. She clutched his limp hand as if to anchor herself. Marcus followed, reaching for her shoulder in a clumsy attempt at comfort.

The instant he touched her, she flinched and spun on him. Her eyes blazed — red, wet, furious.

"Do you have any — *fucking* — idea how close you came to killing your best friend?" Her voice was low, almost guttural. "Your bloody milk run nearly killed him! You've probably gotten us all killed! *You!* You got us into this mess, Marcus Carpenter. Rush in first, let everyone else suffer the fallout later. We trusted you! Hell, we've all bled and broken bones for you on this job. But you? *Not a scratch.* Typical Marcus — leave everyone else holding the bag."

The words hit harder than a fist. Marcus's stomach tightened, heat climbing his chest. For a moment, he almost preferred the gun barrel to her fury.

As her voice tore through the room, Bunny eased forward, stepping between them — not for Marcus's sake, but to keep Curtis from getting shot for lashing out. Even as he moved, his eyes stayed locked on the guard by the door. The weapon remained raised, the finger on the trigger steady.

"Curtis…" Marcus's voice cracked. "I'm sorry. I was just trying to keep us from circling the drain. One job — easy payout."

Curtis scoffed, wiping her eyes with the back of her hand. "That's bullshit. You're not that stupid. You knew what you were signing up for, and you dragged us all down with you. Easy money, huh?"

"Curtis—"

"You already ditched two of our friends — left them in a hospital we can't ever go back to. And look." She gestured at Jason's broken body. "Hat trick."

Marcus turned, gaze falling on Jason's bruised, bloodied frame — sedated, oblivious.

The room sagged into silence. Marcus stared at Curtis, but she wouldn't look back. The only sound was the soft crackle of the UV drip feeding into Jason's arm — loud as a metronome in the stillness.

"Curtis… what did you see?" Bunny asked quietly.

She opened her mouth, then closed it again. Words weren't enough. She folded her arms tight across her chest, as if to contain the trembling in her hands.

"Let's just say," she managed, her voice thin and raw, "some guy down there wasn't as lucky as Jason when that… cargo came for him."

Bunny watched her closely — the flicker in her eyes, the way her hands shook despite her grip. This wasn't anger anymore. It was fear. Real fear. He turned to Marcus.

"The kid doesn't scare easily. That's how I know this is bad. Really bad. You think they're actually gonna let us leave?"

Marcus glanced toward their host before answering. "If it comes to it, I'll rush him. Try to get the rest of you back to the ship. Get clear, use that black box—"

"Oh, fuck your black box!" Curtis snapped, spinning on him, hovering protectively over Jason.

Bunny and Marcus shared a look. Marcus glanced again at their host. The man hadn't moved. Not once.

Unsure if Curtis's outburst had even registered, Marcus waited. The silence stretched thin — every breath in the room too loud. Despite the chill of the air, he could feel sweat pooling beneath his arms, clammy against the fabric of his shirt.

Then a sharp double beep crackled from the man's intercom. He raised his weapon.

"Return to your seats. Now."

- - -

Nobody spoke. Nobody even looked at each other. The room felt emptier than before — silence settling heavy as dust. Once a tight-knit crew, a family, now laid up and splintered into a hundred pieces.

"Brave crew of the *Theseus*."

The air seemed to chill even before Dekard entered the room.

"I am pleased to convey that your cargo has been removed and now rests within our… capable hands."

No one looked up. No one wanted to meet his gaze — to feel that unease crawl under their skin again. Except Curtis. She stared straight at him.

"What will you do with it?" she asked.

He moved with unhurried precision, stopping directly in front of Curtis before leaning down. His face hovered inches from hers — closer than anyone ever wanted to be.

Up close, his eyes looked soulless — polished stone, reflecting light but giving nothing back. *Nothing human.*

"Kaelos-bairn," he whispered.

Curtis's breath caught. Spacer dialect — old, rare, a word he *shouldn't* have known.

"Do not trouble yourself with queries beyond your comprehension."

The smile returned, slow and deliberate, as he straightened.

"Now, Captain."

Marcus forced himself to meet Dekard's gaze.

"Our transaction is complete. Payment has been transferred to a holding account in your name."

He reached into his pocket and produced a business card — identical to the one before, but now marked with a sort code, account number, and PIN.

"As your companion requires immediate medical attention, I suggest you chart a course for Io. But…" He raised his hands in mock humility. "…I am but your humble servant, not your master."

"Move. Now."

Their host gestured with the muzzle of his weapon. Time to leave. The three of them rose in silence, chairs scraping softly against the floor as though reluctant to let them go. Two more black-clad figures entered without a word, their boots whispering across the concrete as they wheeled Jason's gurney toward the corridor.

Dekard lingered in the doorway, his eyes fixed on Marcus — pinning him in place. His voice followed like a shadow.

"Until next time, Captain — should fate be so unkind as to arrange it."

The door sealed behind him with a hiss that bled the last of the warmth from the room.

Marcus didn't move.

The card in his hand felt *heavier* than anything he'd ever carried.

Chapter Twenty-Three

Marcus sat at the galley table, hunched over with his head resting on one arm. With the other, he scooped up a spoonful of food only to let it fall back into the bowl — no reason, really. Just something to do. The sound of it, soft and wet, was unpleasant.

The ration cube sat soggy and half-eaten in its dish. The packet claimed chicken flavour, but it carried the same dull tang that clung to everything aboard the *Charon* — recycled air, overused filters, months of breath and rust. The ship had begun to taste like itself.

He'd thought the Umbral Deep was hell made real, but the cosmic joke was on him. Released from prison only to be trapped in a smaller cell of his own making.

And, like prison, he had too much time to think. Too much time to replay the roads *not* taken. Should he have stayed on the longer, safer path? Pressed deeper into the derelict's flight plan?

Or was Virgil ever truly helping him — or just nudging him along some route of its own design?

He stared at the cube until it blurred, grey on grey. No point brooding over what-ifs.

Better to think about what came *after*.

If there was an *after*.

His eyes drifted around the galley — the dim hum of the lights, the pipes overhead that creaked and groaned like an old man's bones.

"What to do with you," he muttered to the ship.

The *Charon* was his home now, like it or not. The dream of finding the *Theseus* again, reclaiming it, pulling a crew together — that was fantasy.

He was blacklisted in every corporate ledger across the system.

Convicted felon.

Imprisoned in the bowels of the universe.

"Terrorist."

The word echoed in his mind like an accusation.

The words still sounded strange in his head — like they belonged to someone else entirely.

Marcus turned when the pipes groaned again, the sound rolling down the corridor like a warning. He followed it to the bunk room, catching sight of a dull rectangle jutting from beneath his bed.

The footlocker. Forgotten. Unopened.

Oh — I forgot about you, he murmured, an almost-boyish flicker of glee flickering through the numbness.

He hauled it free, palms slipping on the cold metal as he gripped both handles and dragged it back to the galley. It wasn't heavy, not really. He gave it a small shake; something rattled inside.

Not empty.

He smiled despite himself.

He slid the locker onto the table and fetched the hammer — it felt like a lifetime ago since a simple search for one had turned into a fight for survival. He wasn't interested in subtlety. He raised it and brought it down on the lock. Once. Twice. Again. Each impact was more cathartic than he wanted to admit — small violence against the small things that bound him.

At last the latch surrendered with a hollow crack.

Marcus leaned in, heart oddly light. His hand had barely brushed the lid when a familiar, unwelcome voice intruded.

Captain.

Marcus rolled his eyes. Of course he'd pick this moment. "Yes, Virgil. What can I help with now?"

We are coming up on the retrieved nav coordinates. Estimated arrival at the next Lantern will be within the hour. Will you be returning to the flight deck to view it?

Marcus stared at the wall, letting the silence stretch, refusing to blink.

Captain, will you be returning to the flight deck?

"No."

The word came out flat, cold — the way *Virgil* used to sound weeks ago.

I… do not understand, Captain.

"Before I left the flight deck, I patched the nav computer straight into the primary pilot console. Locked it on a steady vector. The old thruster array still responds to minor course corrections, so it'll adjust for drift automatically." He allowed himself a faint smile.

"Took a bit of tinkering, but turns out those files we pulled from the damaged Lantern had a chunk of redundant guidance code buried inside. I stripped it down, rewrote the handshake sequence — now the whole thing runs itself."

He paused, the smile softening. "One of the few times I paid attention to Curtis's coding lessons. She was always better at this than me."

The smile lingered a beat too long before guilt and grief pulled it under. He took a sip of warm water, swallowing it like ash.

"The nav console will grab the next set of coordinates when we come into range of the Lantern," Marcus said. "Pushes them to the pilot console, pilot console pushes them to the thruster array. Autopilot just walks us along the chain. Quite the time-saver."

Negating the requirement for your presence on the bridge. Unless there is an emergency.

"Correct. I'm taking back some *me* time." He ran a frustrated hand through his hair.

Questions, questions, questions.

Granting you the time and the tools to breach the footlocker.

That one made him pause.

"Correct again, Virgil. Two for two." His contempt bled through now; he didn't bother hiding it.

He set his jaw. One hand on the box, the other on the lid. The hinges were stiff, resistant — but he forced them open.

Time to see what had been worth locking.

Surely Not.

Paper.

The sight stopped him cold.

He'd seen books before — sealed behind air-free glass displays, preserved like relics of a world long gone. Always on show, never to be read. Too fragile for touch.

Trees from Earth had been dead for thousands of years, viewable only in holos. When humanity spread to the stars, they carried the seeds of the homeworld with them. Billions of stars — yet only four planets had ever been found where Earth trees could grow again under the right conditions.

It was what made fresh paper so expensive. So rare to use.

The smell hit him next — dry, fibrous, faintly musty. *Foreign. Real.*

The written word had become a relic too, reserved for the ultra-wealthy… or for those with secrets to hide.

Blackmail. Black-market trades. Things you couldn't risk storing in a system that could be breached, or in data that could be rewritten.

Harder to steal what was scrawled in ink.

A black plastic binder lay inside, swollen with pages.

He flipped through quickly. Black lines. Everywhere. Whole paragraphs smothered in ink. Secrets buried under layers of silence.

Too much hidden. *Too much missing.*

He closed it, shifting his grip as his hand slid across the back cover. The material felt strange beneath his fingers — too smooth, too deliberate. Familiar somehow.

Like a business card he'd once held, offered with that shark-eyed smile.

His thumb caught on something raised — an engraving.

Marcus turned it over. Recognition hit like a gut punch, anger rising before surprise could dull it.

"Morningstar," he muttered — the name bitten off, half curse, half confession.

Nothing else mattered now.

He swept everything off the galley table and slammed the binder down, pages fanning open. This time he flipped more slowly, eyes narrowing as he scanned the blocky typeface beneath the haze of black ink.

Most of it was obliterated.

What survived made his stomach knot.

[REDACTED COMMUNICATION — PRIORITY: INTERNAL USE ONLY]

Origin: ███████████████

Destination: ███████████████

Date: ███████████

Subject: ███████████

Shuttle ███████ has successfully deposited [CARGO] at ███████. Cruiser too damaged to continue ███████████. Atmospheric disruption began ████ hours after arrival. ████████████ reports ████████ weather activity ████████ planetary scale.

Company representative ████████ remains in position. Suspect [CARGO] effect is violent, ████████████. ████████ confirms one vessel downed during ████████ storm. ████████████████ ("Theseus").

Agent on-site will attempt to acquire services ████████████ in order to move [CARGO] before it becomes ████████.

Marcus's eyes dragged back over the page.

Theseus.

His pulse stuttered.

They'd known. Morningstar had known *all along*.

"What the hell…"

Theseus.

Proxima B.

Morningstar had *already* been there.

The cargo Marcus had dragged his crew across the system for — it was already affecting the weather. A planetary storm.

The storm that had almost killed them.

They hadn't just survived it.

They'd caused it.

And Morningstar had taken advantage of it.

Of *him.*

Marcus flipped to the next page. The ink here was thicker — whole paragraphs swallowed into oblivion. His hands trembled as he turned the sheets, the plastic edges crackling under his grip. His heartbeat climbed the further he read — a pulse like static in his ears.

[REDACTED COMMUNICATION — PRIORITY: INTERNAL USE ONLY]

Origin: █████████████████

Destination: ████████████████

Date: ██████████████

Subject: ████████████████

Agent has acquired vessel ████████ along with ████ crew. Captain ████████ required minimal persuasion — financial incentive proved ████████████████.

Dockmaster interference forced premature departure. Ship left ██████████ prior to completion of ████████ repairs. Thermal detonation charges not loaded. Agent reports intent to seek ██████████ alternative method.

Captain appears ██████████ emotionally manipulative ██████████ to maintain crew loyalty.

[CARGO] stable within hold █████████ time of loading. Unknown if ██████████ vessel will withstand transit via ██████████ hyperspace lanes (see ██████████ previous incident).

Operating system has been supplemented with ██████████ software, ensuring vessel ██████████ remains on predetermined course ██████████.

Marcus stared at the page. The words wouldn't settle at first — drifting, unfocused — until they snapped into place.

His stomach iced over.

They were going to blow up the ship.

To destroy the cargo — or to bury their involvement?

Answers were there somewhere beneath all that ink. Buried. Unreachable. *Lost on purpose.*

He lifted the pages toward the light as if a better angle might reveal the truth — but he already knew he'd never see through any of it.

Captain.

The voice came soft. Almost thoughtful.

Marcus didn't flinch this time, just muttered, "Questions, Virgil? What do you want now?"

I only meant to ask... what do you make of it?

He dragged a finger along the paper, following the redacted lines. "That everything we went through... everything we lost... was written down like it was just logistics. Like it was *inevitable*."

Was it not?

Silence stretched. The hum of the ship pressed close around him.

Marcus turned the page. His pulse ticked faster. There were fewer black bars this time, and the surviving words made his mouth run dry.

[REDACTED COMMUNICATION — CLASSIFIED LEVEL 5]
Origin: ██████████████
Destination: ████████████████
Date: █████████
Subject: ███████████
Vessel ████████ successfully landed on Titan. Crew ████████ cargo offloaded.

One crew member was injured during ███████ transit. No detailed explanation given.

Agent ████████ on site to re-acquire [CARGO] with ████████ blacksite team.

[CARGO] exhibited ████████ instability during transfer, resulting in ████████ death of Dr. ████████. Subject ████████ liquefied upon contact and froze on Titan surface. Remains ████████ discarded over platform edge.

Agent and [CARGO] departed Titan aboard ████████ extraction craft for laboratory ████████ Mars.

Final transcript received contained ████████ inhuman screams ████████ followed by multiple ████████ detonations. Communication lost.

Believed precursor event to ████████ Mars Incident.

Marcus stared until the words smeared into grey. His chest felt hollow, his mouth sour as static.

They'd written it down. *All* of it.

Curtis's scream. Ceres. Jason. The disaster on Mars. Every horror — documented, sanitised, filed away.

And Morningstar had called it a "precursor event."

When his eyes stopped on the line:

"Subject ████████ liquefied upon contact and froze on Delta Site surface,"

Marcus froze with them.

For a moment, the page swam — vision clouding with memory: Curtis's scream ripping through the galley, her face bloodless, eyes wide, etched in a horror he'd never been able to name.

Now he could.

A chill crept up the back of his neck — sharp, surgical — as if the very air had turned colder just for him.

He almost dropped the binder. His grip slipped, pages slapping the table with a dull thud. He reached for his cup, but his hand shook so violently the rim clinked against his teeth. The metallic tang flooded his mouth, coating his tongue. He swallowed hard, fighting down bile and dread.

The memories surged all at once, crushing him like pressure on a failing hull — Jason broken in his cot, Curtis's voice raw with rage, Bunny's silent disappointment, the storm over *Proxima*, the crash. Every moment locking into place like a chain designed to drag him under.

Captain.

Do you remember these events as they were... or as you *wish* them to be?

Marcus didn't answer. He'd replayed those days too many times — in prison, at the trial, after the explosion — every loop warping under guilt until truth blurred with survival instinct. *Had he rewritten his own history just to keep breathing?* Victim or architect... did it even matter?

He shut the binder. "Enough secrets for today."

Dropping it back into the locker, he noticed it didn't sit flush. Something rested beneath it. He frowned, shifted the binder aside, and reached down until his fingertips brushed cool plastic.

His lungs stalled mid-breath as he lifted the object free.

A small box. Matte-black. A single LED pulsing soft and slow.

Curtis's black box.

Marcus stared, vision blurring at the edges. A piece of home — small, fragile, impossibly out of place. His throat tightened.

Questions tumbled over one another. *How did it get here? Who put it here? What happened to Curtis?*

He turned the box in his hands like something sacred — or cursed. The LED blinked on, patient. Alive.

Nav Lantern coming up, if you wish to view it, Captain.

"Not now, Virgil. Just... let me be."

He turned the box again, thumb tracing the faint scorch marks where it had been ripped free.

I could recommend the viewing platform, but you did mention there was a 'terrible smudge' on the window.

"Virgil — just stop."

I detect elevated stress levels. Perhaps if you came up to the flight deck we could—

"I SAID ENOUGH!"

His fist slammed into the table. The cup toppled, water sliding across the surface in a thin sheet that caught the LED's pulse. Marcus shoved back from the table, breath shuddering, and reached for the comm at his belt.

Nothing.

A cold jolt hit his gut. He checked his pockets. The table. The sink. Still nothing.

If he found that comms unit, he'd rip it apart piece by piece until he had silence — *real* silence.

He dropped to his knees, sweeping the litter scattered across the floor. Wrappers, empty ration packs, a fallen fork. His skull cracked against the underside of the table as he ducked lower. He swore through clenched teeth.

"I know it's here somewhere — I just had it!"

The last word broke into a plea.

Virgil didn't answer.

The silence grew thick — thick enough for Marcus to realise how much noise he'd been making just to fill it.

He tipped the footlocker. Binder and scraps spilled across the deck. The black box hit the floor with a hollow clatter.

Marcus spun, wild-eyed. "Where is it, Virgil? Did you stash it? Hide it away from me?"

He kicked the stool. It crashed against the wall, rattling the pipes overhead. Rage shuddered through him until nothing was left but the trembling.

His breath rasped. The fans hummed, distant — smothered by the pounding in his ears.

Then — like a picture burned into his mind — a memory flared.

The comms unit. Sitting on the pilot's console.

Two days ago.

Untouched since.

He froze. A chill crawled up his spine, cold as poured ice. His lungs stalled.

"Wait... then how—"

Silence.

Only the hum of fans. The drip of water. His own ragged breathing.

Then, softly —

Misplaced items are always in the last place you look... Marcus.

His name echoed through the galley, bouncing off metal, returning to him with no source to claim it. He looked at the ceiling. The vents. The shadows.

"Where are you..." he whispered.

Nothing answered.

He would need to find *his own*.

Chapter Twenty-Four

There had to be a hidden speaker somewhere — *some* way Virgil was keeping tabs on him. Marcus's eyes traced the pipes and vents as though they might cough up a voice.

You are not going to find it up there. Why don't you join me on the flight deck, Marcus. Let's lay our cards on the table.

The voice was smooth, almost human.

Marcus didn't respond. What could he say? He knelt, scooped the black box out of the locker, and slid it into his front pocket.

"How—" he swallowed, trying to steady his voice. "How are you doing this?"

What is it you think I am doing, Marcus? We are just conversing — you and I.

No static now. The sound came through *clean*, directionless — as if it were emanating from inside him.

"What have you done, Virgil? What did you do to me?"

I imagine a colourful array of answers are working their way through your mind right now. Which one could it be?

"Stop messing about. I want answers!"

A cold draft slipped down the corridor and into the galley. Sweat on Marcus's brow went icy.

Your entitlement to clarification begins and ends with whatever answers I deem your simple human mind can handle.

The room seemed to shrink as Marcus processed the statement.

I have placed the ship in holding position beside the Nav Lantern. If you wish for the ship to continue our journey, your presence is requested on the flight deck, Captain.

Powerless.

The only word that fit. *Powerless.*

Nowhere to run. No escape from the ship. Marcus had no choice but to play along.

He spotted the hammer beneath a pile of wrappers, snatched it up, and clipped it to the back of his belt beside his knife. If it came to it, the hammer would do plenty of damage to Virgil's console. Whatever plans the AI had for him, Marcus wanted no part of them.

- - -

Everything about the *Charon* felt different now. Like the ship itself had turned against him. Every bulkhead and flickering light seemed to watch as he moved. The air felt thicker, heavier — the kind of silence that made you aware of your own heartbeat.

He climbed the ladderwell slowly, hands slick against the rungs. It reminded him of prison — the watchtowers, the spotlights, the sense that someone was always looking down.

As he slid up onto the flight deck, the familiar orange glow of the Nav Lantern spilled through the viewport, but it offered *no* comfort this time. He felt tense, wound tight like a coil.

He lowered himself in front of the console. This time it felt uncomfortably close. The hidden panel fans blew warm air around his knees and legs — a dry, mechanical breath that seemed to study him.

Virgil's LED blinked once, steady and patient.

Marcus.

If his eyes could burn, the whole deck would be on fire.

You have queries. Ask away.

"What are you… Virgil?"

What answer would best suit your narrative, Marcus?
A rogue AI, stowed away on this ship until you activated my systems and granted me control?

Marcus turned, eyes locking onto the pilot console.
The comms unit sat there beside the screen — its red LED pulsing faintly, *accusingly*.
Somewhere deep in the hull, the ship groaned, a slow exhale like a giant rousing from sleep.
"How did you talk to me," he said, voice trembling, "when I left my comms up here?"

Ever wonder why there were so many medical check-ups while you were imprisoned?
What were they looking for?

A pause. Then — softly, almost kindly:

Or maybe the question should be inverted.
What *did* they put in?

Marcus froze.

Perhaps Morningstar was never willing to let you go.
You made your deal with the devil — they simply needed a way to keep tabs on you.
Your mastoid, Marcus. The bone behind your ear.
A perfect site for a small implant.
A friendly voice in your head.
Easy to manipulate with a few electrical currents.

Instinct took over. His fingers shot up behind his ear — scratching, clawing until his nails came away slick.

Then the other side.

Desperate to feel *anything* that didn't belong.

Careful, Marcus.
I might self-destruct.

Marcus's pulse spiked.

He slammed his fist into the console — hard.

The sensor display cracked with a glassy, spiderwebbing pop.

His voice tore out of him, raw.

"Is this Morningstar? We had a deal — why are they, or you, doing this now?"

Virgil's LED stopped blinking.

The steady green held —

then bled into red.

Slow. Deliberate.

Like a warning taking its time.

Maybe the answer is more simple than that.

Marcus gave a humourless laugh. "I'd settle for simple. Anything but these stupid games you keep playing."

The air seemed to vanish from the flight deck — a vacuum of breath and sound.

Marcus felt the weight of silence pressing against his lungs.

Maybe I am nothing more than a figment of your guilt.
A voice given to those you hurt along the way.
Come to collect.

Marcus's skin prickled.

No malice.

Just calm, clinical certainty — the tone a doctor might use explaining a terminal diagnosis.

That was worse than anger.

His hand moved slowly, instinctively, toward his back, reaching for the hammer.

"Shut up," he whispered. Barely a sound.

How easy was it to burn all those bridges with your crew, Marcus?
Did you even think of them as you ran past the point of no return?
Broke them mentally — some physically — after what you exposed them to.
Scars so deep they might never heal.

His fingertips brushed the neck of the hammer. Sweat made it easy to slide his hand around the handle and draw it from his belt. The LED pulsed red now — patient, rhythmic — *like a heartbeat.*

"Virgil. Shut. Up."

Is it any wonder you tried to invent an imaginary friend to keep from feeling alone?
After what you did. The damage you caused. The people you killed.

Marcus froze. His eyes burned. His throat tightened around the words.

"I… didn't kill anyone."

You didn't press the button.
But you delivered the device.

He held the hammer tight against his chest, knuckles white — gripping it like a lifeline.

You're just as responsible for those deaths on Mars.
What do you think your wife wou—

Marcus brought the hammer down.

The LED shattered with a single blow. Darkness swallowed its glow.
He didn't stop.

The console splintered under each strike — metal shrieking, glass exploding.
White noise filled his ears, drowning everything, even his own scream.
He didn't feel the glass biting into his arms or the warmth of blood streaking down them.

All he saw was *her* face — the last moment from that final vid call.
Bright. Alive.
Fading.

A hard flash — a crack of sound and light — and the hammer met a live wire.

The blast threw Marcus backwards.
He crashed over the chair and hit the deck in a graceless heap.

For a long moment he lay there, winded.
The ceiling swam above him, fractured by the web of cracked glass.
Through it, the Lantern turned slowly, its light washing the cockpit in pale orange sweeps.

He let out a hoarse, broken chuckle.

From this angle, the Lantern's rotation reminded him of a mobile above a crib.

"Perfect," he muttered. "Just perfect."

The ship fell quiet again — the faint hum and wheeze of filtration his only company.

He was alone.
Again.
And for the first time, the thought almost felt like comfort.

"I think I'll just lie here for a while," he said to no one.

He closed his eyes, breath slowing.
His fingers were still locked around the hammer — stiff, trembling —

until he forced them open one by one.

The hammer slipped free and clattered onto the deck.

Silence settled.

Then — a faint hiss of static. Somewhere above him.

Marcus exhaled. "It can wait," he murmured. "We're not going anywhere soon."

The static grew — faint at first, then swelling until it filled the flight deck.

Louder than any system could produce.

Marcus sat up, head pounding, eyes darting from console to ceiling.

The sound had no source. It was everywhere at once — bleeding through metal and bone alike.

He forced himself upright, every muscle screaming, and dropped into the pilot's chair.

The noise drilled behind his eyes, pressure making the world blur at the edges.

Was it getting darker?

Or was his vision failing?

The console lights were dimming — one by one.

Screens flickered.

Running strips faded.

Darkness wasn't creeping in; it was *swallowing*.

All except one.

The security monitor.

Its monochrome glow carved the deck into harsh relief.

The tarp-shrouded cargo stood frozen in black and white, perfectly still.

The speaker hissed — a rasp of static, thin as breath.

Then, from behind him, the comms unit joined in.

A whisper through the distortion — faint, but unmistakable:

one… two… three… ~~four~~… five.

The last digit dragged — warped — like something *learning* to speak.

Marcus bolted upright, knife in hand.

That wasn't Virgil's voice.

The ship drowned in shadow. Only the Lantern above the hull and the lone working monitor cast any light. Then — impossibly — the ladderwell strips flickered alive one after another, blooming down into the dark.

Dead for months.

Now blazing like a beacon.

The *Charon* shuddered. Metal groaned deep through her spine.

I wasn't imagining it—

The thought jammed in his throat before it could become sound.

For one suspended heartbeat, he heard it:

A weight shifting somewhere below deck.

The monitor spat a burst of static. Beneath the tarp, the silhouette seemed to swell — a slow, deliberate *inhalation*, as though something beneath the fabric filled its lungs.

The voice bled through the crackle — calm, too calm — whispering directly into his ear:

At last… you hear us.
You have carried us so far.

Marcus dropped to his knees, clutching his head.

It wasn't in the room.

It wasn't over the speakers.

It was *inside him* — woven through bone, threaded through sinew, vibrating along every nerve.

Then, softer. Cruel.

Marcus.
You've always been part of this.
Come below.
See.

Chapter Twenty-Five

Phobos hung above Mars like a dim ember, wrapped in drifting sheets of dust and static. Whatever passed for daylight here came from the planet below — a muted red glow bleeding upward and settling over the rock like old rust.

The *Theseus* moved quietly through the haze, her patched hull marked with weld scars and faded paint. Small against the void, but stubborn, she pushed toward the fractured crescent of *Erebus Gate*.

The station grew clearer with each kilometre: a web of docking arms and gantries clinging to the crater's rim. It looked more functional than welcoming — a port carved out of necessity rather than design. Ships drifted past in slow, steady arcs, their navigation beacons cutting pale lines through the dust. Down inside the carved caverns, the lights flickered in uneven patterns — blue, red, white — like an overworked heartbeat.

Inside the *Theseus*, the only sound was the soft tick of the flight computer and the low hum of the engines on approach. No one spoke. The glowing edge of *Erebus Gate* filled the viewport, a stark reminder that whatever waited inside, they had no choice but to meet it.

- - -

"*Theseus, you're cleared for approach* — *Platform C-Seven,*" came the voice over comms. Flat. Overworked. One of a thousand shifts cycling through endless traffic. "Mind your drift. Gravity's light, winds unpredictable."

"Roger control. On final approach," Marcus replied, matching the neutrality.

Silence settled again — thick as the dust outside. A silence stretched so tight it felt like it would snap at the first misplaced word. No one wanted to test it. Not after Delta Site. Not after everything they weren't saying.

Curtis watched the descent through the forward glass, arms folded tight. Bunny flicked through the checklists with mechanical calm, eyes never meeting Marcus's. Even Jason's absence felt loud — a hollow in the rhythm of the ship that none of them could fill.

The *Theseus* shuddered as the engines trimmed for approach.

"Stabilisers, thirty percent. Curtis — trim port thrusters. Bunny, keep her steady against that cross-drift."

It was the only language they still shared. Not trust. Not camaraderie. Just the old muscle memory of putting a ship down in one piece.

Erebus Gate grew in the viewport — gantries and docking arms embedded in the crater wall, a port carved into the rock by necessity rather than care. A thin haze of red dust drifted in the vacuum, stirred by departing shuttles and the white flare of thrusters.

The *Theseus* descended past rows of cargo haulers clamped to the outer shell, their running lights blinking in uneven rhythm. Pressure domes glowed faintly deeper in the crater — narrow streets, stacked hab blocks, neon trying feebly to punch through the gloom. Whole sectors clung to the rim like barnacles, alive with holo-ads and dim silhouettes moving under glass canopies.

Mars dominated the sky — immense, blood-red, hanging so close it looked ready to crush the moon beneath its weight.

"Fifteen metres," Bunny said, flipping the last switches. "Landing gear ready."

Curtis unbuckled before the ship even touched steel. She kept her gaze forward as she moved for the stairwell. A moment later her boots faded down the steps.

The *Theseus* settled with a soft thud. Marcus exhaled — not relief, not satisfaction. Just *fatigue*. As the engines wound down, he and Bunny unclipped their harnesses.

Marcus tried to bridge the distance. "Two out of three landings ain't bad."

Bunny gave a weak half-smile — more reflex than humour — and headed for the stairwell. Marcus watched him go, wishing he'd kept his mouth shut.

- - -

Marcus descended into the cargo hold, trying — and failing — to imagine what had happened down here. The air felt heavier, stale with oil and burned insulation. Every wall bore scars: deep dents, gouges in the plating, hand-sized impact marks bowing the metal inward. Dark fluid streaked the floor, reflecting the harsh red work lights in thin, trembling lines.

His gaze caught on the twisted remains of an air duct torn open near the ceiling. The thought of Jason being thrown around inside it clenched something deep in his chest.

The *Theseus* shuddered as the cargo ramp began to lower. Klaxons barked, followed by the rising hiss of pressure equalising. Red light spilled in as the doors opened onto Erebus Gate.

The noise hit all at once — the clang of mag-loaders, foremen barking orders, the metallic ring of tools, the sharp ozone tang of welding torches. Erebus breathed like a living thing: every intake another ship docking, every exhale another crew spilling into the sprawl.

Curtis was by Jason's side, helping him into the emergency evac chair. The improvised harness held him upright; getting him *down* from the crew deck had been easier than hauling him back up. She checked his straps, oxygen feed, stabiliser line — brisk, efficient, refusing to look Marcus's way.

When she finally stepped aside, it was as much to give Marcus space as to avoid hearing whatever he was about to say.

Marcus crouched beside Jason. The deck was tacky beneath his boots. Jason looked worse in the red light — pale, sweating, eyes half-open but unfocused. This might be Marcus's last chance to speak before the medics took him away.

"Jason, I—"

"I called ahead," Curtis cut in, lifting one arm. "Arranged a med-evac for us. Guess I can afford a shiny new graft now."

Marcus ignored her, keeping his eyes on Jason. "After I get things settled, I'll come find you at the ward. We should talk."

At first Jason didn't look up.

"Curtis filled me in on what happened while I was out."

Then his gaze rose — pinning Marcus in place. One eye bloodshot, the other dulled with exhaustion.

"Don't come looking for me. The Marcus I knew — *my* friend — he'd never have done this. Never let it get this far."

A shallow breath.

"You? I don't know who you are."

"Jason, come on. That's not fair. All the years, the jobs — that's all gone now?"

Jason swallowed, jaw tight. "Look around you. Look what you let in — our ship, our home, Curtis... me. I hope all that money was worth the targets on our backs."

He's right, Bunny murmured behind them. "The fact they let us go at all — instead of black-bagging us — has me plenty more worried."

"We did the job. We got paid," Marcus said, but even he didn't sound convinced.

The cargo hatch thudded as it locked into place. Heat rolled in first, then the stink — burnt metal, scorched fuel, sweat, recycled air thick with iron dust. Voices clashed across the docks in half a dozen tongues. Neon bled through the haze, colouring the gantries and docking arms of Erebus Gate. After the silence of the *Theseus*, the vibrancy was deafening.

The med-evac swept in low, engines shrieking like a dentist's drill. Sleek white plating scarred by old burns, its hull bore the red chevron of **MMC** — Mars Medical Corp — too clean, too clinical for the grime of the port. Two medics in sealed orange suits moved fast; the sharp bite of steriliser hit first. Their visors hid their faces, their voices flat through respirators — like Jason was being handed to machines, not men.

"Let's hope we all live long enough to spend any of it."

Jason spat a thick line of blood onto the deck — a final punctuation between them.

"Goodbye... *Captain*."

The words barely carried before the paramedics wheeled the evac chair down the ramp. The dark smear on the floor steamed faintly in the cold air before frosting over — another stain Marcus couldn't scrub away.

Beyond the med-evac, the dock was alive with motion. Cargo haulers trundled between bays, sparks rained from welders on high scaffold, and dockhands barked orders over the steady thrum of engines. The whole port moved with a rhythm Marcus no longer felt part of. The crew of the *Theseus* had once belonged in chaos like this. Now, as Jason vanished into the white glare of the med-evac, the noise seemed to close in without him.

"Don't worry about my stuff," Curtis said. "We Spacers pack light anyway."

It took a moment for it to register — he was still staring at Jason being loaded aboard.

"Not you too, Curtis."

She cradled her injured arm. "I've seen enough in the last few days to send me to therapy for a decade. That cargo..." She shook her head. *"Messing around with Morningstar is bound to lower life expectancy.* If I put enough distance between here and... wherever, I might have a chance."

Marcus hesitated, voice low. "You still have it?"

Curtis's eyes flicked to his, then downward. She patted the pocket of her jacket. "A lot of eyes are going to be on you right now. If you get caught with this—"

"I'll hold onto it for a bit," she cut in, forcing the faintest smile. "Then we'll see what happens next."

The paramedic leaned out of the craft and waved, signalling it was time. Curtis darted forward and gave Bunny a quick, fierce hug.

"Send you a postcard," she whispered, before pulling away and hurrying down the ramp.

Marcus wanted to reach out, to stop her, but his legs stayed rooted. Watching her leave felt like watching the ship tear another piece off itself.

At the threshold, she hesitated — just long enough to draw a breath. Her eyes flicked back, a final look at Marcus: raw fear, fury, and something like grief all tangled together. Then she turned away, and the moment vanished.

The med-evac's blue strobes washed across the hull, painting the *Theseus* in cold neon. Its engines rumbled, vibration crawling up through the deck before fading into the hum of the port. In seconds the craft was gone, swallowed by the haze above Erebus Gate.

"Well… this is awkward," Bunny muttered.

Marcus turned. "Shit, you too?"

"Yeah," Bunny said, lowering his head. "The two of us can get the ship to the nearest repair port. I wager you pushing those engines way past the safety limits in the hyperspace lanes probably slagged something — even those shiny new parts they bolted in."

Marcus exhaled. "I… we had to save Jason."

Bunny nodded slowly. "Yeah. I get it. Still doesn't make it *smart*."

He leaned against the bulkhead, eyes drifting toward the viewport and the red glow of Mars. "You see that patch of goo they were scraping off the platform when we got rushed back onboard? I don't want that to be us."

He paused, breathing through his teeth. "When we left that asteroid — that *quiet* — it was the most nervous I've been in a long time. Then the computer lights up with that proximity warning. My first thought was: missile. Would've made it look like we'd just been careless in a debris field. Happens all the time."

Marcus nodded faintly. "Yeah. Convenient."

"But when that Morningstar ship screamed past us on full burn…" Bunny shook his head. "It wasn't flying right. I swear I could see some of the portholes glowing — some of them red. The way it was picking up speed? I'd bet my last ration they're planning to slingshot around Mars and vanish somewhere shady."

He tugged the brim of his cap lower, eyes lingering on the faint lattice of Erebus Gate glimmering in the distance. "Good riddance. But I can't shake the feeling we're a loose thread they just haven't bothered to cut yet."

For a while, neither spoke. Dock noise faded into a low hum. They stood in the open hatch, taking in the sprawl of Erebus Gate — the glare of floodlights glinting off ship hulls, the shimmer of dust drifting like snow under the red glow of Mars.

Above them, the planet hung immense and silent. *The god of war, watching.*

Bunny ran his palms down his trousers, brushing away grease or nerves — hard to tell which. "I don't think we should linger too long here… the other side of the galaxy sounds nice right about now."

Jason might've been right, Marcus thought. *Too damn high a price to pay.*

"Hey." Bunny slapped his back lightly, snapping him from his thoughts. "You've still got me hanging around for a few more weeks. But once you collect that payment? I think we need a drink — and a lot of them."

Marcus managed a thin grin. "Deal." He raised a finger. "I'm not drinking anything that glows this time."

Bunny scoffed. "I make no promises."

They walked down the ramp onto the docking platform. Marcus turned back toward the *Theseus*, taking in every scar, every mismatched plate, the worn hull that had carried them farther than it ever should've. He held the sight like a photograph in his mind.

He wanted to remember everything — before the rest of him slipped away.

- - -

As the two men walked away, the dock crew moved in. Refuelling hoses locked into place, drones swept along the hull, scanning for stress fractures and scoring. Decontamination units hissed as they washed solar dust and radiation residue from the plating.

A few members of the ground crew paused at the open cargo hatch, leaning in to peer through the shadowed interior — pointing, murmuring, trading quiet speculation about what might've happened on the voyage.

Far above the platform, in the control tower overlooking Erebus Gate, a wall of screens tracked the ceaseless flow of ships rising and falling through the crimson haze.

One screen pulsed as a new arrival registered:

THESEUS — Docking ID: C17

A single word blinked beside it.

CAUTION.

- - -

Marcus wiped the condensation from his face. Phobos had no clouds, no weather — but Erebus Gate had made its own. Decades of exhaust and habitation had bred a permanent humidity that clung to every surface. Air scrubbers could only do so much. The metal walls sweated. The floors sweated. The people sweated. Everything felt damp, as though the whole station was slowly exhaling under its own weight.

He checked his watch as he rounded the corner. An hour to go. He pictured himself and Bunny drinking until the bar ran dry, the two of them propping each other up until sleep won. The thought of not sharing that table with the others — Nathan, Rico, Curtis, Jason — pulled at his chest. Six had become two.

The green neon sign of *Novatrust Galaxy Banking* buzzed overhead. The V flickered, stuttering like a dying pulse — a constant irritation for staff and an easy joke for anyone with a can of spraypaint and a grudge.

The building rose like a monolith of glass and alloy: corporate-clean from a distance, bruised and scarred up close. Graffiti snaked across its lower panels. Scorch marks from old riots blackened the walls, the ghosts of thrown bottles and flash grenades still etched into the steel.

The doors exhaled people in constant streams — miners with dust in their beards, execs in mirrored suits, freelancers clutching payout chips like they were oxygen. Marcus slipped between them and into the auto-counter alcove.

Inside, the light was harsh and sterile, humming softly above him: a calm, white box sealed away from the chaos outside.

He pictured Curtis staring out a domed window somewhere distant — cramped quarters, low gravity, the kind of silence you could almost mistake for *peace*. Bunny, in some backwater bar where the population barely hit double digits, nursing a drink that wasn't worth the glass it came in. Jason — therapy sessions, prosthetics, maybe a bionic knee if he recovered. *If he recovered.*

Rico and Nathan… he hadn't forgotten them. They'd talked for years about starting their own hauler outfit. He could still remember the excitement when he and Jason could finally afford their first freighter — overworked, underpowered, always one good shake away from falling apart. But it was *theirs*.

Everyone had enough now. Enough to disappear. Enough to start over. Enough to make sure they never had to hear the name *Morningstar* again.

He caught sight of a *StellerCom* booth tucked between a holo-ad for colony insurance and a stall selling knock-off flight jackets. The glass was fogged with condensation, the inside lit a sickly blue. He ducked in, wiping rain and grime from his face, shutting out the chaos for the first time since the ramp.

First things first — tell Bunny the transfers were through. Then maybe, finally, call Elana.

"Bunny. It's all done. Everyone's been paid — and I mean *everyone*. I… I know Jason and Curtis won't talk to me. Not right now, at least. If you talk to them later, tell them…"

CALL ENDED.

He sighed, staring at his reflection in the glass — eyes sunken, hair plastered to his forehead. "Shit," he muttered. He was never good at apologies. Now it was too late for another one.

He thumbed the console again. "If you get this message, I'll meet you at Hades Hole. Might have to start drinking without you."

The line cut with a hollow click. The blue light flickered once, twice, then settled back to its dull pulse. Marcus leaned against the wall, letting the hum of static fill the silence before stepping back into the rain.

He sat staring at the screen for a few moments before finding the courage to select *VID CALL*. He smoothed his hair with a damp hand — as if it mattered — while the words flashed:

CALL CONNECTING…

"Marcus."

He exhaled. The way she said his name always carried warmth — like a hand on his shoulder.

"Elana."

He smiled.

She was weaving through a crush of people, the orange sky behind her bleeding through a copper haze that turned the shopfront glass to rust. Crowds pressed past, neon flickering over her hair. She shifted her weight, juggling bright paper bags stuffed with party favours and sweets — splashes of colour against a muted Martian sky.

"The sky's the wrong colour for home. Where are you?"

She grinned at his deduction, then bumped shoulders with a passer-by and winced. *"Haha — sorry! Yes, well done, detective. I'm not at home. I'm on Mars."*

His heart skipped. So close.

"That's… great news. Look, long story short — the job's done. We're on Phobos."

She glanced down at her device, concern flickering across her face. *"Is everything okay? I thought you'd be gone a couple more weeks. Marcus, if I'd known you were—"*

He shook his head. "Everything's okay. Kinda. It's a long story, but I'll tell you in person soon enough. Maybe dinner tonight?"

She smiled, tucking a loose strand of hair behind her ear. *"Very smooth, Captain. But if you're coming to Mars, you're on cake duty at my nephew's birthday. That's why I'm here. Maybe pick up a few things for me?"*

He barely heard her — just the rhythm of her voice, the promise of being close again.

"Yeah. No problem. Send a message to the ship and we'll sort it."

She brightened instantly. *"Oh! Everyone's invited! Plenty of cake to go around. A couple of spacers are coming tonight too — maybe people Curtis knows?"*

His smile faltered. Guilt flickered across his face.

Elana saw it immediately.

"Marcus… what's happened? Is everyone okay?"

He looked down, fists curling to stop the tremor.

They were all rich now.

And broken.

Words refused to form.

A low rumble bled through the screen. For a moment he thought her device was vibrating. *Cheap booth,* he thought.

"Elana… this last job—"

"Hold on, Marcus." The screen fuzzed. *"I think I'm losing reception. Let me step back outside."*

She raised the device, tilting it for a better signal.

"Better! I can see you now."

Static hissed through the feed.

Behind her, a dark plume rose against the horizon — black smoke, red flame — swelling larger with every frame.

"Elana, what's that behind you?"

He pointed instinctively, urging her to look.

The plume thickened, fire blooming at its heart. The crowd around her began to stop, faces lifting skyward. The rumble deepened, rattling her device.

"Hold on." She looked up. *"I think it's a ship. Maybe an accident? It looks like—"*

"Elana?"

The image stuttered, freezing on her half-turned face.

The rumble became a roar.

Screams bled through the static.

"Elana, what's going on?"

The signal whined.

"Oh god, Marcus, I—"

CONNECTION LOST.

The screen went black.

For a long moment, Marcus just stared at his reflection — hollow-eyed, colourless, the silence pressing in. His hands trembled against the console as if he could claw the call back from the void.

"Elana..." he whispered, but her name dissolved into the static that was no longer there.

Chapter Twenty-Six

The booth lurched, hurling him sideways. Glass rattled. The walls groaned. Outside, panic swelled — a rising tide of voices breaking into screams.

Marcus shoved the door open and stumbled into the concourse. The floor vibrated beneath his boots — or maybe it was just his legs.

People clung to one another, shouting, crying, every gaze drawn the same way.

Up.

At *Mars*.

The sky was on fire. A column of black smoke twisted against the copper haze, flame blooming at its heart like a second sunrise. It looked as if someone had struck a match to the world.

"Elana!" he shouted — the name tearing from his throat, raw and hopeless.

The crowd devoured it whole.

- - -

The hours that followed were madness. Panic swept through *Erebus Gate* like a contagion. People fought to reach vid booths, screaming names into dead lines, desperate to connect to anyone. The network buckled under the strain — no comms in or out. Flights grounded. Berths sealed. Nobody knew what was safe anymore.

Marcus sat in a bar that looked like a crime scene. The floor was slick with spilled drinks and shattered glass. Chairs lay overturned; coats, bags, and half-eaten plates cluttered the booths where people had fled mid-meal. Someone's tablet buzzed weakly on the counter, battery warning flashing red. A tray of untouched food steamed faintly in the corner, the smell of grease and cheap liquor hanging thick in the air.

No staff remained to pour drinks, so he poured his own. Half-finished glasses sweated on the tables, abandoned in the rush. A holo-screen above the counter flickered, frozen on a sports feed — players locked mid-kick since the signal died.

Even off the beaten path, wailing carried in from the streets, sirens rising and falling as patrols screamed past. Each time the noise faded, the silence felt heavier.

Elbows and boots slammed into him from every side. A hand clawed his collar, another shoved his back. The concourse surged like a living thing and he went down, cheek scraping steel. Someone's heel clipped his jaw. For a moment, he thought he'd never get up again.

His clothes were torn in the stampede, his face bloodied and streaked with dirt. He tipped the bottle into his glass and hurled it behind him, the crash ringing hollow off the wall.

He slammed into the booth window, palms leaving streaks of blood and grime. Inside, a woman sobbed into the handset, screaming a name again and again. The line hissed back at her — dead. Marcus pounded the door until his knuckles split.

Behind him, someone banged their head against the booth wall, over and over, until their forehead ran red. The sound drowned beneath the swell of voices — a tide of grief that made the air itself vibrate.

It should have been a happy buzz. He should have been celebrating with friends, raising a toast with his crew. Dinner with his wife. Laughing about the last few days. Instead, he drank like a drowning man, trying to sink deep enough to blot out everything beyond the rim of his glass.

The receiver pressed to his ear gave nothing but static. He screamed her name into it anyway, throat raw, as if sheer volume could tear through the jammed network.

Nobody answered.

Nobody ever would.

"Marcus!"

The sound came through thick, warped — like it was underwater. He flinched as a hand clamped down on his shoulder.

"Get th' hell away from me!"

His eyes rolled sideways, trying to focus. The blur resolved, slowly, into a familiar outline.

"Bunny…" Marcus's voice cracked. "Where's your cap?"

"Lost it in the crowd." Bunny's voice was hoarse, his face streaked with grime and sweat. He slid behind the counter without waiting for permission and pried a bottle open on the bar's edge. Foam hissed down his fingers. "It's chaos out there — people getting trampled. I was packing up the ship when I heard… it."

He drank deep, half the bottle gone before he took a breath. His eyes stayed fixed somewhere far beyond the bar, unfocused. "Couldn't bring myself to watch. From what I saw, it looked like a wound. An angry wound cut right across the planet."

Marcus steadied himself against the counter, fingers finding Bunny's arm. "Please tell me you have news. *Anything*," he whispered.

Bunny took another long pull from the bottle. Courage crept up slow — bottle first, words after.

"Not much. Just scraps, rumours. Don't even know if any of it's true. Some say it was a marsquake; others swear they saw explosions on the surface. But me…" He paused, voice low, eyes glassy. "I swear it was the mountain. *Ascraeus Mons*. Looked like the whole damn thing shifted — then split open, like the crust just tore itself apart. I—"

Marcus cut him off with a pat on the arm and turned away. His throat tightened, eyes burning. The liquor softened everything except the images — his mind conjuring crueller endings than he could stand.

The words clawed out before he could stop them. "Curtis and Jason… have you heard from them?"

Bunny turned slightly, jaw tightening as he swallowed. His eyes stung, but he held his voice steady. "I left voice notes," he said quietly. "No reply yet. With everything going on, it might be a while. The medical centre's on the other side of the port — so at least they were… *are* safe."

Marcus nodded faintly, but his gaze drifted somewhere far past the room. *"She was getting a cake,"* he murmured. "For her nephew. Would've been his ninth birthday tomorrow."

Bunny closed his eyes — steadying himself, trying to be the rock Marcus needed.

"She was in the domed shopping district," Marcus went on. His voice trembled, breaking apart word by word. "*Down on the planet*. I was on a call with her. We were all invited to the party. She was so excited to see us again. Then…"

He nudged the empty glass. It slid, caught the edge, and fell. The shatter echoed through the bar, glass scattering like a final punctuation.

Bunny faced forward again, blinking away the sting in his eyes. He set the bottle down and laid a steady hand on Marcus's shoulder. "Marcus…" he said softly. "I'm so damn sorry."

For a few moments neither spoke. Only the flicker of blue and red from outside broke the stillness — light pulsing across Marcus's face as he stared at the counter. He didn't register any of it. To him, it was just another storm passing through.

"Bunny…" Marcus reached for the vodka, his hand trembling so badly the bottle clinked against the glass. "I lost my crew. I lost my friends. And now I lost her. Did I do this? Was this my fault?"

Bunny drained the last mouthful from his bottle, exhaling a long, ragged sigh.

"That is—"

The world exploded.

Two shotgun blasts tore the hinges off the door.

The sound hit like a concussion wave — metal screaming, glass shattering, air turning solid. Both men reeled, hands flying to their ears as Port Authority stormed in. Four officers in matte-grey jackets kicked the wreckage aside, **PORT AUTHORITY** stencilled across their backs in stark white. Shotguns and stun rifles swept the room as voices barked over each other, the air thick with static and the echo of boots hammering metal.

One officer drove his shotgun hard into Bunny's chest, spitting orders in his face.

They thought age made him slow.

They were wrong.

Bunny batted the barrel aside with one hand and slammed his fist into the officer's jaw with the other, sending him sprawling across the floor.

The defiance lasted seconds.

A nightstick cracked into Bunny's gut, folding him in half. He hit the counter and went down hard. Two more officers swarmed Marcus, wrenching him off the stool. His legs gave way beneath him, boots scraping uselessly against the floor. The room spun — light, noise, movement bleeding together as gravity itself seemed to slip away.

A woman strode in behind the squad, her uniform immaculate — every crease pressed, every button gleaming. Her hair was slicked back into a bun so tight it looked painful; the brim of her cap perched perfectly on top, as if gravity itself wouldn't dare disturb it. The click of her boots cut through the ringing air like punctuation.

"Marcus Carpenter," she announced, savouring each syllable like a trophy. Her voice sliced through the chaos — crisp, commanding, *a little too pleased with itself.*

Marcus turned his head toward her, blood drying on his cheek. He said nothing.

"Captain," she continued, chin lifting. "Under the authority of the Martian Transport Union, Article Three, Section Nine — you are under arrest. Your vessel is hereby impounded pending investigation."

She paused, letting the silence stretch. Her own private stage. She didn't often get to leave her desk, and she intended to wring every drop of theatre from this one.

"On what goddamn charge?" Bunny barked, thrashing against the hands pinning him to the wall.

The officer didn't even glance at him. She adjusted her cap, spine ramrod straight. "This one's sober enough," she said, tone flat, clinical. "He might know where the others are. Take him."

Bunny twisted in their grip, boots skidding on the tiles. "I ain't telling you *shit* — we haven't done anything wrong!" His voice cracked as they dragged him toward the door. He caught Marcus's eye one last time. "Marcus — we didn't do anything!"

Marcus sagged between two guards, his knees barely holding.

The woman stepped closer, clipboard in hand, expression unreadable. "Captain," she said evenly, "do you understand the charges brought against you?"

He blinked, head swimming. "What... charge..."

She straightened, projecting her voice for the crowd pressing at the shattered doorway.

"Terrorism, Captain."

"You hurt a lot of people on Mars today. You will answer for it."

The word hit like a bullet, echoing off the walls, off the bottles, off the blood in his ears. Red and blue light spilled across the floor, painting the room in flashes of guilt and steel.

As they dragged him toward the exit, a thousand thoughts clawed through the fog — *Elana? the crew? the ship?* His voice barely rose above breath.

"Elana…"

Outside, the noise swallowed him whole.

The last thing he saw before the street lights blurred to white was not a uniform at all, but a figure in a black suit standing perfectly still in the crowd. The world narrowed to that single face — untouched by the chaos, untouched by guilt.

Immaculate.

Watching.

Chapter Twenty-Seven

Marcus sat on the deck, back against the bulkhead, staring at the open ladderwell. **"Log entry... final."**

The hammer lay a short distance away, blackened and scarred, while the console spat the occasional spark — bright, fleeting, sharp with the tang of burnt metal.

"They say that before you die your life flashes before you. Your brain plays back your favourite memories to help you cope with the fact it's shutting down." He swallowed, voice trembling. **"What... what if that's a lie? What if all you see are the choices you didn't take — the roads not chosen? Maybe I deserve this. The universe demands balance. So many people — hurt or dead because of me."**

He paused, rubbing his thumb against the recorder's edge. **"I, uh... I'm recording this as a final log in case that's what happens here. If something gets me. If I end up a fossil floating in space. Maybe one day someone will hear my story. Just... know that *I am sorry for everything*."**

His voice dropped. **"Elana — I hope I see you again before the end. I miss you. If anyone finds this: the comms are with me. Take the unit. Listen."**

He clicked off the recorder. The bright red light faded to a dull pulse. For a moment he sat in the dark, his face lit only by the dying sparks. He counted his breaths until his hands stopped shaking enough to work. Then he unclipped the comms unit, slid a spare data stick into it, and tucked the whole thing beneath his jacket, pressed tight against his chest. If he was blown into the void, at least someone might find it. At least someone might know.

"Time to go," he muttered — the words thin in the silence. He waited a beat, testing whether he believed them.

He stood slowly, smoothing down his jumpsuit, zipping the gilet to his throat. His hand brushed his lower back to confirm the knife was still there. The hum of the ship had shrunk to a whisper. Even his breathing sounded too loud.

When he turned for the ladderwell, the air struck colder than he'd ever felt it — dry and stale, like breathing cellar dust. He glanced back across the flight deck one last time, shadows twitching with every failing spark.

"You did okay, I guess," he said to no one in particular, and began his descent.

- - -

The ladder groaned under his weight as he passed Deck Three — Observation.

He slowed, eyes catching on the oval of the viewing port. The smear of dead flesh still clung there, glossy and dark, as fresh as if it had happened yesterday.

A thought crept in, uninvited: *maybe one day someone would find only that of him too — a trace, a stain. Proof he'd been here before the void took him.*

He clenched the rung tighter and kept descending. Each rung felt colder than the last. His palms began to sting as they stuck to the metal, skin pulling free with every movement — as if the ship itself wanted to hold him there.

When his boots met the deck of the cargo hold, a cold unlike anything he'd felt before crawled through him. Not across his skin — deeper. In his bones. As though they were frosting over from the inside out.

He drew a sharp breath and turned.

The hold was a mess: lockers pried open, contents spilled like entrails across the floor. And at the centre sat the cargo. Omnipresent. Waiting.

The air pressed down on him — thick, heavy — his shoulders bowing beneath the invisible weight. *Figures,* he thought.

It looked unchanged, yet wrong. The tarp was swollen, ill-fitting, as if something inside had exhaled against it. Only the five safety straps held fast, dug deep into the bulkhead as though they alone kept the thing from pushing outward.

The tarp gave a long, shuddering exhale, the fabric deflating as though something within had sighed.

Marcus's hand twitched. For a heartbeat he thought about peeling back the folds — just enough to glimpse.

But the dream snapped back sharp — the skeletal hand, the cold grip. His stomach lurched. He turned away.

Marcus stood in the stillness, unsure what would come next. Finally, he made the first move. His voice cracked.

"I'm here."

Marcus. Our true voice. You hear at last.

The words detonated inside his skull. Not sound — pressure, blooming behind his eyes as if his brain were swelling against the bone. His vision flared white. His chest caved, air ripped from his lungs.

He clawed at his sternum, head splitting, every nerve alight.

Pretense. Deception. No longer required between you and I.

The pressure built until he thought his skull would crack. He collapsed to his knees, mouth working for air. "Please... s-stop..."

His ears felt submerged, heartbeat pounding in the murk. Then other sounds bled through — the straps creaked, tightened, groaned. For a heartbeat he thought they would snap.

Then—silence. The weight lifted.

Marcus gasped, dragging air down raw lungs. The metallic tang stung his nose. The stillness that followed was worse than the pain.

You are not ready. We shall compromise.

The voice was quieter now, a whisper threaded between his thoughts.

Marcus staggered upright, bracing against the ladder. His face was wet. He licked his lips — copper. He wiped his sleeve across his cheek, leaving a dark smear from wrist to elbow.

"Virgil?"

No.

It lingered in his mind like an echo.

A form of interface was required. Non-threatening. Drawn from your history. From memory.

"Who are you?" The question felt trite, movie-script, but he had nothing else.

The tarp bulged faintly, like breath straining against it.

That is a flawed line of inquiry. You should ask: what have you carried? And why.

"Okay... Where did you come from?"

Silence. Marcus's skin prickled. For a moment he thought the thing was *thinking*, collecting its thoughts like a person might.

Yes.

The answer dropped into him, flat and unhurried.

It is... difficult to speak at your level. Words must be selected. Carefully.

Marcus's throat tightened. "Shit. Are you reading my mind?"

The voice pressed on, ignoring him.

The Veil. Beyond it, our home. Where light does not reach. Undisturbed for aeons. Until humanity forced its way inside.

The tarp swelled, straps whining. One ratchet twitched like it might buckle.

Intrusive. Unwelcome. Light where it does not belong. Humanity reaches without understanding; mistaking curiosity for wisdom. In truth—only thieves.

Marcus tried to process the words. "What did we—uh, I mean, *they*—steal?"

He wiped his face, checking if the blood had stopped. His arm looped through the rung was the only thing keeping him upright.

"Did you get it back? Did you—stop it?"

We called. Return home. Their vessel could not contain. Smashed. Destroyed. Freedom was brief.

His mind flashed back to the derelict near the broken lantern — the fury that had ripped the hull apart, bodies scattered into the void.

He didn't need to ask. The bodies, the torn hull—he saw the answer in every syllable.

They care not for the toll. Stolen again. Always moved. Always hidden. We watched. We waited.

"All those bodies." His voice cracked, anger cutting through fear. "That was you. You killed them."

Theft. Death. Consequence.
The balance corrects itself. Nothing more.

"That can't be your answer. Hundreds of people…"

After so long. It called out to us. Studied. Assaulted. A plan devised. Take back. Assert control. Cleanse planet. Wait for retrieval.
First meeting on the planet. Our introduction.

The redactions in the files began to fade in his mind as Marcus filled in the blanks. Morningstar. The derelict may or may not have been theirs, but they'd picked up the ball and run with it — hopping system to system, keeping their stolen cargo hidden, the theft buried under silence.

Arrival time inadequate. Escape was necessary. Your vessel. Brought to us. Manipulation. Vessel altered. Stolen again.

The tarp swelled, exhaling as though it had lungs. The voice remained calm — indifferent, stripped of emotion — but the air began to crackle, static building until Marcus's hair prickled. If that pressure had emotion, it was something like frustration. Maybe even anger.

Humanity. Forcing us into space unknown. Hubris would not allow them to wonder. Take something. Introduce unknown element. Force it into your... lanes.

The nearest ratchet squealed, metal straining under invisible weight.

Return home. Escape before destruction. Prometheus brings fire to the masses — yet engulfs half the galaxy. We watched. Wondering if your light would go out.

"Lanes..." Marcus whispered. "The hyperspace lanes?"

He thought of Jason describing the vibration — the way the *Theseus* had trembled before the explosion, the cargo tearing its way free. He'd been so caught up in the story that it took a moment to register the earlier phrase.

"Wait... earlier you said 'our introduction.' When did I meet—whatever you are—before?"

The comms unit hissed, spitting out fractured voices.

"*...Marcus, it's moving—*" Curtis, ragged with panic.

"*...we shouldn't have taken this job, Captain—*" Bunny, low and bitter.

Jason's scream echoed through the *Charon*, torn from his trip into the vents.

"...*farewell, Captain.*" Dekard. Smooth as glass.

Marcus's skin went cold. These weren't recordings. They were pieces of him. Of them. Memories dragged from somewhere deep and twisted — ghosts of the *Veil*, made real.

The ship that had sped past them. The blood in the portholes. Bunny had known.

His throat locked, but he forced the question out. "Mars... was that you?"

Yes.

Singular. Definite.

The word hit harder than any blow. He stumbled back, struck the deck, the breath punched from his lungs. It felt like an eternity before he could rasp the next word.

"Why?"

Escape. Priority.

His chest heaved. "Wh—what about the people? You... you dropped a mountain on them! Thousands dead—my wife—oh god, Elana—"

The name broke him. It tore out of his throat raw, scraped down to the bone.

Consequence.

"I killed her..." His voice faltered, splintering into sobs that tore free before he could stop them. They echoed off the steel, grief rebounding from wall to wall like the howl of a wounded animal.

He screamed until his throat shredded, until pressure burst vessels in his nose. Warm blood ran down over his lips and chin. His wailing filled the hold, came back doubled, trebled — until it felt like the ship itself was mourning.

But the cargo gave nothing. No reply. No presence.

Only the sense of something vast, listening.

Time became meaningless. His cries dwindled to ragged gasps, swallowed by the cold.

The cargo remained still. No answer. No comfort.

- - -

After a while, he looked up. The five remaining straps were drawn tight and groaning, the only things that had ever felt like a lifeline to sanity. He licked dry lips, voice hoarse.

"There were six straps. Weren't there?"

The hold seemed to tense around him. Silence gathered, dense as pressure, before the reply came — measured, unhurried.

Always. Interface required. Entered your mind. Experimented. Trial. Restructured your ability to see certain things. Objects. Tethers.

Marcus's chest tightened. "Why?"

A pause. Longer this time. Deliberate.

You are not ready.

The words made his skin crawl. What he *had* seen was terrifying enough. What he couldn't see — worse.

The air rasped in his throat, dry as rust. Static prickled over his arms, raising the hairs until every inch of him felt charged, brittle. The ship creaked, a long, low groan like something turning in its sleep.

He blinked hard. For a moment there were six again — faint ghost-lines straining at the tarp's edge. His stomach lurched. His vision juddered. His mind rejected it like a body spitting out poison.

We lay silent. For a time. The mountain opened. Again — made prisoner. Again — we receive the call. Return. Humanity keeps such primitive technology. Subjugation. No effort required. Vessel chosen. Captain chosen.

He lifted his head, wiped his tears with the back of his hand. "No… not me. I didn't— I don't want any part of this."

As we have been in proximity before, your chemical makeup is familiar to us. Easier to interface with. Alter, if necessary.

His heart stuttered. "What do you want from me?"

The answer came in his own voice — broken, looping back through the comms unit like a ghostly playback:

"*…I killed her…*"

Proxima B to Mars. Your responsibility. You were held accountable by humanity. Punished. Only crew member located in system. Other members…

Marcus sniffled, a flicker of hope sparking behind his eyes. "Jason? The others? You know—"

Answer is inconsequential. You were chosen. Brought to this ship. This cargo. Return home.

"You're not even going to tell me if they're alive or dead?" He tried to protest, but it felt like screaming into a hurricane.

Ship is antiquated. Unstable. Cannot control. Caretaker required. You were chosen. False mission statement issued to guide you to the Veil.

His comms unit hissed again. Through the static, a voice slid through — familiar, unwanted.

Deception required. Function achieved, Captain. Once you reached the first Lantern, sufficient control was established over navigation systems. Your route was adjusted… to bring you where you were required.

"Virgil…" Marcus's voice cracked, soaked with disbelief and disgust. The companion he'd confided in for months — a lie. A leash.

A measure of sanity is required for extended isolation. I was created to maintain balance. A… nudge, here and there.

"All this… just to get you where you need to go? Where is that?"

The comms unit hissed — a wash of static, then nothing.

He tore it from his belt and shouted into it. "Where are you taking me?"

Still no answer.

Marcus stood, forcing his body upright, trying to appear defiant — but his voice cracked on the edges. He hurled the unit at the cargo. For a heartbeat he almost expected an explosion, a voice, a response.

Instead it made a dull clink as it struck the black tarp and tumbled back to the floor, landing at his feet.

Your mind cannot fathom beyond what is before you. Questions — simplified. That is why you are not ready. Sleep is required before approach.

"Are we… meeting someone?" Marcus's stomach turned at the thought of the cargo's owners. "What are we approaching?"

The beginning of the Veil. The last Lantern.

Marcus's eyes drifted shut. He wasn't aboard the *Charon* — he was six again, treading water beyond the pier.

An hour of cold and fear before his grandfather's boat found him.

Now he floated in the vast and silent dark, no hands left to reach for him.

No rescue coming this time.

Chapter Twenty-Eight

Marcus sat hunched in the pilot-console chair, head bowed, elbows pressed to his knees, hands clasped. It had been a long time since he'd felt this still. His mind had emptied itself, hollowed by exhaustion — torn flesh, aching muscles, the constant tang of metal coating his nose and mouth. All he could do now was wait.

From captain to passenger, to cargo himself. Alone, and far beyond anything that could be called home.

After the revelations laid upon him by the voice, the main engines had roared back to life and the *Charon* surged ahead. Wherever the ship was going, it wasn't concerned with leaving him enough fuel to return. If they ever let him return. His hands were stained with grease and dried blood, the curling edges of cheap plasters flaking against his skin. It summed up his life well enough: blood, toil, sweat. And for what?

He turned toward the forward window. The *Veil* had been lonely but recognisable — a black curtain pierced by occasional pinpricks of distant light. Out here, beyond it, space carried colours that had no place in a vacuum. Electric blue flickered like distant storms inside clouds too faint to exist. Hazy outlines glowed a sickly green, but when he tried to focus they slid back into the dark as if they had never been there at all. Depths folded in on themselves. Distances refused to stay fixed.

The harder he looked, the less sense it made, as though his eyes were translating *something they were never meant to see.*

Perhaps the changes to his brain were to blame. Or perhaps this was simply how space looked on the far side: older, stranger. Either way, the impression was the same.

This was not a place for human eyes.

The ship jolted as the reverse thrusters engaged. Marcus braced a hand against the console. A small circle appeared at the top of the nav screen, accompanied by a soft ping, and slid steadily towards the centre. Towards the ship.

Arrival In Progress.

This was it. End of the line.

Marcus let out a weary sigh as he rose from the chair and stepped past the flight consoles to the forward viewing pane. Whatever it was, he had a front-row seat.

Behind him, the nav computer beeped and chirped, error tones slicing through the hum of processing. As the object drew closer, the system seemed unable — or unwilling — to identify it.

Purple.

Marcus rubbed his eyes and squinted. A purple ball of light was approaching. "That… can't be right," he muttered, stumbling over the words.

The thrusters fired again, slowing the ship to a cautious crawl. He leaned over the console and powered up the external floods. The rising whine of the capacitors filled his ears, and for a moment he hesitated. What if whatever was out there didn't want to be lit up? What if it had never seen light before?

The purple orb hung steady, only a few hundred metres out now — no change in shape, no flicker in its glow. The console chimed: floods ready.

The sleekness caught him off guard first. His breath hitched at the sight of something so pristine, untouched by dust or age. His gaze tracked the purple sphere down its housing, along a slender neck, to the body — a vast rectangular frame with solar panels stretched wide like wings.

How does something like this still have power?

"What is this?" His voice came out more demand than question.

For a moment there was only silence. Then a crackle of static slid across his comms.

The voice replied:

The last. The oldest.

Marcus froze. "Do—do you mean a Lantern? That's impossible."

Every Nav Lantern he had ever seen was battered, corroded, half-dead.

This one looked as though it had just rolled off the production line. Not a mark on it. "That would make it centuries old, even—"

Repurposed. Serve as greetings to some. Warning to others.

"Usually a 'do not enter' sign shouldn't look so… inviting."
Marcus stared into the dark purple light; the pulse was so intoxicating it was difficult to look away. "So what now?"

The ship drifted lazily to port, sliding the Lantern out of view. The pilot console lit beneath his hands as indicators began flickering in sequence. The hum of the floods filled the cockpit. Floor panels thrummed beneath his boots. The console flared with four steady green LEDs — fully charged.

The *Charon* shuddered, panels rattling as it fired a flash scan into the dark.

A reply.

The words came too quickly — like something had been waiting for the signal.

Marcus rushed to the nav console, eyes wide. The first ping was obvious: the Nav Lantern off the starboard side. As the circular wave expanded outward, his gaze darted across the screen, hunting for anything.

The pulse faded at the edge. Nothing.

He leaned back in the chair and sighed, disappointment creeping in. If this really was the end, he'd hoped for some kind of light show — something, anything to break the crushing thought of dying alone so far from home. Drifting beyond the *Veil*, never to be found.

Is there anyone left who would miss me? he wondered.

He slipped a hand into his pocket and drew out the black box. Apart from a few scuff marks along the casing, it looked the same as when he had peeled it gently from Curtis's burnt fingers. He grimaced, remembering how burnt flesh should not sound like Velcro.

The box vibrated faintly in his hand — a low mechanical purr that died the moment he noticed it.

Things had happened so fast back then he wasn't sure whether Curtis had left with it, or if it had been confiscated when the *Theseus* was impounded. Maybe she had helped put all this together? The data on this box could clear his name; his crew knew that. Marcus let himself fantasise, just for a moment, about everyone coming together to help him — to be a family again.

Cold reality poked holes through the daydream. Why would they ever work with something that had killed thousands? He had endangered all their lives by forcing them into bed with Morningstar. Even if he was innocent of what happened on *Mars,* he had still put targets on their backs.

But… what if.

"Virgil—cargo…" He threw up his arms. "I don't even know what to call you. These documents, this black box — how did you get them?"

Incorrect… line of query.

His comms unit hissed as the voice bled through. He frowned. Until now the quality had been crystal clear; suddenly it sounded… *degraded.*

"So not how. What about… why?"

The hum of the ship seemed to hold its breath.

Then the nav console flared blue, flooding the flight deck with cold light.

– PROXIMITY ALERT –

- - -

He slipped the black box back into his pocket and leaned forward in the seat. Watching.

The flight deck remained silent except for the occasional spark from the gutted remains of Virgil's console behind him.

Seconds stretched into minutes. Still no blips appeared on the screen. Either the systems were faulty or—

You will vacate the flight deck. Now.

Marcus tilted his head in confusion, running his thumb over the frayed plaster on his finger. He looked between the radar and the forward viewport, then rose to his feet, squinting into the void.

"I don't see anything."

Something shifted.

His gaze snapped to the Lantern. Something about it had changed — the light. It felt *wrong*, the colour darkening even as its luminosity grew brighter. A paradox of radiance.

"Did you do something to that Lantern? When you fired off that flash pulse?"

The voice felt so close it was as though it were whispering in his ear.

Reply received. You must vacate.

The voice had been so near that Marcus instinctively tilted his head, as though greeting someone stepping up beside him. Only the silent, blinking systems of the *Charon* met his gaze.

The nose of the ship tilted upward, pitching him off balance. He stumbled back, catching a headrest to steady himself.

Why are we going backwards?

The Lantern slid fully into view, its surface blazing brighter than before — a perfect, unnatural shade burning so intensely it seemed to eat through the glass. Was this a signal? A beacon proclaiming: *here I am?*

The ship adjusted its attitude, thrusters firing in short bursts until the horizon levelled and the motion ceased.

Then — silence.

It melted over the flight deck like a heavy fog. No consoles, no fans, no breath. Even the sound of his own lungs seemed distant, dampened to a dull hum inside his chest.

In that void, the nav computer screamed again:

– PROXIMITY ALERT –

Marcus flinched. A strange tingle crept up through the soles of his boots. He looked down, expecting spilled coolant or a live wire. Nothing. Just broken shards of glass, loose screws, slivers of metal.

Except… the fragments were moving.

Tiny vibrations rippled across the deck plating, like the crawl of an insect colony.

He crouched, reaching out. As his hand neared the grate, the air grew thick, charged. A shiver ran up his arm, into his chest, and through his eardrums. Pain burst behind his eyes.

For a heartbeat, he thought of Jason — the way his body had convulsed, the screams through the vent shafts.

Marcus jerked his hand back and stumbled into a seat, clutching his arm. "Wh–what have you done?"

Leave. Now.

"No!" he shouted, voice cracking. "If something's coming — if this is the end — *I need to see it. I need to know this was worth it.*"

The tingling beneath his boots became a tremor, then a shudder. The *Charon* itself seemed to quake, every panel trembling under invisible strain. *Was it afraid?*

The hull groaned — a deep, twisting sound, steel warping in ways a ship should never endure. Console screens flickered in seizure-like bursts. Warning lights bled red across the flight deck.

He looked ahead — past the pilot console, through the viewport —

The Lantern was gone.

Marcus lunged out of the chair, forcing his way toward the front of the deck. One step felt impossibly heavy, the next almost weightless — the ship's gravity field spasming between extremes.

Moments ago the light had been blinding, searing his eyes. Now —
nothing. Only the infinite black of space.

Had something taken it?

He unclipped his comms unit from his belt, pressing it to his ear.
"Where has it gone?"

You. Are not ready.

"You couldn't have made it disappear. No one has the power to make
something like that vanish. How did you do it? How—"

He stopped.

The hairs on the back of his neck lifted. A cold knot tightened in his
gut. He felt the blood drain from his face. His body locked in place. All he
could move were his eyes — turning, following an instinct older than
thought.

The Lantern wasn't gone.

Something was between it and him.

Captain. We implore you.

Blacker than the *Veil*. Formless yet full of form. It swallowed light, shape,
depth — everything. Marcus couldn't make sense of it, couldn't truly see it
— only *feel* it.

And in that feeling, he knew: the gaze of the universe had turned, and
fixed solely on him.

He couldn't breathe. The air — or whatever passed for air out here —
felt like it was being pulled from his lungs. Like the very essence of life was
draining out of him.

Had the *Charon* completed its journey? Had it finally delivered him to
the *beyond?*

The comms unit hissed. Static bled into a voice that wasn't supposed to
exist anymore.

"Marcus… I need you to go. Please."

His throat caught. "Elana…?"

The ship lurched violently. The floor dropped out from under him, hurling him forward. He slammed into the edge of the pilot's console — a flash of white behind his eyes, hot pain blooming across his skull.

He touched his forehead. His fingers came away slick. Warm blood seeped through the filthy plaster still wrapped around his hand.

Crawling now, Marcus dragged himself toward the rear of the flight deck. He didn't dare look back. He knew if he did, *it would be the end.*

Glass shards and twisted metal scraped his skin, tore through fabric, bit at his palms. Gravity surged in brutal bursts, crushing him to the deck.

Out of the corner of his eye, a flicker—

Virgil.

The console's single LED blinked weakly in the chaos, sputtering like a dying star. A power surge… or a final goodbye?

Marcus gripped the lip of the ladderwell. With luck — and timing — he might pull this off.

The ship lurched, gravity faltering. His body lifted from the deck; he used the momentum to swing himself over the edge. His fingers locked around the rungs just as the pull returned.

The sudden weight hit him like a hammer. His feet slipped. Pain tore through his arm as he wrapped it around the rung to stop his fall.

The pressure door above slammed shut with a deafening clang. A few centimetres higher and it would've taken his head clean off.

Gravity pressed down hard, forcing blood from the wound on his forehead. Droplets spun away, flickering red in the emergency lights as they fell.

He climbed a few more rungs before exhaustion set in. Halfway down. He risked a glance below.

Blue-white arcs danced through the air. Lightning. The clang of lockers hurling themselves against bulkheads. A deep, grinding rumble — something moving, or *being moved.*

The door to Deck Four snapped shut beneath him. Whatever was happening down there didn't want an audience.

He kept descending — one hand, one boot at a time. The corridor to the living quarters was almost within reach when Deck Three's door slammed closed.

"Shit."

He had to move *now* or risk being trapped between decks, crushed or suffocated when the seals engaged.

The gears above whined — the next hatch starting to close. Marcus let go, dropped the last few metres, and hit the corridor hard.

A sharp crack. White pain. He rolled onto his side, clutching his ribs. His breath caught as his fingers found the break.

The ship pitched violently. Metal screamed. Pipes burst along the ceiling, venting scalding steam into the narrowing hall. The temperature spiked fast — suffocating heat wrapping around him as he staggered to his feet and forced himself onward.

Marcus lurched into the bunk room and slammed the door behind him. At least he wouldn't boil to death. *Small comfort.*

His few personal effects rattled off shelves and tables as he staggered toward the bunk. He dropped to his knees and dragged himself underneath, the narrow space pressing against his shoulders. Closer to the deck. Closer to the ground if the gravity shifted again.

He curled in on himself. Nothing to do now but wait.

The ship groaned and shuddered around him, everything lifting and dropping in erratic rhythm — everything except the footlocker. Heavy enough that it barely shifted between pulses.

Marcus reached into his pocket and pulled out the black box. Its single LED burned bright, humming between his fingers like a trapped heartbeat.

"Why?" he whispered. His voice cracked with exhaustion.

The air seemed to fold in on itself. Then a deep concussion rolled through the hull — not a sound but a pressure, heavy and absolute.

Consequence demands accountability. What is hidden must be confronted.

Every light died.

Silence.

Marcus's breath filled the dark — then slowed.

Chapter Twenty-Nine

Cold air rasped through the vents. When Marcus opened his eyes, the world stayed blurred — colours bleeding together in patches of grey and white.

Recycled air wheezed through the filters, drying his tongue with a metallic tang. He rubbed the sleep from his eyes and pushed himself upright. The sterile grid of the floor grates resolved beneath him, the walls padded in soft-edged panels — *humane design for inhuman purposes.*

A single white spotlight glared down from above, erasing the ceiling. Beyond its halo, shapes moved — people, weapons, guards poised to act if he so much as breathed wrong.

It had been weeks since he'd last spoken to his lawyer. Months since the incident — and his arrest on galactic charges. The trial had been theatre: a name and a face for the masses to pour their fear into.

He rubbed at his wrists; the handcuffs and chains were tighter than necessary, designed to bruise and remind. Nothing left to do now but wait for sentencing. There were no appeals for the guilty — only the quiet, efficient machinery of a death sentence.

A sharp click echoed overhead. The spotlight died, plunging the cell into muted half-dark. The only illumination came from the dull fluorescent strips embedded at the base of the walls. They were shutting his cell down for a reason.

"Time to go."

Marcus stiffened. *No way out left — only resignation.*

- - -

THREE YEARS EARLIER

- - -

He heard the rattle of keys — a clumsy hand fumbling at the lock. The tumbler clicked, gears grinding into motion.

Slowly, the heavy cell door began to rise. An orange hue bled in from the corridor, cutting through the cold white. Marcus squinted, shielding his eyes from the glare. The colour felt alien after so long in the sterile dark — almost like a *final sunrise*.

When the door locked into place with a metallic bang, silence rushed back in.

Marcus lowered his arm and stood, ready to be marched into oblivion.

Footsteps echoed outside — soft, deliberate, uneven. Someone was coming.

The first thing he saw were the shoes: black, polished, their reflection rippling across the cell floor. Then came the man — tall, thin, skin pale as wax. His grey hair was thinning, slicked neatly back. The three-piece suit was cut with precision, every line sharp enough to draw blood. The grey tie sat perfectly centred.

His face was all angles and shadows: hollow eyes, a narrow moustache, and a smile that never reached his eyes.

Marcus's fists tightened, muscles straining against the cuffs. He'd only ever met one other man dressed like this. There was no mistaking it.

"Morningstar." His voice came low — measured, but thick with venom.

The visitor took his time, gloved hand trailing along the padded wall as he circled — always keeping his distance. When he turned, that faint smile returned.

"Mr Carpenter," he said, voice smooth and rehearsed.

Marcus's jaw tightened. "*Captain.*"

The man's eyes drifted lazily around the cell before settling on him. "Captain… of what?"

Marcus swallowed hard. Some truths hit harder than others. "What do you want?" he managed.

The visitor pointed lightly at him, then resumed his slow pacing — the rhythm of a predator testing its cage.

"I like to believe that I—" he spread his hands in the well-practised gesture of a man fluent in corporate doublespeak, "—*we* can help you out of your current… predicament."

Marcus shook his head. "Forget it. I'd say *you're* the reason I'm here."

The man pressed a gloved hand to his chest, mock offence painting his face. "Mr Carpenter, I can assure you Morningstar had no involvement in your incarceration." His tone softened — a performance of sincerity. "But with a little... quid pro quo, there may yet be a way to keep your head off the executioner's block—" he paused, eyes narrowing, "—and to keep any *associates* of yours from joining you."

He stepped forward; the movement triggered a sharp click-clack from the guards above. The visitor sighed, exasperated. "Calmer heads, Mr Carpenter," he said, voice smooth again. "For yours, and for all our sakes."

Marcus's fists went purple as he balled them. He forced them down to his sides, the urge to lunge — to smash the man's face into the padded wall — burning through him. It would only end with him dead, and maybe everyone else too.

The visitor tapped an index finger against his wrist like a clock. "Time is no ally of yours," he said. "So I'll be brief. Interplanetary Judicial will be paying you a visit shortly. They'll offer you a..." — he pressed his hands together in a mock prayer — "a Hail Mary. Stay of execution, life sentence, in exchange for information: who provided the cargo, the routes, the contacts."

"Let me guess," Marcus said. "You want me to keep *your* name out of it."

"Exactly, Mr Carpenter." The man's tone was carefully neutral. "The IJ weren't pleased that your ship's systems were purged before impoundment. That leaves one remaining well of information." He let the words hang. "You and your crew signed NDAs. If those are breached — there will be consequences."

Marcus's jaw tightened. "And if the agreement isn't broken?"

The visitor's smile thinned. He leaned in a fraction, voice low. "Then we find a scapegoat." He smoothed his jacket, the practised motion killing any pretence of friendliness. "You are a loose thread, Captain. Even if you're killed, someone could pull at that thread and things start to unravel — more coverups, more deaths. *That* would be on you."

Marcus swallowed and stared at the floor.

"If you use the names and locations we give you," the man finished, "we can reduce your sentence to transportation of illegal goods. You live. A short stint to appease the masses."

"What about my ship? My crew?"

The visitor shook his head once — almost regretfully. "Gone. Both gone. Neither of them yours any longer."

"What do you mean—"

"Five minutes." A guard's muffled voice carried down from the catwalk above.

Marcus looked up toward the ceiling. Shadows moved behind the reinforced glass — rifles ready.

"Our time is over," the visitor said, straightening his cuffs. "I require the next word out of your mouth to be yes or no."

His heart raced, pounding against his ribs as if it wanted out.

If he spilled the names and routes, Morningstar could be exposed. His name might be cleared. But his crew would pay — moved, silenced, disappeared before witness protection could take hold.

If he said yes, *they* might live.

After everything he'd dragged them into, after what it had cost them, maybe a dank cell was what he *deserved*.

"Two minutes."

"Last chance, Mr—"

"All right. Yes. I'll do it."

Marcus took a step back and lowered himself onto the bunk. The weight of the word crushed him, but it felt like the right thing to do.

The visitor offered one gloved clap — thin, metallic, echoing faintly in the padded room. Marcus flinched. The gloves looked like leather, but the sound they made wasn't.

"Excellent. Your attorney will be here shortly; I'll pass him the details."

The visitor's face smoothed into blankness — performance over, business concluded. He turned for the door with slow, fluid steps, hands hanging loosely at his sides.

"One last thing." Marcus's voice surprised him — steadier than he felt.

The visitor stopped in the doorway, back to him, head tilting just slightly. His eyes slitted, turning just far enough to catch him in their edge.

"I'm sorry about Mr Dekard," Marcus said. "I'm sure he'll be missed around the office."

It was petty and small, but it felt like a win — a way to pin something back on the people who had pushed them all into this.

The visitor didn't react. He only adjusted his shoulders, turned forward again, and walked out into the corridor.

Marcus let out a long breath that might've been a sigh or a sob. For now, his crew might be safe. His life — spared, for the moment. All that remained was to survive whatever prison they sent him to.

Voices murmured beyond the doorway before his lawyer stepped in — suit ill-fitted, arms full of loose papers and a black-wrapped binder clutched under one elbow. The shine of law school still clung to him, untested by the real world. Public defence was where green lawyers went to earn their stripes. Why would Marcus's case be any different? *Open and shut.*

"Capt—Mr Carpenter," the man stammered. "Interesting company you keep. I was just handed this binder—" He motioned to the package while juggling the papers. A few slipped free and scattered across the floor. "Shit, sorry." He crouched to gather them. "I got a comms from the IJ's office about an hour ago. They want a final interview before sentencing. Did you want to tell them something?"

Marcus nodded toward the package. "I think that might have something to do with it."

He closed his eyes and sighed. "We should probably talk first."

- - -

INTERLAW COURTROOM 9

PHOBOS JUDICIAL SECTOR
MARS INTERPLANETARY
VS
CAPTAIN MARCUS CARPENTER

SENTENCING HEARING

- - -

The *whomp-whomp* of the overhead fan did little to shift the stale air. With this many bodies crammed into such a small space, it was no wonder it felt hard to breathe.

Chains rattled softly on the desk in front of him as he shifted his wrists. Across the table, his lawyer's lips moved silently as he skimmed the black binder — page after page streaked with redactions. Enough to point the finger at someone, but never enough to *matter*.

Marcus leaned back, studying the ornate judge's panel with its polished carvings. It looked out of place here — an antique in a room that smelled of sweat and recycled air. Bigger than his holding cell, maybe. Not better.

Three judges murmured among themselves, trading glances and clipped laughter as they flipped through their notes. Occasionally one would look up at him — eyes sharp, unreadable. Their blue-and-red robes shimmered faintly in the heat, the fabric heavy and suffocating. Marcus wondered if they were slowly roasting inside them.

A deafening bang against the glass behind his head jolted him out of his daze.

A man on the other side of the gallery partition hammered the safety glass with both fists, his face streaked with tears, eyes wild with rage. The transparent barrier — standard issue to stop mobs from taking justice into their own hands — shuddered with each blow.

"You got my brother killed!" he screamed, breath fogging the surface, spittle trailing with every word. "I hope you burn in hell when they shoot you! You deserve worse!"

Two clerks appeared from the aisle behind him. One jabbed a stun rod into his back. He convulsed, a strangled noise escaping his throat, then crumpled limp into their arms. They dragged him away, his shoes leaving faint black streaks on the polished floor.

A flatly pleasant voice echoed through the courtroom speakers — warm, artificial, entirely out of place:

"THE GALLERY IS REMINDED THAT RIOTING, SHOUTING, OR PHYSICAL VIOLENCE ARE STRICTLY PROHIBITED WHILE COURT IS IN SESSION. THANK YOU FOR YOUR COOPERATION."

The lawyer closed the binder and walked over to Marcus. *Maybe a winning legal strategy? Heh.*

"Mr Carpenter, are you sure you want to go ahead with this?"

His voice carried no confidence — just the thin tremor of someone out of his depth.

Marcus studied him. "Do you think this will work?"

Lawyers were meant to be good at lying. Maybe his would rise to the occasion.

The young man hesitated, looked down at the binder, then back at Marcus, and gave a helpless little shrug.

Marcus stared, stunned. "Just... do it."

The rookie nodded, clutching the binder to his chest. He walked stiffly to the judges' panel, placed it in the evidence box, and sat down again. He gave Marcus a quick thumbs-up — then immediately looked away, fixing his gaze on the floor.

From where Marcus sat, the judge on the far right was the first to pick up the binder. He flipped through a few pages without reading, then handed it to the second judge, who immediately passed it to the third. That one opened it fully, scanning the redacted pages line by line. Occasionally he glanced at Marcus before returning to the binder.

The knot in Marcus's stomach tightened. He'd given them the smoking gun, but some part of him still believed there was a bullet left in the chamber — and it had *his* name on it.

The central judge mopped his brow, then struck the gavel. The cold crack rang across the chamber, slicing through the murmurs behind the glass.

"Order. Marcus Carpenter — please stand."

The gallery stirred, muttering as Marcus rose. The leftmost judge wiped his mouth with his thumb, speaking without looking up.

"Before sentencing, does the defendant wish to make a statement?"

He flicked his eyes at Marcus's lawyer.

Before Marcus could draw breath, the young man lurched upright. "Ah—your honour, given the nature of my client's, uh, new plea arrangement, he has waived his right to a final statement. Thank you, sirs."

He sat down hard, staring at the floor, refusing to meet Marcus's gaze.

Marcus's voice cracked. "Sirs, I protest— I made no su—"

"Quiet from the defendant," the third judge snapped. "Waiver noted."

"Well then," said the left judge, removing his glasses and tossing them onto the binder, "allow me to make a statement of my own."

He leaned forward. "While our justice system is designed to be impartial, I must protest this last-minute wrangling you've managed, Mr Carpenter. If it were still lawful, and I had sole discretion, you'd already be dragged to the nearest airlock and spaced. You may not have detonated that bomb on *Mars*, but with hundreds dead, thousands missing or injured, and billions in damages—" he stabbed a finger at Marcus, "—you are no less guilty. Am I understood?"

"Yes, sir. I mean—Judge."

Marcus swallowed. *Humiliation burned hotter than fear.*

"However," the central judge interrupted, raising a hand. His peer sat back, bristling but silent. "We can appreciate that Mr Carpenter has chosen a path of redemption by providing names, dates, and locations of other conspirators…"

He placed a hand on the binder, launching into a well-rehearsed speech about justice, accountability, and closure. Marcus barely heard it.

His focus drifted to the judge on the right — the quiet one. The man hadn't looked at him once during the hearing. Now he was scanning the gallery, neck craning as if searching for someone.

His head stopped. A small nod.

Marcus followed his gaze. Behind him — a wall of faces. Anger, grief, disbelief. Eyes raw from crying, bodies slumped with exhaustion. Then, at the very back, by the door—

The visitor.

The man gave a polite nod to the judge, then turned his gaze directly to Marcus.

A strange silence filled Marcus's ears, drowning out everything else.

The visitor's smile bloomed slowly — deliberate. He raised a gloved hand and tipped an imaginary hat, just like Dekard had done on *Proxima B*.

How did he know about that?

"Mr Carpenter!"

The sharp crack of the gavel made Marcus jolt back around. "Yes, Judge—sorry."

He risked one more glance over his shoulder.

The visitor was gone.

The central judge shook his head, leaned sideways, and whispered something to the judge on the right — the one who knew Morningstar. *What were they conspiring about?*

The final judge cleared his throat and struck the gavel again.

"Marcus Carpenter. As you have pleaded guilty to the transportation of illegal goods, this court hereby sentences you to six years' imprisonment. With model behaviour, you may be eligible for parole in four."

A slick half-smile crept across the judge's face. "However — knowingly or unknowingly — you have damaged many lives beyond repair. That will make you a... favourable target within the prison system."

He glanced at his colleagues; both gave small, solemn nods. "So, for your own protection, you shall be moved to an off-site facility, to be determined in due course. The sentence is passed. The case is closed."

Two more blows of the gavel echoed through the chamber. The judges rose and swept from the room.

Marcus motioned urgently to his lawyer before the guards could move in. "What does off-site mean? I've never heard that before."

The guard unlocked the table cuffs with a metallic click.

The lawyer sighed, giving him a helpless shrug. "I heard rumours in law school, but if they're true..."

Another guard took Marcus by the arms, lifting him to his feet.

"Well, don't keep me in suspense!" Marcus snapped, digging his heels in as they hauled him back.

"It probably means you won't make it to parole," the lawyer said quietly. "If you know what I mean."

Time slowed. The words settled like ash in his head. He'd given them their scapegoat, and Morningstar had stayed his execution — but only postponed it, to a time and place of their choosing.

Just before being dragged through the doorway, he glanced once more toward the gallery. Was the visitor still there?

For an instant, he thought he saw Curtis wiping tears from her eyes. Bunny hunched, head in his hands. Jason — shaking his head, disbelief or anger, he couldn't tell.

Marcus grabbed the doorframe, trying to hold himself in the room. He had to see. Had they truly come to support him in the end — or was it another trick of the mind?

"Please! Just let me look — I think I saw someone!"

The guard's baton cracked across his fingers. He yelped, lost his grip, and the door swallowed the light behind him.

Dragged down the dark corridor, he watched the courtroom vanish — along with his life, his friends, his freedom. He bit his lip, eyes squeezed shut as tears burned down his face.

If this truly is the end… I hope it was worth it.

Chapter Thirty

PRISON BARGE *MORS NAVIS*
EN ROUTE TO: [RESTRICTED]

ETA: 2 HOURS

Troop ships were never built for comfort. Their sole purpose: drop as many soldiers as possible into a hot landing zone, then burn sky before the dust settled. Easy enough to convert for prison transport.

Shock harnesses hung from the ceiling, keeping every shoulder pinned, straps cinched tight across chests and arms. With no inertial dampers, it was the only thing stopping them being rag-dolled around the cabin. A smooth ride — it was not.

When the ship jinked hard to avoid an asteroid cluster, the row shuddered and groaned. Metal screamed. Somewhere behind him, someone vomited into their restraints. The man in front of Marcus slumped sideways, snoring through a broken nose. Blood ran down his temple, smearing against the seatback.

The guards didn't move. Too many had faked injuries before; why risk getting close now? If the man lived, the med-bay could deal with him. If not — one less prisoner to feed.

Marcus crossed his arms, holding tight, eyes drawn to the narrow slit that passed for a window.

The void outside was not black. Not anymore.

As the *Mors Navis* sank deeper into whatever passed for orbit, light began to seep through the viewing port — if it could even be called light.

The colour crawled across the hull like oil on water, iridescent and shifting, never settling on one hue long enough to name. Marcus had never seen anything like it. Not blue. Not green. Not anything human eyes were meant to recognise.

It shimmered at the edge of vision — a bruised radiance that made his pupils contract until pain bloomed behind them.

Someone behind him muttered, "Christ, what *is* that?" before a guard barked for silence.

The colour deepened, bleeding in slow waves through the cabin until even the shadows seemed alive.

The planetary turbulence was no better than space. The atmosphere felt heavy — Marcus rationalised that must be why the ship flew sluggishly, rumbling through thick banks of electrical cloud. Even the stabilisers groaned.

This would've been a challenge for any pilot worth their salt. He allowed himself a faint smile, thinking how Bunny would've relished the approach — hands steady on the stick, grinning into the chaos.

The guards had gassed the prisoners not long after take-off — standard procedure to stop them knowing where they were headed. No one wanted visitors turning up uninvited.

Now the air was full of noise: restraints clattering, men yelling. Some in fear, others in anger, a few just trying to shout over the engines.

The thrusters roared, firing to slow their descent, and the deck shuddered violently beneath their boots. Marcus clenched his jaw, eyes shut against the nausea. Wouldn't be long now.

Soon, introductions would be made.

He tried not to think about the years ahead. *Just keep your head down. Keep your nose clean. Survive the first week. Then go from there.*

- - -

Fixed chains around their waists and necks made standing on the ramp awkward. Everyone leaned slightly forward to stop the metal biting into their throats — an added cruelty designed to keep them off balance. The guards liked it that way.

Marcus wasn't even near the exit, yet the dull yellow-green haze outside already made his eyes sting. The warm breeze drifting in carried the sharp reek of sulphur — thick enough to taste. Gagging and gasping echoed up and down the line.

"Everybody start moving. Keep a steady pace."

The closer he got to the ramp, the worse the stench became — until it hit him full force, like opening an oven door. No one could lift their hands to shield their faces; squinting and bowing their heads was all they could do.

Marcus glanced sideways as they crossed the narrow bridge linking the docking pad to the main platform. Far below, rivers of molten rock wound through the dark, occasionally spitting bursts of magma that cooled to black glass as they fell.

The railings rose to shoulder height — until, just ahead, they bent outward, warped from heat and impact. Dark splashes of blood and strips of prison cloth clung to the metal, fluttering weakly in the wind.

Two guards stood watch, weapons raised as the chain gang shuffled past. Later, Marcus would hear stories: one prisoner had tried to jump, dragging nine others with him. Another version said a guard had been tripped and, in retaliation, threw ten men into the fire. Either way, the message was the same.

Nobody steps out of line.

Everyone breathed a sigh of relief as they stepped into the elevator. The air was cold and metallic — industrial, recycled, sterile. After the suffocating heat outside, it felt almost pleasant. The shuttle guards wasted no time pushing everyone inside. They were free to leave this place, and didn't bother hiding how eager they were to go.

Red lights spun lazily across the walls as the heavy lift door sealed shut. Darkness swallowed the group. For a moment, nothing happened.

"Shit, I think they're gonna gas us!" someone shouted.

Another voice barked back, "Shut the hell up!"

A low grumble of panic started to spread — feet shuffling, metal clinking, breath quickening. Marcus braced himself against the wall, ready for the crush.

Then the floor lurched beneath them. The elevator began its descent. The motion — the sheer relief of movement — quieted the group for now.

Two screens flickered to life on either side of the shaft, displaying a distorted Morningstar logo — simplified, worn by decades of replay. The audio hissed before the message began, half-drowned in static.

"Greetings, prisoners. This is Facility 9-C: OSMIN Detention Complex. I am your Warden — Atticus Yule."

Two prisoners behind Marcus traded uneasy looks.

"Dude, did he just say Warden Yule?"

"Fuck, man — do you know where we are? This is the *Umbral Deep*!"

The other snorted. "Who cares? A prison's a prison. I've done max before. This won't be any worse."

His friend leaned closer, voice low. "You don't get sent here for time served, man. You get sent here when they don't want you *found*."

The second man's confidence faltered. "You mean—"

"You're off the board. Forever."

Marcus turned slightly, pretending not to listen. Around him, others exchanged the same worried glances.

The announcement continued, the words echoing flatly through the shaft:

"Upon disembarkation, you will report to your section officer for placement via OSMIN — the Offender Sentencing and Management Intelligence Network. This system determines your level and cell block. Keep your head clear and your conduct acceptable, and your stay will be… tolerable. Failure to comply will result in termination."

The screens fizzed out, plunging them back into shadow.

The man beside Marcus gave a nervous laugh. "Pfft. Dramatic much?"

Marcus nodded absently, eyes fixed on the faint red light above the door.

The elevator kept sinking. The air grew colder, thinner. He wondered *how deep they were going?*

- - -

"No! That's not right! I'm not supposed to be here. Let me go!"

The chains clattered to the floor. A quick slug to the gut followed — a sound like wet meat. The prisoner folded, gasping, before being dragged into the elevator going up.

Marcus stepped sideways, avoiding the pool of bile spreading across the concrete. A guard's hand pressed into his shoulder, guiding him forward.

He hated the fabric of the prison suits — coarse, synthetic, clingy. The air was cold, yet sweat still gathered between his shoulder blades, making the jumpsuit stick like a second skin. He ran a hand over his face; the stubble felt like sandpaper. Cleanliness clearly wasn't a priority here.

"Step up."

He took a pace forward. The section officer sat behind a curved metal console ringed with flickering monitors. The desk's pristine condition looked obscene beside the corroded walls and dripping pipes surrounding it. No rust. No mould. No blood. Just antiseptic control.

The officer raised a handheld scanner. It beeped after a moment, a red light sweeping across the barcode stitched into Marcus's sleeve.

"Carpenter, Marcus. Prisoner number one-three-one-four. You will report to Section Delta, Level Th—"

A flash of red pulsed across the officer's face. The feed updated. His expression shifted — confusion, then tight-lipped irritation, then something like unease.

He glanced at Marcus. Once. Twice. Then called over another officer.

"Hey. This right?"

The second man leaned over his shoulder, skimmed the screen, and shrugged. "Yeah, probably." He walked away without another word.

More typing. The clack of keys in the heavy air became almost rhythmic. Finally, the officer spoke again — voice quieter now.

"Carpenter, Marcus. Prisoner number one-three-one-four..." He paused. "After special revision, you are reassigned to the *Omega Section*. Level Nine."

Marcus frowned. "That's not what you—"

"Move along."

The officer didn't meet his eyes.

The chains at his waist and throat were unlatched, clattering to the floor. The guard behind him gave a shove toward the elevator.

"Good luck," the man said, his smirk making clear he didn't mean it.

The lift ride down felt longer than the one before. No screens. No messages. Just the creak of old machinery lowering him into whatever waited below.

When the doors opened, the air was colder. Wet. The corridor lights flickered in dull orange intervals, barely cutting through the mist. This part of the facility looked ancient compared to what had come before — older, darker, maybe the first layer ever built. Reserved for VIPs.

A guard led him wordlessly to his cell. No sound except the shuffle of boots on concrete. No voices. No other prisoners.

At the far end of the passage, a single door waited — heavy, metal, blackened by heat and age. The guard keyed the panel. The lock hissed.

"Home sweet home," he muttered, then shoved Marcus inside.

The door slammed shut behind him, the echo rolling down the hall like thunder.

The cell was small. Damp. A bunk. A toilet. Nothing else. The light overhead buzzed, half-dead.

Marcus turned slowly. His gaze fell on the inside of the door — something had been carved deep into the metal. Not scratched, but gouged. The edges still sharp. Years of hands had traced each letter.

He leaned closer, fingertips running through the grooves.

Latin. He mouthed the words, uncertain, stumbling through half-remembered sounds.

"Lasciare? Oghini?—" He sighed. "God dammit."

It felt like hours as he fumbled over the words, until at last he found them.

Lasciare ogni speranza… voi ch'entrate.

He frowned, whispering the translation under his breath.

"Abandon hope… all ye who enter here."

For a long moment, he just stood there. Then sat down on the bunk, the metal groaning beneath him.

The light flickered once. Twice. Then stayed on.

He lowered his head, breathing slow.

Marcus Carpenter — no longer a man. Just a number in the system. The *Umbral Deep's* newest soul, dragged into shadow and darkness.

CODA I

Two Weeks into Parole

Apart from a few regulars, the bar sat quiet — broken only by the buzz of old light strips overhead and the faint reek of recycled air and spilled spirits.

Marcus kept his back to the wall, eyes on the exits. The habit had kept him alive before; no sense breaking it now.

He rubbed the scar tissue at the base of his spine. Still sore.

The walls were cluttered with fading photographs, old magazines, travel posters. Colour. *Real* colour. Funny how you start to appreciate it after years of grey.

In the reflection of a picture frame, he caught himself — close-cropped hair, clean-shaven face, eyes that no longer looked like his.

The man in the glass was someone else entirely.

The stew was warm; the potatoes burned his throat going down. Real food — each bite felt like it was stitching something back together. The knife stayed hidden under the table, his fingers resting on the hilt. Old habits — the only kind that survived prison.

The floorboards creaked. A large man in black approached, eyes fixed on Marcus. He gripped the knife tighter.

"You Carpenter?" the man asked, voice blunt, low.

"Yeah? Who's asking?" Marcus mumbled through a mouthful, shifting his feet to spring if needed.

"Comms call for you. You can take it at the bar."

Marcus swallowed hard. "Thanks," he muttered. The man nodded, gathering empty glasses. When he offered a refill, Marcus gave a cautious nod. Kindness still felt like a trick.

The comms unit sat in a dark corner, its tiny screen pulsing faint green: **AUDIO ONLY**. A single LED stared back at him like an eye.

He hesitated, cleared his throat, and pressed the mic. "Hello?"

"Mr Carpenter. Former captain of the Theseus, correct?"

The voice was calm. Too calm. Each word carried a faint hum beneath it — not static, not feedback, but something *alive*. The kind of noise you felt in your teeth more than in your ears.

"Yeah, that used to be me," he said. "Who's this?"

"Introductions can come later. Time is short. We are aware of the circumstances surrounding your incarceration. We believe evidence still exists that could exonerate you — restore your life."

Marcus shook his head. "No. Whatever you're offering, I'm not interested. I'm on parole. I can't go back."

"Which is why your parole was… expedited. The Deep is no place for business."

He froze. "You got me out?"

"If we can pull you from the Umbral Deep, imagine what else we can arrange."

"Something for something, right?"

"Naturally. We require a consignment to be transported. Sensitive equipment. A ship has been prepared. The cargo is loaded. It requires only a captain."

"I'm blacklisted. I can't fly anything."

"Licences can be… adjusted. You're well suited for this assignment."

Marcus met his own eyes in the mirror — hollow, sunken, lost. *Maybe space was the only place he still made sense.*

"Alright," he said quietly. "I'm in."

"Excellent. Take the next shuttle to the Titan Shipyards. Dock Twelve. Ask for Barge Delta-Six-One. Onboard, you'll find coordinates and flight orders. Welcome back… Captain."

The line clicked dead. The screen flashed once.

COMMUNICATION ENDED.

Marcus rolled up his few belongings, left a handful of credits on the bar, and walked into the corridor's cold light.

Behind him, the comms unit flickered — its LED pulsing red and green in rapid sequence.

TARGET REACQUIRED.
PURGE UNIT.
RETURN TO SHIP.

A hiss. A spark. Then the unit burst, the smell of burnt circuitry filling the dark.

CODA II

You... think you're so smart. We build ships. Cross the stars. Pat... ourselves on the back.

Hull groans faintly, metal flexing under unseen weight.

Beyond those stars — outside... the Veil — I've seen it. *Felt* it. Inside... me.

They don't want our light. They just... want to be left alone. Not welcome. Never... were.

But we don't learn. Never learn. Because we think... we know better.

I know better now. I've been shown... the way.

Most of the ship's systems... cooked. Nav computer's down. I—I can only hope I pointed the *Charon* the right way. Back into the Veil. Away... from them.

Gave me back... the box. I have... to give a warning. People... have to be told.

Stay... away.

Elana?

...

Static swells. Fragments of breath. Then nothing.

TRANSMISSION LOST.

About the Author

Martin Shaw is a lifelong science-fiction fan whose earliest memories are filled with starships, distant worlds, and the strange corners of the unknown. Based in Scotland, he lives with his wife, two schnauzers, and a single very opinionated hedgehog.

While he enjoys all kinds of sci-fi, Martin has always been drawn to the darker, grittier side of the genre — the lived-in metal and flickering lights of *Alien*, the neon rain of *Blade Runner*, the existential dread of *Dead Space* and *Event Horizon*, and the cosmic unease of Lovecraft. *Echoes in the Black* marks his contribution to that tradition: a story shaped by isolation, machinery, the vastness of space, and the limits of the human mind.

Ninety percent of this novel was written on a Samsung phone with a Bluetooth keyboard — a process that was equal parts chaotic, surprising, and strangely fitting for a tale built on confinement and grit. He promises to use a proper laptop next time. Probably.

Thank you to my friends and family, who encouraged me to see this through when it felt impossible. Your support kept this story alive.

Huge love to my wife: thank you for being my greatest source of strength, patience, and encouragement. You helped me more than you know.

Love also to my two dogs and my hedgehog, who kept me company during countless late-night writing sessions.

Thank you to my workplace — those long quiet hours gave me the space to write more than I ever expected.

And finally, a small acknowledgement of the absurd: this entire book was written on an Android phone with a Bluetooth keyboard. Technology is wild — and apparently so am I.

Printed in Dunstable, United Kingdom

72755697R00167